Magnolia Tree

Magnolia Tree

The Crossing Trilogy, Book 1

June V. Bourgo

Published 2019 by Next Chapter
Cover art by CoverMint

Acknowledgements

I wrote this book for all the believers in magic. We live in a world that can, at times, confuse, disappoint, and leave us fearful. But there is always the magic—as you, the reader, perceive it to be: albeit through spiritual belief, science, religion, or simple instinct.

As always, I thank Anne Marsh and Heidi Frank, my creative and grammatical readers, who carry me though the initial trials of writing a story. They address my doubts and insecurities in my ability to create a new project.

I am ever grateful for the support from my husband, Dennis, whose creative input and personal support never waivers.

A big thank you to my Next Chapter Publishing family, who work hard to make my story the best that it can be.

A heartfelt thank-you to Annie Kagan, Author of The Afterlife of Billy Fingers (aka William Cohen) for allowing me to quote her brother's words at the beginning of this book.

And to Billy Fingers aka William Cohen, for his ethereal testament to the magic. Thank you for sharing your experience with your sister, who in turn has shared your words with the world.

Where I am I see the light
In you as well as in me
Billy Fingers aka William Cohen

(from *The Afterlife of Billy Fingers* by Annie Kagan)

For all the believers…
Never forget the magic

Prologue

September 21, 2000...

Elizabeth Grey awoke with a start. Her eyes popped open. A feeling of dread passed through her. She glanced to her left and noted her husband's absence from their bed. The LED digits on the alarm clock read eight a.m. Elizabeth sat up and stretched. She shook off her unrest. *Must have been a dream I don't remember.* She padded to the bathroom, washed her face and hands, put her housecoat on over her nightgown and entered the hallway. A voice could be heard coming from her granddaughter's bedroom. She stopped at the doorway and leaned on the frame.

Four-year-old Sydney sat on the floor with her tea set spread in front of her. "Would you like some sugar in your tea?"

Elizabeth smiled. Sydney had an imaginary friend. Elizabeth wasn't worried about it. A lot of children have them, especially when they have no siblings and live rural without other kids to play with. *It's just a part of her development.* Frank, her husband, on the other hand, thought it was weird and believed Sydney had issues. An opinionated man who once he held a belief could not be shifted, she was tired of arguing the point. Elizabeth sighed.

Sydney looked up. "Hi Nana, my friend, Candy, is having tea with me."

"Good morning, hon. Say hi to her for me."

"She's not very happy today. She looks very sad."

"I'm sorry to hear that. Maybe your tea party will cheer her up. What would you like for breakfast this morning?"

Sydney looked at her invisible friend. "Hmm...what should I eat today? What about pancakes?" She looked at her Nana. "Yup, Candy is smiling."

"Pancakes it is after I have my coffee. I'll call up when it's ready."

Elizabeth descended the stairs and went into the kitchen. The aroma of a full pot of coffee beckoned. She poured herself a cup and looked out the back window towards the barn and equipment building. Both doors were closed. *Frank's probably out for his walk.* Elizabeth padded to the front door to claim the swing and enjoy her coffee on this beautiful warm morning.

She stepped onto the verandah and came to a cold stop. With a sharp intake of breath, her free hand flew to her chest and she gasped "Omigod..." The full cup of coffee in the other hand hit the floor. Splintered shards of porcelain scattered across the porch while hot coffee splashed up over her white floppy slippers.

"Omigod..." she gasped.

Frank lay face down on the wooden floor. Elizabeth kneeled beside him. "Frank? Frank..." She shook his shoulder. No response. She tried to push him over onto his back but only managed to get him half on his side. Frank's eyes stared back at her, glazed and lifeless. Her hands covered her mouth. "No, no," she whispered. Elizabeth put her fingers to his neck. *No pulse.* Her hand moved to his chest. *No heartbeat.* His body was feeling cold to the touch. *How long has he been laying here?* Elizabeth knew he was dead. There was nothing she or anyone else could do for her husband. A state of shock froze her body to the spot.

She had no idea how long she kneeled there staring at her deceased husband. She stood and went inside. After making a call to the police, Elizabeth called her friend and neighbour, Carol.

Five minutes later, Carol walked Sydney out the backdoor on an adventure through the meadows, to end at Carol's house for pancakes.

Elizabeth returned to the porch and swept up the broken cup pieces. She placed a pillow under Frank's head and covered him with a blanket. He appeared to be sleeping. A silly gesture to be sure, yet a comforting one. She sat on the porch swing. There were no hysterics, no tears. Only a numbing acceptance...and she waited.

Chapter 1

Seventeen years later…

The old two-story farmhouse with boarded windows, peeling paint and overgrown gardens appeared nothing like the house she remembered from her childhood. Sydney Grey stood on the gravel sidewalk that led to the sagging steps attached to a porch covered with leaves, dirt and broken tree branches. Her eyes scanned the windows on the second floor, resting on one window in particular. *My bedroom.* Her mind filled with childhood memories of swimming in the small lake behind the house and playing hide and seek in the grove of magnolia trees. She loved the smell of the magnolia flowers; a heady, intoxicating scent with a touch of cherry, lemons, and a hint of vanilla.

An uneasiness that started in the pit of her stomach and pushed its way through her body made Sydney frown. She had no idea why. Feelings such as these plagued Sydney her whole life. Usually, they occurred before something happened. She shrugged it off. That's because she didn't yet know that she used to talk to a dead person.

A quick perusal of the roof over the porch and the house showed curled shingles and a few missing tiles. Sydney blew a wisp of blond hair out of her eyes. "Shit," she murmured. *A new roof needed for both.* She opened the notebook in her hand and wrote some notes. The windows were intact on the second floor. Regardless, they were slotted to be replaced with a row of picture windows, along with the intent of turning the whole top floor into one open studio. She stepped onto the porch. *At least the floor's intact.* The suspended swing she'd loved to sit on in the cool of the evenings hung lopsided, one of the chains broken. She leaned against the porch posts. *Solid.*

The interior of the house was in better shape. However, the air inside was hot and stale. She left the door ajar and opened each window as she wandered throughout the rooms. The carpets were frayed which mattered not. There was wood underneath and a good sanding and staining would bring them up nicely. She took in the yellowed linoleum on the bathroom and kitchen floors. *Gone—a complete renovation for both rooms.* Her eyes perused the kitchen, resting on an old-fashioned pantry room with a broken door. *The pantry stays.*

There were three bedrooms on the main floor. The largest would be her room and her office. She envisioned an electric fireplace with an armchair, with lots of room to add an En suite. Sydney stood at one of the bay windows and took in the grove of magnolia trees spread out to the left of the lake. She smiled at the small dock leading into the lake, remembering the swimming lessons her grandmother started before she could even walk. *Nan called me her water baby.* The second bedroom would serve as her Nan's whenever she came to visit and the third as a guest bedroom. *Easy upgrade for them.*

Moving back to the living room, she took in the fireplace set into one whole wall of inlaid stone. If the chimney proved certifiable, a glass front pellet stove insert would be appropriate since she loved the beautiful stone wall. A door slammed upstairs. Sydney's head shot up. "Uh…" *Probably a gust of wind from the open windows down here.* Still, it gave her a start.

The natural wood door jams would stay. *Love those.* She noted the wooden staircase and railing to the upstairs would be beautiful with a sanding and rich stain.

The upstairs housed a storage room and two more bedrooms. Wandering into the one that had been her bedroom, Sydney envisioned removing the inner walls to join the bedrooms and hallway as one open yoga studio for her clients. Pillars could replace the one load bearing wall. She opened a door in the hallway and walked into a storage room. *Perfect size for a two-piece bathroom for clients.* A wooden stool stood in the corner. She glanced up at the ceiling, noting the trap door to the attic. Memories of her grandfather standing on the stool and pulling down the door panel flooded her mind. A set of wooden steps pulled down for access. She smiled, remembering that she'd been too short to stand on the stool and pull the door panel down and longed for the day when she'd be tall enough to explore the secrets of the attic room above. If she hadn't moved to the city with her Nan, it may have become another hiding place.

The sound of a vehicle drew her out of the room and back to the bedroom window. She looked down expecting to see the contractor who was coming to inspect the house. A tall, thin woman got out, wearing a ball cap, her long dark hair in a braid down her back. Sydney headed downstairs to the veranda.

She stepped through the doorway onto the porch and met the woman at the top of the steps. "Hi, can I help you?"

The stranger looked her up and down. "Syd? Is that you?"

Sydney tilted her head. Only her friends called her Syd. Her grandmother refused to because it made her sound like a man. To her Nan, Sydney was bad enough but that was her birth name. *My Nan's old-fashioned that way.*

"I'm sorry. Should I know you?"

The woman laughed and reached out her arms. "It's me, Jessie."

Recognition came instantly. "Omigod … Jessie?"

The two women embraced. "I can't believe it's you," Sydney said. The two had met in pre-school. During kindergarten, her grandfather passed. She and her grandmother moved to Kelowna when the school year finished. The girls had only seen each other a few times over the years and lost touch in high school. At twenty-one they'd both changed considerably from their last visit as tweeners.

Jessie pushed her back. "I love that hair style. You look gorgeous." Sydney's straight blonde hair hung in a layered bob a couple of inches below her chin, parted in the middle with long wispy side bangs she was forever blowing out of her eyes. "It makes your blue eyes pop."

"Thanks. You look wonderful." Sydney took in her height. "So tall. You could be a model."

Jessie pulled a face. "No thanks. I like the quiet life in our little town."

"I guess it still has a small-town flavour but it's grown so much since I lived here. How'd you know I was here?" Sydney asked.

"Mom lives next door to your possible contractor. He mentioned a family member had returned to the farm. I thought I'd check it out, hoping it was you."

"Yes, Rhyder Contracting. I'm waiting for someone to meet me here this morning to go through the house."

"Awesome. They really are the best contractors around."

As if on cue, a white van with Rhyder Contracting graphics pulled off of the quiet road into the dirt driveway. The two women walked down the steps to greet the young man who exited the driver's door. Sydney took in his strong, slim build, white fitted t-shirt, and tailored blue jeans with well-worm cowboy boots. *Whoa! If all the country boys around here look like this one...*

Jessie spoke first. "Hey, ghost. Haven't seen you for awhile. How's it going?"

"Hi, stranger. I was working on a big job out of town but Dad's been away for a couple of weeks. I left the foreman in charge and came back to run the office. It's good to be home." His gaze turned to Sydney. He gave her an obvious up and down stare. "I'm looking for Sydney Grey."

Their eyes locked and Sydney felt drawn into his expressive blue eyes. She stood frozen to the spot. The young man tilted his head with raised eyebrows, waiting for her to respond. Breaking out of her stupor, she rushed forward a little too quickly and almost stumbled. She extended her hand. "Uh ... that's me. I'm Sydney Grey." *What a dork I am.*

"I'm Jax Rhyder, Rhyder Contracting" He gave her a wide smile and shook her hand. He held it a little longer than usual, his eyes searching her face.

She pulled her hand away. *Hmm... seems a little sure of himself.* "Nice to meet you. I'm really excited to see what you have to say about the renos."

Jax took in the old building. "Me too. I love refurbishing old farmhouses. It's my passion. Hopefully, we can come together and make it work."

Jessie cleared her throat. "Well, I should take off and let you get to work."

As the pair turned and looked at her, Jessie laughed. "Wow—look at you two. Don't you make the cutest couple?"

Sydney's mouth dropped open and her eyes got big. She mouthed the word "What?" She gave Jax a sideways glance. He laughed and his eyes held a glint of amusement.

Jessie snickered and shrugged. 'I mean, you're both blue-eyed blonds with that same Keith Urban hair style thing going on. You made me think of those couples that look alike."

Jax laughed. "Same old Jessie. You always were blunt in school. First thing that comes to mind, first thing out of your mouth."

"That's me. So Syd, why don't we meet for dinner tonight at Carl's Steakhouse and we'll fill each other in on our lives. It's on Third Street."

"I'd love to. How about seven o'clock?"

"Great. See you then."

Chapter 2

Sydney and Jax watched Jessie walk to her car and drive off. She turned to Jax who was grinning at her.

"Do you know Jessie well?" He asked.

"Not entirely. We were best friends at ages four and five before I moved to Kelowna. We exchanged letters for a few years and had some visits but eventually lost contact. It'll be great to get to know her again."

"She's good people. You can't go wrong with her as a friend."

"That's good to know. So... do you want to start out here or inside?"

"Let's start out here with the foundation."

For the next two hours Jax crawled under the house and inspected an equipment building on the property. Inside the house, he searched through cupboards, studied ceilings and pulled up carpeting to inspect the wood floor beneath. They talked flooring, appliances, windows, doors and roofing. On the second floor, he asked to see the attic.

Sydney led him into the storage cupboard. After they discussed a proposed two-piece bathroom, she stood on the stool and opened the attic door. "I'm coming up with you. This is exciting for me. Ever since I was little, I've wanted to explore the attic." As she pulled the stairs down, a cloud of dust and spider webs came with them. She sneezed.

Jax reached up and helped her pull the stairs into place and locked the keepers for stability. He started up first. Half-way up the stairs, he looked down. "There are probably more than a few spiders up here."

Sydney followed behind him with determination. "I like spiders. They eat the bad bugs."

He grinned down at her. "Gutsy lady. I like that."

"I'm not a girly girl if that's what you mean."

There wasn't much to see. *A dusty empty room.* Since there was no power at the farmhouse as yet, the small oval window cast a dim light throughout. She laughed. "I don't know what my grandparents kept up here, but this is a disappointment. Back then, my curious five-year-old mind conjured up all kinds of mysterious images."

Jax laughed with her. "Do you have any plans for the attic?"

"No. I have no intention of hauling things up here for storage." She thought about the back door downstairs that entered the mud room off the kitchen. They'd already discussed sharing it as a laundry room. "I was thinking about the mudroom/laundry room and how big it is. Perhaps we could incorporate some built in cupboards and shelving for storage."

"That's a great idea. And what I'd suggest for the attic is to change the window into an air vent. These old farmhouses lack adequate venting. There's a new system that is solar powered that comes highly recommended for controlling heat build-up, moisture and ventilation. An easy install with the new roof. We'll upgrade the insulation up here. Another inadequacy of old farmhouses."

"Okay."

"I think we're done. Let's go back downstairs and go over my notes."

They left the attic to sit outside on the steps.

Jax looked over the pages on his clipboard. "I really think we can do something here. The foundation is solid and the roof structure appears sound. We'll shore up the squeaky floor boards or replace them. You're catching the roofing just in time. Another season and you'd probably have some leaks. I'm surprised at the overall condition, considering no one has lived here for a number of years."

"My grandmother rented it out for a long time to a family that worked the hay fields. Nan paid the husband to maintain the farm. When he became ill and died, his widow took the kids and moved closer to family. The farmer across the road leases the hay fields and keeps an eye on the place. It was always Nan's intention to give me the farmhouse and she didn't want it to become ramshackle."

"She's been lucky not to have squatters or vandals." Jax stood and stretched his back.

Sydney joined him. "We were lucky I guess. But with the neighbour working the fields, there's probably too much activity on the property. And this road isn't as remote as it used to be."

"Fifteen years ago, this area was rural. But the town has grown so much you're now at the edge of town. So—how about you meet me here day after tomorrow? Ten o'clock? I'll have a quote ready for you."

Sydney nodded. "I'll be here."

"You have some great ideas for this old place. Some retro and some modern touches. It'll be fun to make them blend. Meanwhile, I'll do some sketches for the laundry/storage room, the bathrooms, as well as the kitchen where there's lots of room to expand cupboards and put in an island."

"I can't wait to see them." She walked him to his truck.

Jax leaned across the driver's seat and pulled out a box. He placed it into her arms. "Here you go. Something to keep you busy until then. Some paint samples, indoors and out, a ring of coloured tin roof samples for that tin roof you want, and more rings of wood flooring stains and tile samples."

Sydney's heart began to race. She smiled up at him. "Oooh…this looks like fun. I'm so excited. Thank you."

Jax beamed back at her. "I really hope we get to work together. This place would be a dream job for me." He climbed into the van and started the engine. He turned and gave her a wink. "And so would working with you. See you soon."

Sydney dismissed his flirtation and said goodbye. After he disappeared down the road she smiled. He was an awesome specimen of maleness but he knew it too. Women probably chased him. But this was business and she didn't want to cloud the arrangement. Romance was not on her current to-do list. She didn't need or want the complications.

Somehow, she knew they'd be working together. Rhyder Contracting came highly recommended to her by a number of people in town. It was known for fast, quality work. She'd been told they weren't cheap but you always got what you paid for. And she liked the ideas he'd thrown at her for the past two hours. They were like-minded in that respect.

Sydney took another stroll through the house, holding up tiles and paint samples. Earth tones with some dark muted colours and bold splashes of colour held a certain appeal and she couldn't wait to get started. As Sydney stood in the master bedroom working out colour schemes, she felt a sudden chill. She walked to the window and looked up to the sky. She crossed her arms across her body and rubbed her hands over the goose bumps on her arms. *Strange. The sun is still shining bright and hot.* Her eyes scanned the lake and grove of magnolia trees. One tree stood at the back of the grove apart from the others. Sydney watched the branches move in the wind, the leaves twisting and turning to the point that some of the flower petals floated down and landed under the tree. A memory flashed through her mind. She saw herself as a small child sitting on a lower branch hidden next to the trunk.

"Sydney, where are you? It's time for your lessons". She held her body tight to the trunk and giggled. This was her favourite place to hide from her grandfather. Here she could talk to her imaginary friend as her Nan called her. But Sydney knew she was real. Here she felt safe. This was her happy place.

At this point, Sydney noticed that none of the other trees were blowing in the wind. They were still. *Maybe it's one of those circular gusts and it only hit that lone tree.* She looked beyond the grove to see if other trees were affected. Her eyes scanned the area but all she could see far into the distance were open hay fields. Sydney looked at the lone tree once again and the movement stopped. The tree was still. The room suddenly felt warm again and her goose bumps disappeared. *Weird.*

She locked up the house and got into her jeep. Driving back into town, her thoughts returned to the memory she'd envisioned. *Imaginary friend? I'll have to ask Nan if I had one as a child.*

Chapter 3

Sydney hurried down the street to the steakhouse. *I'm late.* A couple coming out of the restaurant held the door for her. She smiled at them and said thank-you as she rushed past them into the entranceway colliding face first into the chest of another customer leaving. He grabbed her shoulders to steady her as she bounced back off-balance.

Sydney looked up into the face of a fortyish man with greying hair at the sides. "I'm so sorry. I wasn't paying attention."

The man stared at her hard. He never uttered a word. She peered past him, noting that people were waiting behind him to exit the restaurant. "Oops... we're blocking the doorway." *Still nothing.* He appeared rooted to the spot. Sydney side-stepped the man and mumbled her apologies again. She proceeded at a slower pace to the Maitre d' standing by a podium. A quick glance back shocked her. The man had re-entered the restaurant and stood a couple of feet away watching her, his expression blank.

The Maitre d' interrupted her thoughts. "Can I help you, Miss?"

"Yes, I'm meeting someone here. Jessica Farrow?"

"Follow me, please."

Half-way to the table, she looked over her shoulder but the man had disappeared. *That was creepy.*

"Syd. You made it."

"Yes, sorry I'm late. Nan called me just as I was leaving wanting to know all about the renos."

"No problem. I was late too and just sat down. It's a zoo here tonight."

"It's rib night," the Maitre d' said. He handed them both a menu and cocktail list. "We're always busy when we serve our rib specialty. Your waiter will be with you shortly."

The waiter arrived a few minutes later. They both decided on the ribs and a bottle of dry red wine. Once he returned with their wine and appetizers, Jessie held up her glass.

"Here's to renewed friendships," she said.

Sydney tapped her glass against hers. "Renewed friendships and new adventures."

"So how did you make out with Jax today? Are you going with his company?"

"It went well. The farmhouse is structurally sound. That says a lot. He understood my vision and offered some great ideas. We're meeting in two days to go over his blueprints and costs. My senses tell me that he's the right person for the job."

"I've seen his work on other homes. It's exceptional."

Sydney held her glass up this time. "Here's to successful renos and my future home."

Jessie reciprocated and popped a nacho with melted cheese and salsa into her mouth. Between bites she threw another question at Sydney. "Talking about homes, where are you staying in the meantime?"

"I've got a cabin at River Road Resorts on the Okanagan River—the south end."

"I know the place. You could have stayed with me and saved some money."

"That's kind of you but I'm fine. You know I've never lived alone before, always been with Nan. So this is a new thing for me."

The waiter brought their ribs. "Enjoy your meal."

"Wow. These taste amazing. I can see why the place is so busy," Sydney said.

"Mmm…aren't they though? By the way, how is your Nan?"

"She's doing well."

"Will she be moving back to the farm when it's ready?"

"No. Her life is in Kelowna now. She has her friends there and she's not ready to retire yet. She'll have her own room when she comes to visit but I don't think she'd come back full time. There are too many bad memories for her."

Jessie sat back and sipped her wine. "I guess it wasn't the same for her after your mom disappeared…" Her friend hesitated. "I'm sorry. Should I have said that?"

Sydney shook her head. "It's okay. Really. I think that's part of it. Nan never talks about those days. Once in a while, when I was a kid, I'd ask some questions and she'd get guarded. My mother was her only child and I think when she left, Nan felt abandoned and betrayed. She said something to that effect once when I was about twelve. She harbours a lot of anger towards her daughter."

"And you've never heard from her after all these years?"

"No, nothing. I stopped asking years ago. I don't remember my grandfather much. Except that he could be really strict and Nan was always quiet around him. My feeling is that they married young and she stayed with him out of duty. I don't think she loved him anymore."

Jessie pushed her plate back and poured them both the last of the wine. "I can see why she wouldn't want to come back. So tell me, why did you move back?" Jessie asked.

"Well, Nan was holding onto the farm to leave me in her will. She saw it as a good investment that I could sell at a good price one day. She never thought of me wanting to return here. But I wasn't happy where I worked and decided to start my own business. And Kelowna was getting too big for me. I wanted to live more rural. I checked around the whole Okanagan Valley to see where my competition would be and where I thought I could make a go of it."

"And you chose Stoney Creek?"

"I did. It showed the greatest growth potential in this part of the valley and I have no competition between Osoyoos and Okanagan Falls. Nan was shocked that I wanted to come back here. But my enthusiasm won her over. A few days later, she came in from work excited and handed me an envelope. It was the deed for the farm."

"Oh wow."

"I couldn't believe it. She said it would be mine when she was gone anyway and if I wanted to move back and renovate it as a home and business, I should have it now. She gave me the money she'd been saving from renting the hay fields for the renos. That means I can use my savings to set up the business. Her only request was that she wanted a bedroom that was hers so she could come and visit."

Jessie leaned forward. "I'm really happy for you. Another toast. Here's to a successful business." They raised their wine glasses. "And what is your business by the way?"

"I'm a Yoga instructor. I intend on gutting the upstairs and building an open studio. Next, I'm converting the equipment building into bedrooms and showers for guests who come for retreats. I'm also an Earthing instructor."

Her friend's eyebrows shot up. "A what?"

Sydney laughed. "Earthing. The short description is to connect to the earth's natural energy; the transfer of energy being a natural healer. The lake behind the house has a natural sandy bottom, perfect for water exercises in season and I intend on planting a patch of grass between the house and the lake for Earthing practices and meditation on the grass.

"I love it. But good luck with the grass. In case you haven't noticed we live in a desert area."

"The lake is formed from a natural underground artesian spring. There's plenty of water. So enough about me. Let's talk about you,"

Jessie sighed. "After high school, I moved to Vancouver and enrolled in nursing school. I got my LPN, Licensed Practical Nurse and stupidly got married far too young to a lab technician. We both worked out of the Vancouver General and it lasted about nine months. I decided to move back to Stoney Creek last year and I'm working at the hospital in Oliver."

The waiter came and took away their plates and returned with coffee.

"Any boyfriends in your life?" Sydney asked.

"Nope, like you I'm living on my own for the first time and I'm happy. How about you? Any boyfriends?"

"No. I recently broke up with a really solid guy in Kelowna. He wanted to move forward in the relationship but something was missing. I couldn't make the leap based on nice, so I ended it."

"Hey, now I have someone to go clubbing with. Most of my friends from school are living in the city or have babies."

"Nan never remarried after Papa died and she's quite content with her life. She told me unless I want babies, don't bother."

They laughed. Sydney's gaze travelled around the room and into the lounge area with a bar and stools and some small tables for people who weren't eating meals. Her smile froze as she stared into the face of the same man she'd run into at the entranceway. His features were still rigid and his eyes unblinking.

She diverted her eyes back to Jessie. "Hey, without making it obvious, take a look into the lounge. There's a man at the end of the bar. Tell me if you know who he is."

Jessie spun around in her chair and looked directly towards the lounge.

"Omigod...you call that subtle?" Sydney groaned.

"What man? There's no one at the end of the bar."

Sydney looked past her friend. The seat was empty. "Damn. He's gone again. I'd think he was a ghost if I hadn't physically run into him at the front door." She described the incident to Jessie.

"It's creepy all right. But maybe he was just into you. You're a beautiful girl and a new face in town."

"Fresh meat? You don't make points with a person by acting like a stalker. Besides, he's got to be in his forties. I'm twenty-one."

Jessie laughed. "Huh...all the more appealing to some men."

The girls finished their coffee and Jessie insisted on paying the bill. She walked Sydney down the street to her car. They exchanged cell numbers with the promise of getting together soon.

Sydney drove across town to the river, checking behind her in the rear-view mirror to see if she was being followed. The strange man really unnerved her. Once in the cabin, she bolted the door, making sure the windows were closed and locked. *Thank goodness for air conditioning.* It wasn't until she'd closed all the curtains that she felt safe and relaxed.

Chapter 4

Jax stretched out in the chair in front of his father's desk. "So when did you get back?"

"Yesterday afternoon about fourish. I was up early and came in a couple of hours ago. You've done a great job looking after things while I was away. Good job, son."

"Thanks. How did the trip go? Did you make a deal?"

Wes Rhyder reached for some papers on his desk and smiled. "You bet I did." He waved the sheets up and down. He'd been travelling through the Okanagan Valley looking at land development in the bigger cities. "Not only will we be taking on a new bank building, we have an opportunity to get in on the ground floor of a new hospital. A state of the art project that will keep us pretty busy."

Jax grinned back at his father. He recognized that sparkle that lit up his father's face whenever a new development project arose. His father was an architect first and flourished in the design process long before construction starts.

"We'll have to open a new office in Kelowna. Hire more staff. This means a big expansion for Rhyder Construction. This will bring us closer to my goal of turning us into a major land development company and moving solely into commercial projects."

"I'm happy for you, Dad. You've worked hard to get this far. I have no doubt you'll get the company where you want it to be."

His father stretched his hands apart above his head. "This requires a name change from Rhyder Construction to Rhyder & Son Developments. But for now, let's take a look at our current projects."

The two men spent the next hour going over their work load and projected finish dates. Wes picked up the last file. "I see you've been working on a farmhouse renos. What's that about?"

"It's the old Grey farm on the edge of town."

His father's head shot up. "The old widow finally sold the place then. Who are the new owners?"

"No new owners. A relative has moved back to the property from Kelowna. Her names Sydney Grey."

Wes leaned forward. "The granddaughter?"

"That's right. Have you ever met her?"

"No. She and her grandmother left Stoney Creek a couple of years before we moved here." Wes sat back in his chair and rubbed his chin in thought.

"Dad? I've lost you. What are you thinking?"

" Umm…we have a rather full plate at the moment. Perhaps we should pass on this one."

Jax shifted uncomfortably in his chair. "You know these kinds of renos are right up my alley. I really want this job."

His father stared at him. "I know they're your passion but we have to think about what's right for the business."

It wasn't the first time they'd had this discussion over projects that his Dad thought they shouldn't do. Jax always listened to his father and gave his words merit. In the end, he'd do what Wes Rhyder thought was best. But this time, he intended on fighting for it and wouldn't compromise.

"Look, I'm pretty much finished with my project in OK Falls. The foreman is more than capable of bringing it to closure. The other projects are covered as well. I've got the time to work on this one."

Wes stared at the file in silence. Jax waited for him to speak first, determined not to give in. "You know the growth of this company is taking us through a transition. We're moving away from residential work to commercial. That's the new vision that I see for the company. Perhaps it's time we discuss the role I'd like to see you play in this new direction."

Jax shifted uncomfortably. He knew this day was coming. He'd always avoided conflict but the moment had arrived to let his father know his true feelings about their work together. "All right. Tell me about your vision."

His father leaned forward. "We've built quite a reputation in the valley over the years. Since you joined me two years ago, I've left you to deal with the residential projects and I've moved into the commercial side. What I see is you taking over this office and moving strictly into commercial construction. For myself, I think it's time I moved to Kelowna and work with the land development and commercial endeavours there and eventually, within other major cities in the Okanagan."

"Wow." Jax felt overwhelmed. "That's quite a vote of confidence in a twenty-two year old."

"You've proven yourself. You have a good work ethic and the ability to tackle problems with quick logic. I'm proud of you, son."

Jax felt torn. He didn't want to disappoint his father but his 'logic' told him he had to follow his own path, not the one his dad wanted for him. "Dad, I'm really excited for you on this and I'm pleased you've been happy with my work. But the truth is your dream isn't my dream."

Wes Rhyder's face clouded over. "I don't understand. I thought we had a plan for you to work with me and run the company together."

"We did. But that was back a few years before you decided to expand and become a big developer. My passion lies in residential housing projects. Preferably renovations. I'm not really interested in commercial ventures. You know that."

"There's no money in house renovations. At least not the kind we can make going commercial. I'm doing this for you, son. One day it will all be yours."

"On no, don't lie that on me." Jax rose and paced in front of the desk. "You did this for you and only you. And that's okay. But if it was for me, you would have asked for my input and what my dreams were."

His father stood and leaned on his desk; his face contorted in rage. "I don't believe this. I thought you trusted my judgement and what's best for the company. This in turn, is what's best for you."

Jax sat back down in the chair. He knew this confrontation wouldn't be easy which is why he'd avoided it for months. *Stay strong.* "If you believe it's best for the company, then it is. And that makes it best for you, Dad. But not necessarily for me. I have my own dreams."

Wes sat, leaned back in his chair and the two stared at each other, once again silent. "Okay. Tell me what you see for you?"

"I'd hoped you would keep the residential division and let me run that. That's where my expertise and my interest lie. I'm not a building architect like you are. That's your skill and your passion."

"I know that. I don't expect you to be an architect, just run the development projects. I trust your instincts and you've proven yourself as a 'boss'."

Jax rubbed his fingers against his forehead. "When I was a kid, you always told me to be true to myself. You and granddad didn't see eye to eye when you told him your aspirations. Do you remember what it was like to stand up to his expectations and say no?"

"Hang on." Wes Rhyder stood and left the office. He returned with two cups of coffee. He placed one in front of Jax and returned to the chair behind his desk. After a few sips of the black liquid, he put it down.

"I can't argue with anything you've said. My argument is that the company can't grow into commercial projects and stay diversified with residential projects. Running two offices and potentially more in the future can no longer support the residential aspect. So from purely a business perspective, we either stay where we are and forget the expansion, or move forward and leave the other behind."

"And I get that. It's the right thing to do for the sake of the business and the direction you want to take it in. You have to do what is best for the business. Dad, you have a fire in your belly and you should go with it. What's left is to decide how I fit into it all. What you're offering me is enormous and believe me, I am appreciative. But housing is what lights the fire inside me."

Wes sighed. "Don't get me wrong. You can make a living in residential. But you'll have some good years and bad years where you'll struggle. I've already done that, son. I wanted to spare you that and build on our existing business side-by-side."

Jax stared into his coffee cup, weighing his next words. "I know you're disappointed. The answer for you is to follow your vision…without me if necessary. And I don't know where that leaves me but I'll figure it out. You say I have good instincts so let me trust in myself and follow my own path. And there's something else for you to consider. You have qualified people here in the office that have been with you for years. Don't you think they might resent me suddenly becoming their boss? They deserve what you're offering me a lot more than I do."

His father picked up the renos project file. "Tell me about this project. What time schedule do you see on this?"

"Well, there's more than the farmhouse here. There's a conversion of the equipment building into a dorm for weekend retreats and a barn upgrade. I'd say two months tops."

Wes opened the file and glanced through. He smiled. "You haven't done the quote yet but I can see this will be a lucrative project, regardless that it's renos. Here's what we'll do. You take this project on if the client agrees to your terms. Two months gives me time to get preliminary things worked out in Kelowna. Meanwhile, there's no reason to decide on anything right now. Let's both think on our conversation here today and we'll talk about this again down the road. Okay?"

Jax let out a big sigh and beamed. "Okay. And thank you."

"Damn. Look at that excited expression on your face. You're too much like your old man, you know that."

"A chip off the old block. You raised me." They both laughed.

"Now get out of here, I've got a hundred calls to make."

Jax went to his own office and sat down at his drafting table. He hadn't been this excited about a renos project before. He set to work building a quote based on the blueprints he'd adapted the day before with his suggested changes. The thought of his future with his father's company was troublesome, but at least his Dad was listening to him. He pushed away negative thoughts and lost himself to his work.

Chapter 5

Sydney leaned over the blueprints spread across the kitchen counter. "I love your ideas for the kitchen and mud room. You've utilized the space well without the rooms appearing much smaller."

"Here's the blueprint for upstairs. I've added something to the new bathroom up there," Jax said. "See the storage room at the end of the hall, here." He placed a finger on the spot. "Once we take the bedroom walls out, there's a bedroom closet on the other side. I'm thinking we should take it out, move the bathroom door entrance around to that side, widen it in the hallway to a larger bathroom and include a corner shower stall. You never know what future plans you might have for the upstairs down the road and you'll have a complete bathroom. The rest of that back wall in the hallway can house storage cupboards and shelving from the new bathroom wall to the stairwell. You can store all your yoga gear there."

"Hmm…so that leaves the solid side-wall for full-length mirrors. I like it. You've really captured my vision for the house. Let's look at the equipment building next."

"Okay, here I've made some changes yet again from what we discussed. I know you wanted six rooms with full private bathrooms for clients on weekend retreats. But the room isn't there to support that. And the town bylaws won't allow it. Because of space restrictions, your plan would only give you four rooms with partial bathrooms. My plan shows two shower rooms; one for men, one for women. Each room has two shower stalls with privacy doors and this counter has four sinks for wash-up. It saves a shit load of money and even leaves room at the end of the hallway for a laundry big enough to house a washer and dryer and a closet for linens. Each of the four bedrooms can house two single beds."

"I guess wanting private baths was a bit fanciful." Sydney was a little disappointed. *It's not Jax's fault that the building didn't hold up to my wants.* "I like the laundry room idea. Originally, I thought I'd bring the laundry into the house but that's a lot of wear and tear on the house appliances. But four rooms from six and four shower stalls total…I don't know."

Jax pulled another blueprint out from under the first. "I thought you might have concerns about the shower traffic so I drew up another plan. How about this one instead." The new plan showed five bedrooms without partial bathrooms and added another stall to each shower room and three toilet stalls.

"That could work. Nice." She paused. "Done."

"One last thing to cover. We never discussed the barn. I know it's leased out along with the hay fields beyond the lake. And your grandmother replaced the barn roof three years ago. But the exterior walls could use a paint job and maybe the odd board replacement. Do you want to include that in with the other renos?"

"Absolutely. It would be nice to colour co-ordinate all the buildings," she mused.

Sydney looked up at Jax and caught him smirking at her. "What?"

"Careful, your girlie-girl is showing."

"Come on. The barn is faded red, the house is green and brown, and the equipment building is white and grey. Pretty ugly, I'd say."

Jax threw his arms out. "I'm teasing. That brings us to the paint samples and tiles etc."

They spent another hour discussing colours for walls, flooring, and trim. The barn roof was a charcoal grey tin. Sydney decided to match the other roofs and paint the exterior walls of all the buildings in a deep rich red called Autumn Maple Leaf with white trim.

"I think we're done. I've got a quote here, which will change a few hundred here or there because of your choices."

Sydney studied the paper. "That's fine. Draw up an invoice with the correct amount. I'll pay you the down payment amount now. When can you get started?"

Jax beamed. "My schedule has opened up. I'm dedicated to your property for the next two months. When I get back to the office, I'll put a team together and we'll begin tomorrow. Is that soon enough."

"Absolutely. I'd like to move in as quickly as I can but I don't want to be in the way. Is it possible for me to live here at a certain point during remodelling?"

"Well, I'd like to do the roofing first, on both buildings. Then, we'll shore up any soft spots in the foundations and replace any exterior wall boards. The exterior painting, trim and accessories can wait until last after you've moved in. We can do the house interior next. You should be able to move into the house in about four weeks; as long as you can stand the noise once we start converting the equipment building. We'll sub-contract the plumbing work and water connections.

"That's awesome. I could start setting up the studio. And don't worry, I won't be hanging around anywhere getting in the way." She wrote Jax a cheque for the down payment and gave him keys to all the buildings.

They walked out the back door and down to the lake. Jax turned his back to the lake and studied the back yard and areas between the home, barn, and equipment building. "There's lots of room back here to unload materials and still space available to work in. That's a real plus." He turned back to the lake.

A soft breeze carried the scent of the magnolia trees in full bloom. Sydney drew a deep breath. "I love the smell of the magnolia flowers. They'll continue in flushes right into the fall."

"You certainly have a beautiful spot here."

"Thank you. I'm happy that I'll be in around the beginning of June so I can enjoy the three warmest seasons."

Sydney turned towards Jax and noticed he was staring at her. Their eyes locked. Jax broke the spell. "Uh... well, I better get back to the office and set up my teams and order some supplies. If you want to meet me here tomorrow, I'll have the invoice updated for you."

"I can do that and then I'll leave you to it for a few days. I'm heading to Kelowna to see my Nan and I'll be in and out of town for the next few weeks shopping for furniture and studio equipment. If you need me at all, you've got my cell number. Otherwise, I'll pop out in a few days to see how it's going."

"Okay, see you tomorrow."

She watched him disappear around the corner of the house.

Sydney walked towards the magnolia grove and wandered through the trees. They needed a pruning. She made a mental note to look for a gardener to help her plan the maintenance and upgrades she wanted to put in place for the front and back grounds, as well as the beachfront to the lake.

The lone magnolia tree drew her to its base. Sitting out in the open by itself, it was a beautifully formed tree with nothing to interfere with its growth or steal from its nourishment. She walked around to the far side and stared across the hay fields. Soon it would be time for the first harvest. *Another scent I love—fresh cut hay.* Sydney turned to the tree and noticed a faint impression in the bark. She moved closer and ran her fingers over the imprint. The darkened letters had been carved into the tree many years before. *C & C. My mother's name is Chelsea. Did she make these markings? But who's the other C?*

A ruckus further up the tree caught her attention. She glanced up to see some yellow-breasted chats flying out of the branches amidst a series of caw notes and squawks. Something caught her attention peripherally and she turned her head in that direction.

"Uh…" she gasped, jumping backwards. Her heart pounded and her throat constricted. Her hands clutched at her chest. It all happened in seconds. A girl in her late teens sat on Sydney's favourite childhood branch. Sydney swallowed hard and snapped her eyes shut and open—the girl was gone.

She couldn't tear her eyes from the spot for several minutes as her brain processed what her eyes had seen. *It makes no sense. Did I really see someone in the tree?* She closed her eyes and tried to envision the image. She opened them quickly in case the girl had returned. *No one there. How could I make it up?* The girl had blue eyes and long hair—pink hair. *That's right. Pink hair?* Sydney picked up on the clusters of pink magnolia blooms within the tree and smiled. Perhaps it was only the flower clusters and a vivid imagination. Then, something else struck her. There was more than a face to what she saw.

Why did I see a girl in blue jeans, a white t-shirt and bare feet?

Chapter 6

Elizabeth Grey returned the coffee pot to the counter stand and joined Sydney at the kitchen table. She sipped her coffee. "Umm...a little strong." She got up and turned on the electric kettle.

Sydney laughed. "Sorry, Nan. I forgot you drink your coffee black."

"One day you young girls will regret drinking those fancy milk and sugar coffee concoctions. You're skinny now but once you've had babies or get into your forties, it all changes." She leaned back against the counter.

Sydney smiled at her Nan. She'd been hearing this argument for years. *Sugar is the devil.*

Her grandmother frowned. "Don't give me that patronizing smile. For someone who's into yoga, spirituality, and 'our bodies are a temple'; I don't understand why you still drink those fancy drinks which are more crap than coffee."

"You know I'm careful what I eat and put into my body. But my coffee is my one vice. I don't drink much alcohol or do drugs. My coffees are my way of relaxing and pampering myself."

"Humph...they certainly don't relax me. A couple of those elaborate brews leave me jumping out of my skin." Having said her piece, her grandmother changed the subject. "So, tell me about your shopping day."

"I went to my old work and they sold me some of the older stock they were replacing. I got some pillows and mats that still have life left in them. And then, I ordered some bolsters, blocks, chairs and benches from the wholesaler in Vancouver. They're blowing out stock for their new summer line. They're holding onto my purchases until I've moved into the house."

"That's wonderful, dear. What's next on your agenda?"

"Tomorrow, I'm going to an auction of that hotel that went into bankruptcy in Westbank. I'm hoping to get duvets and sheet sets for the residency."

The kettle whistled and her Nan topped up her coffee cup. She sat down opposite her again and took a sip. 'Ahh...just how I like it. It sounds like you're organized. You can store some things here you know. The spare room will hold them until you move in. Did your contractor give you a date?"

Sydney pushed back from the table and brought her feet up onto the chair next to her. "Yes. Four to five weeks. The house interior will be finished and the roofing is being done now. I can work on setting up the studio and furnishing the house while they work on the equipment building and exteriors."

Her grandmother was studying her. "What?" Sydney asked.

"I haven't seen you this happy for a long time. I'm happy for you."

Sydney reached forward and took a hold of her hand. "I am happy. And I can't thank you enough for this."

"I'm happy too. It's fun watching you do all this. If they're able to, I think more people should give family members their inheritance while they're still alive to share the joy it brings to them. It's something you and I can share without the grief of losing a loved one."

Sydney squeezed her Nan's hand. "Talking about sharing, how do you want your bedroom decorated at the farm?"

"Which room is mine?"

"The room in the back of the house, at the end of the hallway, next to the bathroom. It has a bay window and looks out on the lake."

Elizabeth smiled. "That's a nice room. What colours are you planning for the interior.?"

"Mostly neutrals; champagne, beiges, slate green, burgundy, and bold splashes of colours in accessories and furniture."

"Hmm...neutrals are nice for my room. You know my favourite colour is green. All I need is a small dresser, and a bed. You can pick what you want for furniture and I trust you to pull it all together. Surprise me. All I ask is no abstracts."

Sydney laughed.

Her grandmother groaned. "I know...abstracts are in and you love them. But if I'm going to sleep in a room that's my own, you know I like flowers."

"Flowers it is."

"When do you plan on opening your business?"

"The contractors won't be done until the end of June, then I need a landscaper and I want a fence built across the front. I'm thinking the first of September. I need to do some pre-marketing before the doors open."

Elizabeth took the empty cups to the sink. "I must say I miss having you here, but it was time for you to follow your own path."

"I miss you too. You could still come live with me back on the farm. Wait until you see it finished. You'll love it."

"What would I do there? I have my own business here."

"You could set up a mobile hairdressing shop there just as easily as the one here. I checked it out you know. There isn't a shop in Stoney Creek. Everyone goes to Oliver or Osoyoos."

They talked about it for a few minutes and her grandmother looked excited. Then the spark went out of her eyes. She put her head down and when she looked up at Sydney she looked sad.

"Oh, Nan. I wish you could let the past go. When I was little, you told me of happy times at the farm."

Elizabeth walked over to her granddaughter and put her hands on her shoulders. "I had my time at the farm. Now it's your turn. I'll come visit but that's all."

Sydney dropped the subject. She'd like nothing more than to see her grandmother living back on the farm but she couldn't push her into it. "Why don't you freshen up and we'll go out for dinner. What do you say to Greek food?"

"I say yes. I'll be ready in ten minutes."

It was a beautiful warm evening as they walked along the lakefront in downtown Kelowna City Park.

"I'm stuffed," Sydney said. "I need to walk off that delicious food, but all I can muster is a stroll at a snail's pace."

Elizabeth snickered. "I hear you and believe me, I relate." Once they reached the marina, they sat on a bench and watched the activity on the docks.

"Guess who I've reconnected with in Stoney Creek?" Sydney asked.

"Let's see. Since you were only five when we moved, your world was pretty small and insular. Someone from school?"

They both laughed. "Yes. Jessie Farrow. We had dinner the other night."

"How nice you reconnected. I'm surprised she stayed there. Most young people can't wait to leave village life."

"She did leave once to go to nursing school in Vancouver. She got married and divorced within a year and moved back home to the Creek. She works at the hospital in Oliver."

"Well, I'm glad you have a friend all ready."

"Yes, so am I." Sydney looked at her grandmother out of the corner of her eye. "Talking about friends, can I ask you something about my childhood?"

"Sure. What is it?"

"When I was really little, did I have an imaginary friend?"

Her grandmother looked at her in surprise. "As a matter of fact you did for awhile."

It was Sydney's turn to look surprised. 'Really? Huh..."

"Why/"

"I had a memory pop up about an imaginary friend...but that's all I remember. Did I have a name for her?"

"You said her name was Candy. Gosh, I hadn't thought about that for years."

"How often did I talk about her?"

"Lots. Your grandfather worried there was something wrong with you, but I told him lots of kids have imaginary friends, especially when they're an only child stuck out on a farm with no immediate friends."

Sydney stood. "We'd best start back. The sun's set and the air is cooling down." As they walked back through the park to the car, Sydney thought about her imaginary friend, Candy. "Did I ever tell you what we talked about?"

Elizabeth laughed. "She never talked. You told me she was mute. According to you, she'd sit on the floor with you and pretend to drink tea with your tea set, or she'd smile as you told her about your day at school. I remember walking by your room and you'd be doing all the talking, showing Candy your dolls and asking what clothes you should put on them that day."

"If she never spoke, I must have made up her name. I wonder why I called her Candy?"

"You did tell me once that she smelled like magnolia flowers. Perhaps that reminded you of sweet candy."

"How long was she with me?"

"I'd say about from age three through five. But when we moved to Kelowna you gave her up. School and dance filled up your time and I guess you didn't need her anymore."

Sydney thought about that as they drove out of the parkade and headed to her grandmother's house. *So that's what I envisioned at the farmhouse. And if I used to hide in the tree from Grampa, and talk to my imaginary friend, that's who I was remembering sitting on the branch of the magnolia tree. She was just a memory from the past.*

Chapter 7

"Wow!" Sydney stood in the driveway staring at the farmhouse. "The roof looks great." She walked around the side of the house with Jax. The equipment building had a new roof as well, and the damaged boards on that building and the barn had been replaced. Jax's crew were using a backhoe to pick up discarded roofing and wall materials from the ground, dropping it into the bed of a dump truck.

"We're hauling away the roofing debris. Tomorrow, we have a couple of commercial dumpsters coming in and we'll be able to clean up as we go." Jax said.

"Even unpainted, the buildings look better already. You got a lot done while I was away."

"How was your trip?"

"Very successful. I accomplished a lot. So what's next?"

"Even though the foundation is sound, we discovered the house is slightly tilted towards the back. Over the years, the ground and house settled in that direction. It's quite fixable, using jacks and levelling it off." Jax shuffled through a folder and pulled out a paper. "Here, this is the additional cost for the work and materials."

Sydney studied the paper. "That's fine. I was fully prepared that there could be more costs involved with an old house like this one. And it certainly needs doing."

"Okay. We'll get started on that this afternoon. When that's finished, we'll move into the house and start with the attic."

"I'd like to go in the house and take some pictures before you get started. It would be so awesome if I could have an album following your progress."

"Go ahead. The house is empty right now."

Sydney headed to the front of the house. A horn honked and she looked to the road to see a pick-up driving out of the driveway of the neighbouring farm. She waved at Arne Jensen. He'd lived on that farm his whole life, having been born and raised there. He'd worked the land; first with his parents who were gone now, and then with his wife, Mary. Sadly, Mary had died years ago from a fatal heart attack. Arne still worked the farm. It was all he knew.

Arne pulled into her driveway and opened his window. "Well, well, haven't you grown up since I saw you last."

"It's been a long time for sure. How are you, Mr. Jensen?"

"Please, it's Arne. I'm well, thank you."

"I was so sorry to hear about Mary. It must have been a difficult time for you."

"That was a long time ago, dear. Life goes on. Your grandmother was a good friend to my Mary. Back in the day, we were the closest neighbours to each other."

"I guess, it was all farmland with huge acreages. I'm glad when they allowed owners to subdivide agricultural land, they put five and ten acre lot restrictions in place."

"So how is your grandmother. Is she moving back to the farm?"

"Nan's fine. She's not moving back but she'll be down to visit once I'm moved in. I'm sure she'll pop over to see you."

A door slammed shut inside the house, which startled Sydney. She glanced towards the house perplexed, knowing it was empty.

Arne drew her attention. "It would be nice to see her again." He nodded at the house. "Big renovations going on."

She looked back at the old farmer and smiled. "Yes. I'm really excited about the progress. I can't wait to move in."

"You planning on living here on your own then?"

"I am. And running a home-based business. By the way, the house is now in my name. I'll get the lawyers to draw up a new lease on the hay fields. Same terms if that's what you want."

"Sure thing. It'll be nice to have a neighbour again. If there's anything you need help with, anything at all, don't you hesitate to call me. Okay? Now I'm off to an appointment in town."

"Thank you. Talk soon."

Sydney watched him leave and waved back at his arm extended out the window. She entered the house and wandered around taking pictures. Another door slammed shut upstairs and she climbed the stairs. "Hello?" No answer. When she reached the hallway, she noted the bedroom doors were shut. She opened one and stepped into the room that had been her mother's many years ago. Instantly, the door closed hard behind her.

Sydney spun around, heart in throat. *What the hell?* She opened it and peered into the hallway. No one there. *Okay. There's a reasonable explanation for this.* She went back into the bedroom and stared out the open window. *Of course.* Sydney rummaged through her shoulder bag. "Where are you? I know you're in there…aha."

She took the pencil lying at the very bottom of the canvas sack and turned away from the window. She bent down and placed the pencil on the floor. It rolled in the direction of the door just as Jax entered. "Oops, watch out for the pencil."

Jax stopped and looked down. He raised his head up and stared at her in surprise. "Were you checking up on me to make sure I was telling you the truth about the tilt? I assure you that Rhyder Contracting has a high standard and a great reputation in this community."

Sydney felt her face get hot and knew she was blushing. "Oh Jax, don't be ridiculous. Of course I believe you. I heard doors slamming up here and I was trying to figure out why. I realized the doors and windows are all open and there's a breeze blowing through. It didn't seem enough to slam the doors, so I was seeing how big the tilt was as a contributing factor."

Jax looked at the door. "I see your point. Definitely, with the door on a tilt, it wouldn't take much of a wind to slam it shut."

"Mystery solved. I was starting to think the house was haunted."

They both laughed.

"I came up to tell you that the dump truck is gone. I'm heading to town to pick up the jacks and materials we need for the foundation repair. I was wondering if you'd like to join me for lunch first."

Sydney hesitated. "Jax, I don't want to blur the lines between us. Right now we have a business arrangement and ... "

"I'm talking lunch not a date. I'm on my lunch break right now and you will probably head home to eat something too." Jax threw his hands up. 'This is just about food...and I'm starving."

She laughed. "Okay. I'll follow you back to town. Where do you suggest?"

"The Rattlesnake Grill, it's on the river a couple of blocks south of where you're staying. They have the best salads and grilled meats."

"I know where it is. If we get separated, I'll meet you there."

They descended the stairs and headed out the door to their vehicles. Jax pulled out of the driveway and drove down the road. Sydney felt good. Reconnecting with Jessie and her neighbour, Arne went a long way to make her feel right about returning to Stoney Creek. She thought of Jax. We can be friends like he is with Jessie. She smiled. *He's pretty easy on the eyes too.*

She turned the rear-view mirror towards her head to check out her make-up and hair and caught the glint in her eyes. Instantly, she reset the mirror and pursed her lips. *No, no and no.*

Sydney took in the decor of the restaurant while waiting for the server. "I love the brick red, turquoise and mustard yellow colours. So southwestern." There were big clay pots of ferns and cacti affording the tables some privacy. The huge room appeared smaller and cosy.

Jax looked out the glass windows."It suits our arid climate." He nodded towards the Okanagan River flowing south. "The river is really high and deep at this time of year."

"Do people tube down it to Osoyoos like everyone does in Penticton?"

"No. They are different sections of the Okanagan River but they are like two different rivers. This end is far too dangerous. Have you ever done the Penticton run?

Sydney smiled. "No. But that sounds like my kind of fun."

"There are places along the way to stop for picnic lunches. Tell you what, come summer I'll arrange a group of friends. We'll float down the channel, stop for lunch and have a swim in the lake when we get there."

"But how do we get back to our vehicles?"

The waiter arrived and Sydney ordered a Mediterranean salad and grilled salmon steak. Jax ordered a garden salad with a t-bone steak.

"We'll leave the vehicles at the entry point. Usually there's one or two who don't do the river. They bring the drivers back to the car park and they return to pick up everyone else down at the lake."

"And what about lunch?"

"The ones who don't do the channel bring the lunch to a designated spot downstream at a pre-determined time. Once we return to Stoney Creek, we usually meet at a pub for a few beers and dinner. Makes for a great day with friends."

Their food arrived and they were silent for a few minutes as they dove into their food.

"Mmm...you're right," Sydney said. "The food is wonderful."

"Told you. So what do you think? Are you up to a day on the channel?"

Sydney looked up at Jax. Making new friends was a good thing. "I can't wait."

Jax picked up his water glass."Here's to a hot summer." He grinned and winked at her.

Warmth spread through her body and she was certain it had spread to her face. She clinked his glass and took a sip of water. Immediately, she dropped her eyes and dove into her salmon. *Damn him with his expressive blue eyes and dimples. He looks like a young Chris Pine.*

Chapter 8

A week had passed and with the attic finished, the crew were now working on the upstairs floor. The walls had been removed, the floor levelled, and three support posts placed. Sydney was pleased with the progress thus far.

She was stretched out on a chaise lounge outside her rental cabin sipping a glass of wine. Jessie occupied the second lounger beside her. It was a warm evening and they were discussing ordering Chinese food.

"I'll let you chose the restaurant since I'm sure you have a favourite," Sydney said.

Jessie reached for her cell phone. "Is there anything you like in particular?"

"Nope. I love it all. Oh...I do prefer low mien noodles to chow mien."

Jessie frowned. "What's the difference?"

"Low mien are skinny, chow mien are shorter and fat."

"Gotcha." Jessie called the restaurant programmed into her phone and ordered their dinner.

"Wow... that's enough food for an army," Sydney said.

Jessie giggled. "I love cold Chinese food for breakfast the next morning."

"What? So do I. Another thing we are like-minded about."

The girls laughed and fist bumped.

"How long did they say it would be?" Sydney asked.

"Thirty minutes."

Sydney stood. "It's my turn to pay. I'll get my credit card."

After retrieving her card, she exited the house in time to see Jax pull up in front of the cabin. She waited by the door until he exited the truck. "We're having wine. Want some? Or do you prefer a beer?"

"I'd love a beer," Jax said.

"All I have is Heineken."

"All good." Jax headed towards the loungers and sat down at the picnic table. He had a wooden box under his arm which he placed on the table.

"Hey, you," Jessie said.

Sydney returned to the kitchen. She opened a cooler bag and put some beer in it with another bottle of wine. She joined the others outside.

Jessie refilled their glasses. "So what's brought you slumming down by the river?"

Jax laughed. "I wanted to give Syd an update on the farm."

That was the first time he'd called her Syd and it didn't go unnoticed. Sydney sat back in her lounger feeling warm all over. And it wasn't from the wine.

"We finished replacing floor boards and put the final touches on the storage cupboards. Tomorrow we'll frame the new bathroom. The electrician was in today. He replaced the old wiring and electrical box. We're running power from a generator for now. Most of it he ran through the walls but where he couldn't he ran it around the room. But don't worry. We'll cover it with molding. You'll never see it."

Sydney beamed. "Still right on track, I see. You're doing a great job."

"Thank you." Jax took a long swig of beer. "Aww…nothing like the taste of a cold beer on a hot night. Oh…" He put down his bottle and pointed at the box. "I brought you this. After we broke down one of the bedroom closets we started pulling up the carpeting. Inside the closet, one corner of the carpeting was already loosened. Underneath, we found a lifted floor board and under that this box sat nestled in the floor joists." Jax stood and carried it over to Sydney.

"It looks like an old jewelry box." She tried opening the lid. "It's locked. The key is long gone I'm sure." She gave the box a shake. "Whatever's inside has some weight to it." She ran her hands over the wood. Sydney looked up at Jax who had returned to his beer. "Which room did you find it in?"

"The one at the end of the old hallway on the side wall. I probably have a tool in the truck to pry it open if you'd like."

Sydney stared at the box. "That was my mother's bedroom." The thought that there could be something inside that belonged to her mother excited and scared her at the same time. "I don't think it belongs to the people who leased the house for a few years. Their children were toddlers. What if it's hers?"

"Your mother's?" Jessie asked softly.

"Yes."

"Why don't we open it and find out? This is so cool. Like we found buried treasure." Jax said.

Jessie gave him a stare that said, 'shut the hell up'. She reached out and touched Sydney's arm. "You all right?"

Before Sydney could answer, the delivery boy arrived with dinner. She handed the box to Jessie and went to pay for the food.

Her friend spoke to Jax. "You want to help us eat some Chinese food? We have more than enough."

"I'd love it, thanks."

"Then come inside and help me get plates and cutlery. We'll eat out here." She carried the box into the house with her.

As they disappeared into the cabin, Sydney heard Jax whisper: "Did I say something wrong?"

Sydney busied herself, opening the various containers, pushing away thoughts about Jax' find. There was more than enough food for three. She smiled. *Should even be enough leftovers for breakfast.* The other two joined her while she opened the second bottle of wine and put out another beer for Jax. They ate and laughed heartily as Jax shared stories about childhood antics. Whatever Jessie told him in the kitchen, no one mentioned the farm house or the wooden box. Sydney knew little about her mother. She didn't remember her and her Nan avoided the subject. There weren't even any pictures of her in her grandmother's home. Nan was a very private person and she'd hidden her pain about her daughter over the years. Sydney got a glimpse once in awhile when she'd pressed her as a teenager and was always left confused by the mixed emotions of anger and pain her Nan would reveal; only to close down and shut her out. The thought that the box may contain things that belonged to her mother or reveal something shook Sydney to the core.

They cleared the picnic table and Jax made a fire in the pit. The three of them settled in lawn chairs around the fire.

"I haven't laughed this hard for ages," Sydney said. She sipped more wine, having had way more than she usually would. *Tomorrow I'll suffer.*

"It's your turn to tell us a funny story from your childhood," Jax said. "And don't tell us you were a good girl who never did anything wrong. Even perfect girls can go rogue."

Jessie snorted. "Ewww...are you crushin' on my friend?"

Sydney laughed. She'd had enough wine to find the whole thing hilarious. "If you think I'm perfect, you're in for a big surprise. Let's see. When I was eight, I wanted to see what Nan had bought me for Christmas."

Jax interrupted her. "What? Didn't you still believe in Santa at eight? I know I did."

"I did until a couple of weeks before Christmas that year. A girl at school found out from her older sister. They had a fight and her sister wanted to get back at her and spilled the beans about Santa not being real."

"What a little bitch," Jessie said.

Jax and Sydney stared at her.

"A little harsh, Jess. She was a kid," Jax said.

Jessie giggled. "Sorry, that's the wine talking. Continue your story, Syd."

"I saw Nan hiding some parcels in the garage. So one night I snuck out of bed and down the hallway to the door into the garage. Nan had fallen asleep in her chair watching a movie on television. I'd slipped into the garage and started to snoop around when I heard her footsteps in the hall. She'd woken up and was heading to bed. I heard the deadbolt on the door to the garage lock."

Jax and Jessie laughed. "And you were locked in the garage," Jessie said.

"I was too. I heard her go into the kitchen and bounded out the door that exited to the driveway. It was snowing hard and I ran around the back of the house in two feet of snow, in my pajamas and slippers. I'd let the cat out and knew the door wasn't locked yet."

"Did you get back in?" Jax asked.

"I carefully turned the handle and opened the door. Just as I crept in, the cat ran from outside between my legs and I stepped on his tail. He let out a yell and took off running down the hallway. Next thing I know Nan comes running to check out the noise and catches me in the open doorway."

Jax hooted. "Uh-oh, caught red handed."

"Yup. I tried to lie. Told her I woke up to pee and heard the cat on the stoop."

Jessie interjected. "Let me guess. She didn't buy it."

"How could she? There I was standing in the house with snow in my hair and the bottom of my pajamas and slippers caked with snow. She knew I'd been outside. I told her the truth."

"Did she punish you?" Jess asked.

Sydney laughed. "No, because when I saw how disappointed she was in me and how mad she was that some girl had spoiled my belief in Santa, I told a lie that I did get away with." She pointed at Jax and giggled. "When you hear it, you'll know I'm not perfect and can lie with the best of them."

Jax grinned that big dimpled expression that always had an effect on her. "Tell us. What'd you say?"

"I told her I still wanted to believe in Santa and didn't want to give him up. If what she'd hidden in the garage were the same presents left under the tree from Santa on Christmas morning, then I'd be sad but would know it was true."

"Clever girl," Jessie said.

"So you're not just a pretty face, you're smart too,: Jax added.

"You better believe it, cowboy. She felt so bad for me that she went into the kitchen and made me hot chocolate while I changed my pajamas."

They kibitzed back and forth until they all stared into the fire; each lost to their own thoughts. A moment later, Sydney jumped up. "Okay. It's time. Let's do this."

The other two stared at her and then at each other.

"Huh?" Jax grunted.

"Do what, Syd?" Jess asked.

"I'm getting the wooden box and Jax you're getting a tool to break it open."

Sydney raced towards the cabin before she could change her mind. The box was on the kitchen table. She picked it up and hurried back to the picnic table. Jax had a small screwdriver in his hand. She looked over at Jessie who was still sitting by the fire. "Come on Jess, gather 'round. We're going to find out what this has been hiding all these years.

Jax pried the box open and slid it over to Sydney to open. She glanced at Jess and then at Jax, took a deep breath and lifted the lid. Sydney stared at the contents. Her friends stood on the other side of the table and couldn't see past the hinged lid.

"What's in there, Syd?" Jessie asked in a whisper.

Sydney picked up the first item. "It's a journal. There's three more in the box." She opened it up to the inside cover and read aloud slowly. "Property of Chelsea Amanda Grey, Grade 11." She leafed through the book, filled with handwritten notes. With shaky hands, she picked up the other three journals. "Property of Chelsea Amanda Grey, Grade 12; Property of Chelsea Amanda Grey, Starting My Life; Property of

Chelsea Amanda Grey, Baby and Me. Sydney sat down hard on the bench. “These are my mother’s. All the entries are dated and addressed to Dear Self.”

Sydney put three of the journals back in the box carefully. The fourth one she held in her hands and rubbed the cover. She carefully opened it and reread the inscription. “The year1997 was the year she left.” She looked up at her friends and realized her eyes were blurred with tears. “She’s in here. Her life; her inner thoughts, and me–I’m in here too.”

Jessie came around the table and sat beside her. She placed an arm around her shoulder. “And maybe the answers to all your questions are in there.”

“Maybe.” Sydney stared at Jessie. “What if I don’t like the answers? What if I hate her?”

Jax busied himself putting the fire out while Jessie comforted her. “What I think is that these pages will help you understand who she was and why she did the things she did. She’s given you an opportunity to know her inner most feelings at the time. And it’s straight from her. No gossip or lies. However hard that may be to read, it’s going to be for the best.”

Sydney placed the last journal in the box and closed the lid. “You’re probably right but not yet. I’m not ready.”

Jax cleared his throat. “I’m off for home, ladies. Thank you for the food, beer and fine company. Tomorrow morning comes early and if I don’t show up for work, my client might fire me.”

Sydney wiped her wet cheeks with the back of her hand and stood. “Fat chance, cowboy. You’re not going anywhere until you meet your contract obligations.”

“Okay, boss.” Jax turned to Jessie. “Do you want a ride home. I don’t think you should be driving.”

“No thanks. I’m bunking here tonight with Syd.”

Sydney forced a laugh. “Yes, she is. We have a breakfast date…cold Chinese food.”

Chapter 9

Sydney carried their empty plates to the sink. "That was delicious. Love cold Chinese food."

"How's your head?" Jessie asked.

"Fine now that I've eaten." She carried the coffee pot over to the table and refilled their cups.

"Thanks. So why don't we go to Kelowna for the day? There's some great spring blowout sales. We can start buying things for your new home."

"Sounds like a plan. I can't buy too much though. I still have a few weeks before I can get in. Not much room around here to store anything."

"Not a problem. I've got a spare room we can fill up." Jessie stood and downed her coffee. "This is going to be so much fun. My mother helped me get my stuff last year but we didn't always see eye to eye. She'd of had my house looking like my grandmother's. You and I however…" Jessie ran to the bedroom to get her things and left Sydney still drinking her coffee.

Sydney laughed and finished clearing the table. It really was cool to have a close friend to share her new adventure with.

The two-hour drive to Kelowna flew by fast. Once there they spent the afternoon filling Jessie's car with kitchen dishes, cutlery, glasses and pots. Then they hit a linen sale and bought towels and bathroom accessories. Sydney checked out bedding for her Nan's bedroom. She settled on a scalloped floral duvet in greens and blues which reversed to shades of green and blue stripes, matching a striped skirting. There were matching curtains, pillow covers and solids for throw pillows. They visited her Nan at her home and they all went out to dinner.

By the time Sydney and Jessie returned to Stoney Creek, it was dark. Jessie dropped Sydney off at the cabin and took her purchases to store at her place. Sydney closed the curtains and noticed a dark SUV parked in the road by her driveway. It caught her attention because it was still running. She turned off the lights in the cabin and peeked out of the curtains. The door opened and a man got out. He stood staring at her cabin. An eerie feeling passed over her. She knew he couldn't see her but still, his gaze bore right through her. He climbed back into the truck. Sydney could make out his profile in the glow of the inner light. He turned towards the open door and reached out to pull it shut. Her heart began to pound. It was the man from the restaurant. She was sure of it. The one who stayed and stared at her. He started the engine and drove away. *Okay. Now you're stalking me.*

She checked all the window locks and placed a kitchen chair on two legs with the back jammed up under the door handle. There was only one way into the cabin and no one would get in through this one. She flipped the outer porch light on to light up the place. She had no idea who this man was or what he wanted of her. *Maybe, he's harmless. But he has no right scaring the bejesus out of me. Maybe I should report him. Tomorrow, I'll figure it out.*

Sydney showered and crawled into bed ready for sleep. But her nerves were still jangled. Sleep evaded her. Then the wooden box and its contents came to mind. She rolled over to the bedside table and turned on the lamp. She lay still staring at the box. Her mixed feelings about the journals weren't getting any better either. The only way to resolve her dilemma was to take action. *Do it.*

She propped herself up with pillows and retrieved the box. She opened the lid and picked up the top journal. She flipped the pages and noted it was three quarters full. This was the last of the four books. The urge to turn to the final entry and see what it said welled inside her. Sydney ached to know how close the last entry was to the date her mother left. She fought the impulse. *No, I might be upset at what I find in those final pages. Start at the beginning and get to know her.*

She replaced the last journal with the first one, when her mother was sixteen to seventeen years old and settled back into the pillows.

Grade 11, 1993-94

September 9

Dear Self,

Back in school, Grade 11. Got the teachers I wanted. Yay! Pam's in most of my classes. Can't wait to start volleyball this year and modern dance. W is in my home room class. He still likes me… barf. Of course, he sat right beside me. He's such a dork! (I know, Self, be nice).

September 17

Dear Self,

Wow, homework is all ready heavy this year. Mr. S (history) is hilarious. Studying WW1I and he acts out the battles. Maybe I'll like history this year… not. Got into drama though. So excited.

October 2

Dear Self,

So pissed. I'm sixteen and finally allowed to date. B asked me to the movies and Dad says he wants to meet him first. I'm not a kid anymore… hello. How embarrassing. No way I'm telling B that so I asked him to come over tomorrow to listen to my new Cyndi Lauper album. Finally got it. Oh girls just wanna have fun… oh ya!

October 13

Dear Self,

B and I went to see the romantic comedy, He Said She Said with Kevin Bacon. Love him, loved the movie. B kissed me and stuck his tongue in my mouth... yuk. Don't think I'll date him anymore. Besides, he had bad breath.

Sydney smiled. Her mother sounded like a typical teenager. She continued reading the entries which were enlightening and funny. They were an easy read and much to her surprise, she could relate to her mother's teenage angst and troubles. *Just like I was. Only it was my Nan who ruled the roost.*

November 22

Dear Self,

In about four months I'll be seventeen. Can't believe it. Sometimes I don't think I'll reach nineteen. Can't wait to be independent and legal age. Don't laugh but sometimes I don't think I'll ever grow up and be an adult. I think I might die before that happens. Guess I'm a true Aries. We crave excitement, adventure and above all—freedom. Life here on the farm certainly isn't exciting. Oh... and we are impatient... and I certainly am.

November 26

Dear Self,

OMG... I'm grounded. Friday night I had a sleepover at Pam's in town. She had some kids over. Her parents were always there to chaperone when I stayed but this time they went out. Mom and Dad think I lied but I didn't know they wouldn't be there. Worse... I got drunk and puked all over their bathroom. Pam's father called my father at 3:00 a.m. and he drove into town to pick me up. The past two days have been hell.

December 1

Dear Self,

MY LIFE IS RUINED. Dad has pulled me from church now. He says he's disappointed in the church. According to him, they've strayed from the true doctrine and are too liberal and that's what's wrong with kids today. We need more discipline and bible study. Okay, so I don't care about missing prayers and the God thing, it's the socials I'm going to miss. The church serves goodies after service and now I can't go and spend time with my friends. Oh well, at least I can sleep in on Sundays. Yay!

December 3

Dear Self,

So guess who didn't get to sleep in today (Sunday)? Just as I thought my life couldn't get any worse, my father tells me he's going to give me my bible lessons and study. Study? Like I don't have enough homework to do. Not only did I have to read scriptures aloud, then I had to discuss what they meant. MY LIFE ISN'T JUST RUINED…IT'S OVER…

Sydney put the journal down. Her thoughts turned to the bible lessons her mother had mentioned. Sydney closed her eyes and remembered her recollection of hiding in the lone magnolia tree from her grandfather. He was calling her to come and do her lessons. The memories flowed back to her at that moment. She was too young to read, but her grandfather read to her out of the bible. And some of the stories and things her grandfather told her about his God, scared the hell out of her. *So he continued with the lessons even after my mother left. Strange that after he died and we moved to Kelowna, Nan never sent me to church. And I never saw a bible in our house ever.*

She opened the journal and continued reading. There weren't many entries during the winter months. She skimmed through to spring.

April 1
Dear Self,
I made it! Today is my birthday. Yah, I know April Fool's Day. Hey, that makes me unique right? One more year and I'm out of here. Pam and I have plans to move to Kelowna and share a place.

May 10
Dear Self,
It's really hot these days. Early spring. Working with Dad preparing hay fields. One thing I learned, bitching about it just gets him mad. Do the work, get it done and get back to my own life. It makes living with Dad easier. I've noticed he and mom barely talk anymore. No fights, just co-existing. I think my mom learned the same thing I did. Shut up, take his shit and life runs smoothly. If that's what marriage is, don't want it.

May 20
Dear Self,
Going to the May Prom with T. Have to go with someone. He's okay. Funny how last year I couldn't wait to date. But they're all such babies and all they want is sex. I've had lots of dates but not with any one special. The bitch brigade are gossiping that I'm gay, 'cause no one knows if I'm still a virgin or not. Good thing they all know my best bud, Pam, isn't a virgin or we'd be labelled a couple. Only, the queen bitch, S was overheard once saying that Pam was probably bi. When you don't know, make it up right? I don't care. I'm not gay but what if I was? We don't get to choose our DNA. We are what we are. Right?

Chapter 10

The days passed and Sydney couldn't have been happier. Her time was filled with shopping and online ordering to fill her new home. She hadn't seen the man in the SUV since that night in front of the cabin. She decided to wait it out. He obviously lived in the town and she had nothing to give the cops on him. He'd never spoken to her or even approached her. What he was doing that night at the cabin, she had no idea, but she needed more for them to take her seriously. All she had now was a man who stared at her. Seeing him in front of her cabin was a little upsetting but she had no license number, name, or proof he was there because of her.

Sydney drove to the farmhouse to see how it things were going. She'd talked to Jax on the phone but hadn't seen him since the night he brought her mother's journals. She'd finished reading the first one. It was more or less the same entries throughout. What became clear to Sydney, was that her mother was independent, strong-willed and had very definitive ideas about her life for one so young. Her clashes with Sydney's grandfather were more frequent. Chelsea had dated often but none of the boys met her standards. And that was because they were boys and she felt so much more mature. Sydney had laughed aloud. *Most teenage girls feel that way about boys their age. They're babies still.*

She turned into the driveway and parked to the far side of the house to not block the front of the house. Workers were hauling tools and supplies in and out of the house. She waited on the porch for an opportunity to slip into the house without being in their way. Jax was in the living room with his back to her. Sydney looked past him. "Wow," she said.

Jax spun around. "Hi."

"The pellet stove insert's in. It looks gorgeous." She moved in for a closer look. Jax had stripped the inner guts of the fireplace and ran a pipe right up the inside of the chimney. The insert fit tight. It jutted out enough to expose the hopper for loading pellets and allow access to the covered operation controls. The front of the stove with a glass door sat on the hearth. The shorter sides angled back at a forty-five degree angle, fitting snug against the stone wall. The grouting between the stones had been cleaned and the whole wall looked new. The hearth in front of the wall had been replaced with a natural stone to match the stone wall. "I love it."

Jax laughed. "I wish I had more clients like you. You gush about everything we do and love it all."

Sydney beamed. "Well that's because you get my vision and do such a great job providing it."

"Thank you. Now come and see the kitchen and laundry room."

She followed him into the kitchen. Her hands flew to her mouth but not before she let out a squeal. "Omigod…I love it" Jax was laughing again. "I'm sorry…I can't help it. Look at this." The cupboards and counters had been replaced and more cupboards added to a back wall that used to house a table and chairs. Jax had built a long Island with open shelves underneath. One side extended out with a set of four stools and a stainless steel bar underneath to put your feet on. The cabinets were all white with green floral handles. The counter tops were green granite. Jax bought the stainless steel appliances through his company wholesale account.

The walls were an olive green and the new flooring bore the look of restored wood. "The laminate is called 'Blackened/Natural', Jax said.

"It has a weathered look to it. Nice. The kitchen really does show the effect of an old country kitchen combined with the new. Jax it's beautiful. Wow…I don't deserve this," Sydney said with a sigh.

"What? Of course you do."

"I mean this is a chef's dream. I don't even know how to cook."

"I can teach you."

She looked at Jax who had that cocky look she'd come to know. "You? You know how to cook?"

"You insult me." Jax feigned a hurt look. "My dad taught me. He's a great cook too."

"Is there anything you aren't good at?" Sydney asked.

"I'm sure if you got to know me better, you'd find something." He winked at her and headed to the mud room.

"Again, you've given me what I want in this room. The storage shelves and cupboards on the outer wall are perfect." She looked at a lower shelf by the back door and saw that he'd built a grated holder for wet boots and shoes. The inner wall housed a washer/dryer and table to fold laundry.

They wandered back into the living room. Jax picked up the conversation. 'Tomorrow, we'll finish the bathrooms. Then it's just painting the rest of the walls, restoring the wood floors, and the finishing touches like moldings. How about seven days and you can move in?"

"Yay!" Sydney clapped her hands. "I can't wait."

"One more thing." Jax grabbed her by hand and pulled her back into the dining room area towards the back wall. "See this blank wall?"

"Yup."

"Remember it." He led her through the kitchen into the mud room and out into the back yard. He placed both hands on her shoulders and spun her around to face the back of the house.

He leaned forward over her shoulder and with his right hand pointed to the right. "You know that we decided to run a new deck from the bedrooms at this end of the house all the way across to the other end of the house?"

Jax' face was so close to hers that she could smell his aftershave and it left her a little giddy. "Uh-huh."

He placed his hand back on her right shoulder and lifted his left one, pointing at the opposite end of the house, switching his face to the opposite Side of her head. "See that solid piece of wall?"

Sydney found it hard to concentrate. Being this close to Jax was doing things to her insides she was glad he couldn't see. "I do," she said, breathlessly.

"That is the dining room wall. What if we put a set of French doors right there that open onto the back deck."

Sydney pushed away her personal thoughts. *Focus.* She liked his plan but money had been flying out the window and she wasn't sure she could afford the additional expense. "The idea is a brilliant one, Jax. But I'm not sure I should spend the extra it would take. We haven't done the residence yet and I need to be conscious of my costs in case anything unforeseen comes up."

Jax spun her around, leaving his hands on her shoulders. "Listen up. This project is more than the usual renos we get to do. It's a very lucrative one and when finished, it'll be a showcase. We have another client who all ready paid for the French doors. After we installed them, his wife decided she wanted sliders. Rhyder Contracting would like to put them in for you as a thank you for your business, no charge. Call it my housewarming gift to you."

Sydney was taken aback. It seemed a little extravagant. "That's quite the housewarming gift."

"All we ask is when we're done and if you're happy with our work, give us a written testimonial with photos for marketing purposes. And if you don't mind, let us use your home once in a while as a show home for prospective customers looking for an older home upgrade."

Sydney beamed. "In that case, yes. Let's do it."

The pair stared at each other, their smiles wide and their eyes locked. The world disappeared for Sydney. All she saw was his face. Jax leaned forward and brushed her mouth so lightly, so teasingly that she leaned in for more.

"Boss?"

The two jumped apart. Sydney turned and looked at the man briefly, lowering her eyes when she saw the smirk on his face.

"Yes?" Jax answered.

"Sorry to interrupt." The man looked back and forth between them and his smirk widened.

"What is it, Brian?"

"We have some questions about the shower stall."

She turned and walked a short distance towards the barn while the two men talked, stopping in her tracks. Her farming neighbour was standing in the open doorway of the barn with a pitch fork in his hand. His stare was so intense, it unnerved her. *Did he see Jax and I kissing too?* Sydney raised her hand and gave him a wave. The man nodded and disappeared into the barn with the same blank stare. *Humph... not as friendly as the last time we met.*

Sydney turned back to Jax. Brian started back to the house and Jax stared at the barn. "The old man wasn't too friendly."

"Perhaps he doesn't approve of our kissing. Not that it's any of his business He shouldn't have been spying on us."

Jax shrugged and grinned his crooked smile. "He's a widower isn't he? Maybe it was nostalgia. Remembering when he was young."

Once again Sydney had mixed emotions concerning Jax. "I'd better let you get back to work. Thank you for the doors. Rhyder Contracting is an awesome company." She saw Jax stiffen a little. He probably wanted to resume where they left off. Sydney side-stepped him and headed towards the front of the house. "I'll be back in a few days. Bye." She gave him a wave as she practically ran to her vehicle.

Settled in her bed that night, she closed her eyes and thought of the gentle kiss from Jax earlier in the day. She ran her fingers lightly over her lips and remembered the sensation she'd felt, the warmth of his body close to hers…and his smell. There was no doubt she was attracted to Jax. *No sense denying it.* But she didn't want a relationship right now. Nor was she into casual flings either. *And what about Jax? What was he looking for?* He had a reputation around town as a lady's man. Women loved him and they chased him. Jessie told her that he was always respectful to the women he dated. But apparently, he also made it clear he wasn't looking to hook up with anyone. *Well neither am I, but if he thinks I'm going to be another one night stand…forget it. Ain't happening.*

Sydney picked up the second journal from the bedside table determined to push Jax from her mind and lose herself to the entries.

Chapter 11

Grade 12, 1994-95

Dear Self,

Can you believe this is my last year of high school? So stoked. Can't wait 'til June. FREEDOM!

October 3

Dear Self,

Today is the best day of my life. CHAZ (a nickname) SPOKE TO ME! I've been crushing on him forever. We don't hang in the same circles. His parents are rich and he plays football. When it comes to sports, I'm a klutz. He sits right beside me in English class. School is SO cool now.

October 15

Dear Self,

D is such a BITCH! She heard me and Pam in the bathroom talking about Chaz. Only Pam used his real name. D told him I like him. I'm so embarrassed. Now he thinks I'm a dork.

November 20

Dear Self,

Pam and I are going out to dinner with our parents and I'm sleeping over at her house. Tomorrow, some of us are going skating at the outdoor rink in Woodland Park.

November 21

Dear Self,

Guess what? Chaz was at the rink today and asked me to skate with him. The queen bitch was soooo jealous. We held hands and once he linked his arm through mine. I'M IN LOVE!

December 8

Dear Self,

Dad is driving me crazy. Since I'm dating more and going to more parties, he constantly snoops in my room and tells me to be a 'good girl'. I heard him and Mom fighting. She said I'm a free spirit and he said I'm wild. This morning at bible lessons, he told me to remember that God is always watching me. God sees all. Well, if God's watching me kissing a boy or having a bath, he's a peeping tom. Dad is spouting off more fire and brimstone and heaven and hell stuff. And talking about how God will punish me. For what? I AM a good girl. Dad's God is mean.

January 1

Dear Self,

Chaz and I are dating. Can you believe that? He asked me last night at the town's New Year's Eve party. It's an outside party in the park. Lots of music, skating and dancing. So much fun. Mom wanted to go but has a cold. Dad would never go. Dancing is the devil's work. We aren't telling our parents. His parents have great plans for him. They keep telling him to not get serious with anyone until he's done with school. He'll be going away to university next September. I'm not going to think about that. Just be happy. Dad hates Chaz' family 'cause he says they're hoity toity. But Chaz isn't. Still, I'm not saying anything.

February 14

Dear Self,

Chaz gave me a heart on a chain with a picture of me and him inside. It has a long chain so I can hide the heart between my boobs inside my bra. Dad never notices jewelry. He sure does watch what I wear though. I wish I could dress like Cindy Lauper or Madonna. I love them both. Dad took away my Madonna CD's. He never listens to lyrics but then he heard 'Just Like A Virgin'. OMG...freak out. He listened to 'Oh Father' and 'Like a Prayer' and told me I could never play that music again in his house. At least I got to keep Cindi. I wish I were them. I don't mean pop stars...OMG I can't sing. I mean free spirits like them. I wonder if they ever worry that God will punish them? (That was a joke, Dear Self.)

March 15

Dear Self,

Sorry, I haven't been writing much. Last year of school is harder. More homework and stuff. Dad is making me do more chores on the farm. I hate farm life. I asked Dad why they didn't have more kids. Didn't he want some sons that could work with him on the farm? He got really uptight and then said because after I was born Mom couldn't have more kids. That I'd ruined her insides. I cried myself to sleep last night. No wonder he hates me.

Apr 1

Dear Self,

Happy birthday to me! Seventeen. Can't believe it. Chaz is taking me out to dinner. Dad doesn't know. He thinks I'm meeting Pam.

May 20

Dear Self,

Prepping for exams and grad night's coming up. My feelings are mixed. I'll be out of school soon which is hard to believe but Chaz will be moving to Vancouver to go to University. His Dad is retiring and they have their house up for sale. They're buying a townhouse with a guest bedroom so Chaz can live at home for free while he studies. Chaz has been pressuring me to go all the way sexually. So far we haven't but I'm afraid if I don't he'll forget all about me when he gets to Vancouver. Maybe I should and let him know what he'll be leaving behind. He says he loves me and will come and see me whenever he can. On top of that, A is making me uncomfortable. He stares at me all the time like his eyes are undressing me. I'm keeping my distance from him.

May 29

Dear Self,

I'm heartbroken. Chaz called me tonight to say his parents sold their house. They're moving July 1. I'm devastated. I thought we might at least have the whole summer together.

June 5

Dear Self,

Tonight is our grad dinner/dance. When Dad found out I was going with Chaz, he was furious. But I assured him Chaz was moving to Vancouver with his family so he's letting me go. But not before he gives him a lecture about his expectations. So embarrassing.

June 6

Dear Self,

Last night was so wonderful. After the dance a group of us went to the beach. We went skinny dipping. Chaz and I made love under the stars. Yup! It was exciting and a little scary. The first time it hurt a little and we went for another swim. The second time was so romantic and Chaz was so gentle. I didn't see Dad 'til dinnertime tonight. I was afraid to look him in the eye. I was sure he could tell something was different about me. That his little girl was now a woman. I'm on cloud 9.

June 15

Dear Self,

In the middle of exams. Almost done.

June 30

Dear Self,

NO MORE SCHOOL! Wednesday night we had our grad ceremony. Mom was so proud. Dad said now I have to pull my own weight.

July 05

Dear Self,

I'm heartbroken. He's gone. Every night I cry myself to sleep. We love each other and Chaz says we'll make it work. His uncle came to help them move and Chaz confided in him that he loved me. Know what he said? Listen here, nephew, never, never marry your first piece of tail. I'm so scared I'll never see him again. Mom knows I'm sad and she is trying to make me feel better. Dad is happy Chaz and his family are gone. He doesn't care about my feelings. Chaz says he'll write to me when they've settled in.

July 10
Dear Self,
I'm working part-time at the coffee shop in Stoney Creek and helping Dad on the farm. A is pissing me off. He looks at me like I'm a piece of meat. As far as I'm concerned A is for Asshole. In my spare-time, we kids go to the lake swimming. Every day I wait for Dad to pick up the mail but so far no letters.

July 15
Dear Self,
I'm so ashamed. Last night Pam and I went to the Stoney Creek Summer Fair which included a carnival. The carni that ran the ferris wheel reminded me of Chaz. He was older, maybe twenty-six or so. His name is Danny. He kept flirting with me and made me feel good about myself. When the carnival closed for the night, Pam and I were wandering around the park and he came up to us with some of the other workers. They invited us to party with them. I can't tell you how much I needed last night. But I got drunk and next thing I know Danny and I made out in his trailer. This morning he told me he's married and has kids. What a jerk! But it was my own fault. I feel like such a tramp.

August 8
Dear Self,
I couldn't find the motivation to write to you. Still no letters from Chaz. Six weeks gone. I don't even get pleasure waiting for the mail anymore. Dad says I'm moping around too much and have to forget the rich kid.

He says he's forgotten me because I'm not good enough for his family. Maybe he's right. Maybe I shouldn't have gone all the way with Chaz. Maybe I should have let him wonder what he was missing. And maybe he never loved me at all. Maybe I gave him what he wanted and Dad's right. He'll find someone richer and smarter than me at school that his parents approve. His uncle's words keep echoing in my ears: Never, never marry your first piece of tail. Is that all I am?

August 15

Okay, it's time for me to get over Chaz and get away from Stoney Creek. If he loved me it wouldn't matter if we made love or not. I enjoyed it as much as he did and sex isn't supposed to be used as a pawn. He's obviously moved on. Pam and I are talking about going to Kelowna and sharing a place together. We both want to get more schooling. I think I'd like to train as a lab technician. On Monday, I'm going to make some calls and check out student loans.

Chapter 12

A pounding on the door drew Sydney out of a deep sleep. She groaned and rolled over to see the clock. The time read nine thirty in the morning. *What?* She dragged herself out of bed and padded bare foot to the door. Jessie was standing on the stoop with two large take-out coffees.

"Sorry, Jess. I slept in."

Jessie handed her a cup and followed her back inside. "No wonder. We moved a lot of stuff into the farmhouse yesterday. But we still have time to get you out of here and make the delivery of your furniture at eleven this morning."

Sydney curled up in the easy chair and sipped her coffee. "I'm happy I was able to get most of the furniture at the same store. All I need is the right dining table to seat my residence clients. Big enough for twelve people. I want old country, something in pine. So far I've only found ones in French or Italian. Too ornate and not comfy looking. But the country style sets I've seen are too small."

"You'll find it."

Sydney powered through her coffee and stood. "I'd best get in the shower so we can get out of here."

Jessie looked around the cabin. "What's left to go from here? I'll pack up your car."

"That suitcase and the boxes by the door. Leave the overnight bag on the table. I'll finish packing it after my shower."

Thirty minutes later, Sydney checked out of the cabin and headed to the farmhouse with Jessie following her. Bubbling over with excitement, she couldn't wait to get in and start setting up the rooms. The farmhouse renos were complete inside and the crew were now working on the residence building. She parked off to one side of the driveway and Jessie followed behind her, leaving room for the delivery truck to park by the porch steps. Sydney climbed out of the car.

Jax rounded the opposite side of the farmhouse with a wave and a huge grin. "Welcome home."

"Hey. I can't believe I'm here for good."

He joined the girls at the rear of Sydney's car to help carry in the boxes. Sydney climbed the stairs to the porch carrying a suitcase. She stopped and sniffed the air. "Is that smell of smoke coming from the Washington State fire?"

Jax pointed to the southwest. "Yup, the Cascades fire. The winds changed direction and the smoke is funneling right through the valley. It's still ten miles south of the Canadian border but there are concerns about it heading our way.

Sydney followed his gaze. In the far distance she could see what looked like smog covering the tops of the hills. "We're only about ten miles from the border. That's scary."

"There's a community meeting in town tonight at the community hall. The fire officials were in Osoyoos last night."

Jessie passed them both carrying a box. "I guess we better go to it then."

Sydney followed her. She got busy unpacking her clothes and putting her toiletries in the bathroom. She'd tried to shake off the unease she felt about the fire. Once the delivery truck arrived with her furniture, all else was forgotten. She and Jessie had already decided where each piece should go and the delivery men had the living room done in no time. The men even set the beds up for her. Jax and his crew had installed the window blinds and draperies yesterday.

The girls spent the next thirty minutes in her Nan's bedroom making the bed and rearranging dressers until they were satisfied with the look.

"Your Nan is going to love this room. The greens warm up the room and that white electric fireplace opposite the bed is such a cosy touch."

Sydney took in the whole room, from the white pine furniture, to the slate green walls with the jade sea grass wall paper behind the headboard. Her gaze fell on the window. "I had Jax build a bench in the bay window and the olive green cushion and throw pillows will give her a place to sit and read. But in case she doesn't like the bench, I bought the easy chair." They'd set it up beside the window so her Nan could look out the window or look at the fireplace." Sydney smiled and nodded her head in satisfaction.

"Let's go outside and eat the picnic lunch I brought. Then we'll go create your room. I haven't even seen what you bought for the master bedroom," Jessie said.

They ate by the lake but didn't dally. In no time, they were back in the house and busy at work. An hour later they were finished in the master bedroom. This room was a dream.

"I love the old country flavour. What do you call this bedroom set?" Jessie asked.

"It's pioneer in burnished pine. The donkey beige shade is perfect."

The walls were painted champagne. The headboard wall was done in a burnt orange.

"I have to hand it to you. When you told me plum and orange were your colours…ouch. I couldn't see it. But the headboard covers most of the burnt orange wall. And the deep plum bedspread with some burnt orange throw pillows, and abstract plums and beiges…wow! Your room is a showcase piece."

"Thanks. It took me forever to find the field stone fireplace. I didn't want white or the dark wood. The beige stone is perfect. All I need are some paintings for the walls, otherwise both bedrooms are done."

They headed to the kitchen. As they passed the empty middle bedroom, Jessie stopped. "What are you doing with this room?"

"It's going to be a guest bedroom."

"Great idea."

Jessie and Sydney went to tackle the kitchen next. By dinnertime they were finished with the kitchen and bathrooms. They were relaxing in Sydney's new living room when Jax joined them.

"Wow…this looks inviting. Mind if I wander around and see what you've done?"

"Fill your boots. But you're on your own. We're resting our tired feet.," Sydney said.

A few minutes later, he was back and sat on the fireplace hearth. "Don't want to sit on the new furniture in my work clothes. I love what you're doing with the place. It's really coming together."

"You gave me something awesome to work with. We're a great team." With that said, Sydney and Jax held each other's gaze long enough that Jessie cleared her throat and broke through the silence. "Earth to star gazers."

Sydney blushed and Jax laughed. "We're cutting it short today so we can all attend the fire meeting. I was going to order pizza as a congratulatory gesture; your first night in your new home and all that but we don't have time."

"Aw…nice gesture though," Sydney said.

Jax stood. "I need to get home and shower. I'll see you at the hall at eight o'clock."

"We'll be there," Sydney said. She watched him leave the house and turned to Jessie who was studying her with a raised eyebrow. "What?"

"You two. Something's going on with you both."

"No there isn't." Sydney gave her a defiant stare.

"Oh come on. Jax has never looked at a girl the way he looks at you. Mr. 'Play it Cool' and you, Miss 'I Don't Want a Relationship' are into each other."

"I don't want to complicate my life and he only likes me because I haven't jumped into bed with him yet. I have no intention of being another one of his girls."

"Brian told me he caught you two kissing the other week. Don't you dare try to deny it."

Sydney opened her mouth and promptly shut it. She didn't know what to say.

Jessie laughed. "I think the two of you are in over your heads. You just don't know it yet. It's bigger than you both of you. You'll see."

"It? What does that mean…it?"

Jessie shrugged. "Love, romance, lust…you'll know soon enough."

Sydney stood and stretched her aching legs. *Time to change the subject.* 'I'm going to shower in my new en suite. You can use the main bathroom if you like. Shall we eat in town before the meeting?"

"Sure." Jessie yelled out as Sydney headed to the bedroom. "But remember, you can't wash away those sinful thoughts."

Sydney thought about that as she undressed and smiled to herself. *Good thing Jess can't read my thoughts.*

Chapter 13

The community hall was full. There weren't enough seats for everyone and people stood at the back of the hall and along the sides. There was an information table with brochures by the entranceway that supplied contact numbers for residents in case of evacuation, fire reporting numbers, as well as locations to house evacuees. Enlarged Washington State maps were pinned on the back wall showing the fire's current location. Local area maps were posted marking potential evacuation order locations. To Sydney's surprise, an area just south of the Canada/US border was marked 'Evacuated'.

Sydney and Jessie searched for a place to sit without any luck. They spotted Jax about halfway up the hall. He waved to them and pointed at two seats he was saving and they pushed their way through the crowd of people to join him.

"Thanks, Jax. We would have been standing if you hadn't saved us a place," Sydney said.

"No problem."

She looked around the room. "Is your father here tonight?"

"No, he's in Kelowna on business."

The meeting was called to order. Six people sat at a long table angled to the side at the front of the hall. A screen had been pulled down on the stage directly ahead of them.

A woman stood with a hand mike. "I'm Mayor Givens. I'd like to thank you all for coming tonight. First, I want to introduce everyone here at the table. At the far end, is our local Provincial MLA (Member of the Legislature), Jonathan Brown. Then we have Donna Parsons, Director of the Stoney Creek ESS (Emergency Social Services), Next to Donna is Gordon Summit, the Fire Protection Officer from the Kamloops Fire Centre. Beside Gordon is Kathleen Cunningham, the Fire Information Officer and next to me, Staff Sergeant Roger Reynolds of the Stoney Creek RCMP Detachment (Royal Canadian Mounted Police). Each of us will fill you in on the role we'll play during the current situation. First up is Gordon Summit, our Fire Protection Officer."

"Good evening. I'm the Fire Protection Office in charge of operations here in the valley. What we'd like to do tonight is fill you in on the status of the Cascade Fire in Washington and how that has affected us here in Canada thus far, as well as possible future expectations. If someone could turn the lights down, I'd like to do a slide presentation."

The room darkened and he began. "This is a map of the fire, like the one on the back wall. This fire has been burning for three weeks and due to high winds and mountainous terrain making it difficult to reach by ground crews, it is still uncontained. The rings around the fire shows the expansion of the fire since it originated at this point. Our concern is the northern side of the fire. At the moment it is ten miles south of the Canadian border. Winds have changed direction and it is heading towards British Columbia. If it crosses into BC it will be an interface fire." He changed the slide to a southern British Columbia map. "Should the fire continue to move our way, this local map shows predicted Emergency Evacuation Alerts by area. I want to reference this section west of Osoyoos. It isn't largely populated as it is mainly farms and vineyards. Because of the sudden directional change of the fire, this area was evacuated today." A murmur could be heard around the hall. "The town of Osoyoos has been placed on Evacuation Alert. Should the fire jump the border and continue northeast on its course, Stoney Creek will be next on an Evacuation Alert. Once an Evacuation Alert is put in place, each home will be visited by a triage group. This group looks at roofing materials, out buildings, etc. to determine the most strategic places to set up sprinklers and hoses to protect the town should the fire approach. Rural properties will also be evaluated. At the moment we are set up here in the hall and are available at any time. Our information officer, Kathleen will provide the Mayor and RCMP Staff Sergeant with updated information on a daily basis. She is your liaison. You are welcome to call into a designated number here at the hall or stop in to see her. We will also be posting information on our website which is listed in the brochure. I'll be travelling back and forth between Stoney Creek and Osoyoos daily. Once we have all spoken here tonight, we'll open the meeting up for questions. I'd like to introduce the EMS co-ordinator, Donna Parsons."

Donna stood and addressed the hall. "Good evening everyone. The evacuees from the eastern locale are currently being housed in Osoyoos. Should Osoyoos be evacuated at some point, this hall will provide emergency housing along with the town of Oliver. And in the event that Stoney Creek residents are evacuated, Penticton will be setting up housing locations. I'm available at any time either here in the hall or through the EMP number to address any concerns or answer questions you may have. Should you decide to stay with family elsewhere, we ask that you register here before you leave. In case of evacuation, we need to know that you are safe."

The Provincial MLA spoke to the crowd about emergency funds available in the event of evacuation and in the case of lost homes. The RCMP Staff Sergeant informed the public that they would be calling in additional staff from neighbouring detachments and knocking on all doors should an evacuation be called. He stressed the importance of leaving when ordered to. And if anyone chose to stay behind, they were restricted to their residences. "If you leave your residence at any time you will not be allowed to return." He paused and stared around the room. I'll be very candid here and say that if you decide to ignore the evacuation order, please write your name on your arm with a permanent marker for identification purposes." That brought about an intended reaction of shocked murmurs from the crowd.

The meeting was opened up for questions and the mayor closed it out.

"I just want to add that you can stop into city hall or call at any time if you have questions should the EMP and Fire Centre phones be busy. The last thing I'd like to address is there was the smell of smoke in town today and I understand those living west of town were particularly subjected to smoke filling the valley. It may worsen. I urge anyone who has breathing problems, seniors and those with young babies to consider leaving the area for awhile. You can stop in at the medical centre and discuss any issues you have with our local nurse. And talk to the EMP co-ordinator. We will be holding fire update meetings about every five days here at the hall unless there is an urgency to meet sooner . Check our website, watch the bulletin boards and pass it on to your neighbours. Don't forget to pick up the brochures on your way out. Some are very helpful on what to pack in case of evacuation, For those of you with animals that would need moving, get your name on the list and talk to the Animal Bylaw Officer. Thank you and good night."

"Here's hoping the fire doesn't border jump," Jax said, raising his beer glass. Everyone at the table murmured agreement and clicked glasses. Sydney had joined Jax and Jessie at a local pub after the meeting, Some of their friends had come in and they'd pushed a few tables together.

Sydney observed the group. It was nice to meet some new people around her own age, in spite of the circumstances that brought them together. They appeared to be a great bunch and included her in their midst like she was one of them. They discussed what to pack in case of an evacuation.

Jax pulled a notepad out of his jacket pocket. "Some of the elderly living independently will need some help if they have to leave their properties. And some of them have animals to be moved."

A list was made of the people they knew of and the names split between them. The plan was to visit them all in the next few days and assess their needs should they be forced to leave their properties. They'd taken extra brochures from the hall to give their charges. Sydney asked to accompany Jessie. She didn't want to approach any of them on her own. As a stranger to them, they might be suspicious of her and Sydney knew they would already be on edge and fearful of leaving their properties. She certainly was.

The conversation turned to some lighthearted kibitzing and laughter. The pub was full of people who had attended the meetings, and the synergy was electric. Sydney relaxed and joined in with the group.

"Did you drive into town in your own car?" Jax asked as they were all leaving.

'No. I came in with Jess."

"Do you want a drive home?"

"I'm crashing at Jess' place tonight. But thanks for the offer."

"All right. How about I pick you up at seven. We can have breakfast and I'll take you back to the farm with me."

"Sounds good. See you in the morning." She watched him leave with a couple of male friends, jostling and laughing like teenage boys.

Sydney turned to Jessie who was grinning at her. She leaned into Sydney and whispered in her ear. "Bigger than both of you."

"Stop it. I have to get home somehow." She gave Jessie a glare. "Come on, let's go."

Chapter 14

The week flew by. Sydney and Jessie visited several seniors who lived rurally to educate them on the wildfire and added names to a central list of people who needed help with animals and leaving their properties. All of them were very appreciative that there were people in the community who would come to their aid. The ones who'd lived most of their lives on their acreages were more concerned about the loss of a way of life. Some whose mortgages were paid up years ago, had let their insurance lapse. This was bad. The local insurance company scrambled to provide policies that week to make sure people had coverage. Should the fire jump the border into Canada, the insurers knew the underwriters would refuse coverage on any new policies until the fire was contained.

Sydney was one of those who needed to scramble. She had received inspection approval to move into the upgraded farmhouse and renewed the insurance in her name with the improvements. But the insurance company could only insure the equipment building as it was until the building inspector approved it as a residence. Jax took documents and pictures of the upgrades to the insurer and they allowed for the work done thus far even without the inspector's final occupancy approval. At least it was something.

She sat on the branch of the magnolia tree musing about the past few months. Jax was almost finished with the residence. The new water pipes and sewage pipes had been run to the city line and connected.

Imagine—city water. Her area had been taken into the Stoney Creek Tax Base five years previous. That meant any new buildings had to be connected to the city line. The farmhouse had been grandfathered on septic and well water but Sydney decided in the process to close the well and connect the house to city water and city sewage. Since the old plumbing in the house was being replaced anyway, it was cheaper to do the whole job with the city inspector involved now rather than later.

Jax would be done with the interior of the residence soon and all that was left to do included the exterior painting of all the buildings and landscaping. A smile spread across her face. She was content here and knew she'd fit into the lifestyle easily. *Hell, I all ready have.*

A sudden breeze brought a fresh cloud of smoke through the air, burning her eyes. She looked south at the haze and sighed. Her mood changed. *What if I lose it all in a fire? Would it be worth starting all over again?*

"Hey—you all right up there?"

Sydney looked down to see Jax at the base of the tree.

"Of course. This is my happy place. Wanna join me?"

Jax climbed up to the branch and Sydney wiggled over to make room.

"You didn't look too happy when I walked up."

Sydney laughed. "Actually, I was until that last few minutes when the smoke blew in. Thank god for air conditioning in the house. I was thinking about how close we are to the finish line and then it hit me. What if I lose this whole place to the fire? It's really a scary thought."

Jax took a hold of her hand. "If that were to happen, you'd start over. You're insured. I know it must sound exhausting now, but think of the fun we'd have building a new farmhouse without the restrictions of the old one."

Sydney looked at Jax with sad eyes. "But I like the old farmhouse; a new one wouldn't be the same."

"Then we would duplicate it exactly as you have it now. We'll make it look old but new just like this one."

She saw the sparkle in his eye and smiled. "You do love these projects, don't you?"

Jax stared deep into her eyes. "I wouldn't want to do anything else."

The moment was theirs. He bent down and kissed her. A soft brushing kiss at first. His tongue spread her lips and she pushed back, lost in a series of frantic kisses that left them both breathless.

Jax pulled back and spoke in a low, raspy voice. "The wind has come up stronger. Are we out of breath because of our passion or because we're sucking in smoke?"

They giggled like kids and kissed again. Finally, Jax moved towards the trunk. "Let's go in the house. This isn't healthy."

"Our passion or the smoke?"

"I'll let you know—in the house." Jax climbed down and put his arms up to help Sydney down when she reached the bottom.

They hurried to the house, happy to breath the fresh cool air. Sydney poured them both a glass of water and they sat beside each other on the stools at the kitchen island.

"When I saw the wind was coming up, I sent the boys home a little early. They've been working in this smoke far too long."

"I feel bad for them. No one should be breathing in the smoke that much. I have a new respect for the firefighters."

"Me too. Look, we may have to delay the exterior painting and deck work until the fire is done. There's ash on everything and I don't want it in the finishing touches."

"Makes sense."

"My father has projects in other areas he can send the workmen to. And they'll be smoke free."

Their eyes locked. "What about you? What great project is next for you?" Sydney asked.

Jax frowned. "I'm not sure. My father is expanding the commercial side of the business. That's why he's spending a lot of time in the central Okanagan. He wants to phase out the residential side of the business which leaves me in a dilemma." He filled her in on his father's plans and expectations where his son was concerned. "He let me do this project with the understanding we'd re-evaluate when it's finished."

This time Sydney took a hold of Jax hand. "You have to listen to your own heart. Follow your gut. That's what I had to do when I made the decision to come back to the farm and leave Nan in Kelowna."

"I know you're right but that will hurt my father. But years ago my dad hurt his father and never looked back. I have to be as tough as he was then. I'm hoping he'll help me set up my own company here in Stoney Creek. If not, I'll figure it out, even if I have to run a one man show."

"Then I'd say you've made your decision. And if my opinion matters, I think it's the right one."

Jax stood and put his hands on her shoulders. "Of course your opinion matters. And so do you."

Sydney was in his arms in an instant. Their frantic kisses led them to an instant passion that took them beyond the need for slow foreplay. Jax hands moved all over her body, stroking her breasts and down over her buttocks, while Sydney's hands rubbed his chest. One hand moved down to the swollen member in his jeans. They both fumbled with each other's jean snaps and zippers until they gave up, and raced amidst laughter at a frantic pace to remove their own clothes. "Hang on, one second." Sydney ran out of the room and came back. She handed Jax a condom. He eased her to the floor, his eyes never leaving hers. Sydney raised her hips to meet his heat. "Hurry," she whispered. He entered her and took her to a place she'd never been before. They quickly ascended to the edge of orgasm and released together. They laid in a heap on the floor, gasping for breath.

Sydney stood and grabbed his hand. She led him down the hallway and into her private bathroom. They showered together, washing each other's body, exploring as they did. They took turns drying each other. Jax led Sydney over to the bed and this time, their lovemaking was slow, methodical, aimed to please. Jax knew how to touch her and tease her. He moved from her breasts slowly down her body, touching every inch of her with his hands or his tongue. By the time he reached her sweet spot, Sydney was writhing with need and rolled over on top of him. She eased herself onto his manhood and slowly pivoted her hips until joined together as one, Jax rolled them over so he was once again on top. Their thrusts became rapid and continued until Jax gasped: "I'm coming." Sydney murmured: "I'm ready". They burst together in climax, falling onto their backs, gasping for air.

Jax rolled onto his side and touched her cheek. "Syd? Are you crying?"

She rolled over to face him and giggled. "Tears of joy. Wow. I've never felt what you just made me feel. You took me there and beyond."

Jax leaned forward and kissed the tip of her nose. "I'm glad you're pleased. You were pretty incredible yourself you know. I've been wanting to do this with you the first day we met."

"I know."

He pushed up on his elbow. "You did? How?"

"Your eyes gave you away."

"Really? So did you feel the same way?"

"God no. You were too cocky and self-assured. That may work on the other girls in your life but not on me."

"You're a diva. So when did you want to jump all over my bones and do sweet things to me?"

"About an hour ago." Sydney laughed. "If you could see your face right now."

"I call bullshit. I've caught you checking me out and so have my boys."

Sydney frowned. "You and your boys talked about me?"

"Not about this. But your eyes have given you away too. And more than an hour ago."

"Okay, cowboy. I'll admit to it but I wasn't sure about it until now."

Jax rolled onto his back and pulled Sydney into his Side. "What do you say we shower again, faster this time, and head to the Rattlesnake Grill? I'm starving."

"Okay. I'll follow you in. So you don't have to bring me back."

"But what if I want to come back and make sweet love to you?"

"Mmm... aren't you the stud. No staying over on work nights. I don't want to suffer the looks of your men in the morning when they discover you slept here."

"Maybe I came to work early."

"They're not stupid, Jax. You've already proven that."

"Okay, we'll do it your way. But don't expect me not to show you affection in front of them. They'll figure it out pretty quick—because lady, we're just getting started."

Jax and Sydney walked hand in hand to her car parked behind his truck. They'd had a wonderful dinner full of laughter and stolen kisses when they thought others weren't looking. Not that Jax cared who saw. He was happy. There was something about this girl that was different. People said he was fickle. *I guess I have been—but Sydney? No way.*

"Here we are." Sydney let go of his hand to pull her keys out of her bag. She hit the unlock button and turned to Jax.

He kissed her on the forehead. "I don't want to say good-night. Look, Syd...I don't know what this is but I sure want to find out. You're special."

Sydney smiled and tussled his hair. "Me too. Come for coffee in the morning before you start work. Okay?"

Jax pulled her into his arms and kissed her. She lay her head on his shoulder and they hugged tight.

"I'll be there. Good night," Jax said.

He got into his truck and waited for her to pull out and make a u-turn. He watched in his rear-view mirror until her headlights disappeared. He didn't see a man standing in the shadows across the street—watching. He started his truck and headed to the gas station to gas up. *Rather do it now than in the morning.*

Jax left the station and five minutes later pulled into his driveway. When he got up to his stoop, his father was waiting for him. "Dad? What's up?" He put the key in the lock and opened the door, flipping the light on in the hallway.

"We need to talk, son."

Jax looked at his father and frowned. After what had transpired tonight, the last thing he wanted to do was talk business. "Now? Can't it wait until morning? I can come by the office before I go to work.

His father pushed past him into the hall. He faced Jax. "No. We need to do this now."

Jax weighed the grave expression on his father's face and shrugged. "Okay. Want a beer?"

"Do you have any scotch?"

Chapter 15

Sydney awoke with a start to the sound of the alarm. She reached out and hit the stop button and rolled over to the other side. Pulling the pillow into her stomach, she could smell Jax. Her eyes popped open at the memory of their lovemaking the day before. *Wow! Did I actually do that?* She smiled.

She should have been euphoric. After all, it was invigorating, exciting—incredible. But she had a nagging feeling deep in her gut. Sydney got up and went into the shower. The feeling wouldn't leave even after she'd dried off and dressed. She padded out to the kitchen and hit the start button on the coffee pot. *Something's wrong.* These feelings weren't to be ignored. She'd had them her whole life. Call it psychic, organic, whatever you like. Whenever Sydney felt a tight, unease as intense as this that grew from deep inside her, things happened. And they were never good. The frustrating thing was that she never knew what to expect. The waiting was the worst; the wondering about how bad it would be and when the news would come. She glanced at the clock, shocked at how long she'd been sitting there. *Where was Jax? He was coming for coffee.*

Sydney heard the workers arriving. *No Jax.* She poured herself a coffee and moved to the living room. A few minutes later, a knock came at the door. She swung the door open surprised to see the two people standing on her porch.

"Good morning."

One of them stepped forward. "Hi, are you Sydney Grey?"

"I am."

"I'm Gordon Summit, the Fire Protection Officer for this area and this is Mayor Cindy Givens."

"Yes, I know who you are. I was at the fire meeting. Come in." She led them into the living room. "Would you like some coffee? It's made."

"Not for me," Gordon Summit said.

The Mayor smiled. "I'd love one please. A little milk?"

"Please, sit. I'll be right back." Sydney topped her own cup and returned with both coffees.

"Thank you," Mayor Givens said. "I love what you've done here. This room is beautiful."

'Thanks. I'm pleased with the results. Rhyder Contracting really came through." Sydney sat down. "What can I do for you?"

"The fire has jumped the border. It's heading northeast at the moment. More people have been evacuated between Osoyoos and the previously evacuated area."

"Omigod...that's terrible." *Here it was, the cause of my 'gut feeling'*. She hadn't been kept waiting long.

"We're opening the Community Hall in Stoney Creek to house them. Which means the Fire Control Centre personnel need a new area to set up. Your place was recommended. We understand you have a studio upstairs that we could utilize as an office for our daily meetings and a residence that could house some of our personnel. You have a huge meadow that could hold tents for our firefighters. The Fire Centre will pay you for all of this."

Sydney looked at the Mayor. "But I'm still in the renovation stage. I don't have my final building inspection. Legally, I can't set up for business."

"That's why I'm here. And the building inspector," Mayor Givens said. "He's with the Rhyder employees inspecting the residence. If he deems it useable, he'll issue a temporary approval and we'll get you a business licence."

She turned back to the Fire Protection Officer. “So how would all this work?”

“We’ll set up portable bathrooms and showers for the firefighters tenting outside. We’ll supply the tents and bedding and garbage bins.”

“I do have bedding for the residence and towels for the showers, but I haven’t bought the furniture for the bedrooms yet.”

“Not a problem. The Fire Centre can supply cots. If you can supply the sheets and pillows, we’ll bring the blankets. We aren’t looking for four-star rooms.”

Sydney stood. “Would you like to see the upstairs?”

“Please.”

The three of them climbed the stairs to the studio.

“This is perfect. I see you’ve utilized the old wood flooring. Beautiful,” Gordon said. “You’ve put a lot of money and effort into the renovations here. Understand that we will return your property to you exactly as we found it. Any damage done to anything, and that includes the property outside, will be fixed and paid for by the Fire Centre. I don’t want you to have any worries there.”

The Mayor added, “The town will provide eight foot tables and chairs for up here.”

They left the house and walked towards the residence. “How many did you want to house? And what about food?” Sydney asked.

Gordon addressed her questions. “The firefighters are on an allowance. They’ll eat in town. As for the administrative personnel, there would be myself, our information officer, and a couple of staffers full-time. The MLA would come and go, and a few from Kamloops when needed. Let’s say four permanents and three part-timers. Can you provide meals for us, or would you rather we eat in town as well?”

Sydney laughed. “You wouldn’t want to eat my cooking but if you prefer to eat in the dining room and the Fire Centre will include the cost of me hiring a cook, it could work.”

“Done, we work long, unpredictable hours sometimes. It would be nice to work, eat, and sleep in one place,” Gordon said.

"I'm still searching for a table that will seat my guests when I'm open and operating." Sydney addressed the Mayor. "Can the town provide an extra table and chairs for my dining room as well."

"We could do that," Mayor Givens said.

They joined the building inspector in the residence. The shower rooms and the laundry area were complete. It was the bedrooms that were left to finish. The walls had been painted but the floors were bare wood. The baseboard moldings weren't yet installed, nor around the windows. The cupboards had no doors.

"These rooms may be unfinished but they are liveable," Tim LeFavre, the Building Inspector said. "I have no problem issuing the permit. But I suggest when the public works boys bring out the tables and chairs, they also supply some barricades. There's going to be a lot of vehicles parked on this property and you need to block off where the underground pipes run. You don't want any one parking on them."

"Good," Mayor Givens said.

Sydney shook her head. "There's so much to consider, I'm glad you all know what you're doing."

"Okay then. What do say, Miss Grey? Are you willing to let us invade your life?"

"It's Sydney. When did you want to set up?"

"As soon as possible. I'll return to town and get Kamloops to fax me a contract. I'll be back before lunch. And if you approve and we get you signed up, we'll return to start setting up this afternoon."

"All right. I'll be here."

After they left, Sydney sat at the kitchen counter with pen and paper. There were still some items she'd need to pull this off. She wrote them down while they were fresh in her mind. When she finished, she thought about Jax. She hadn't seen him out back with his men. Her gut ached and her hand unconsciously moved to her stomach. Intuitively, Sydney knew the fire was just the beginning. It wasn't over. *There's more coming.*

She went searching for Brian, the Foreman. She found him in the back yard, cutting molding. "Busy place this morning," he said.

"Hey, Brian. Do you know why Jax isn't here today?"

"He's gone to Kelowna on business for his father."

"Oh? Do you know when he's coming back?"

"He's not."

"What's that mean...he's not?

Brian shrugged. "All I know is his father called me this morning and said he was sending Jax out of town indefinitely and as Foreman, I was to finish up this project."

Sydney felt like someone had punched her in the stomach. *Sure something could have come up in Kelowna he needed to deal with. But he could have called her.* Her senses told her there was more to it.

"Can I help you with something else?" Brian asked.

Sydney focused on the issue at hand. Jax would have to wait.

"Uh...yes. If the Fire Centre people do set up here, I guess we'll be suspending the rest of the work until after the fire."

"Makes sense. Besides, when they start setting up fire breaks, they'll probably hire Rhyder Contracting and our equipment to work for them. We've done it in the past and they'll need some of us there."

"Okay. They're bringing me a contract to sign later this morning. If it's satisfactory, you'll probably finish up then. But I'm wondering if I could use you and a couple of the guys to help me get some things needed to set up? Like a washer and dryer for the residence. Jax was going to provide them later but I need them now."

"I know where he gets them. We could do that."

"I'll need some shower curtains for the shower rooms, a couple of eight food table clothes for the dining room. I don't care what they are or where you get them, thrift store or dollar store, whatever. They'll work for now."

"Gotcha'."

"And if someone could use the vac to clean up the residence. I'll scrub out the shower rooms. Oh, I need five blinds for the bedroom windows. Again, I don't care what they are. I can replace them later. I've got a list you can pick up before you go."

"No need, we have them in stock. Jax already ordered them in. When we go back to town to fill your list, we'll pick them up at the shop. And don't worry about the shower rooms. We'll scrub them up. I'm sure you have a lot of other things to do."

Sydney smiled. "You guys are awesome. I really appreciate this."

"We aim to please. You've been a dream customer, Sydney. We've all enjoyed working for you."

"Not for me, with me."

Chapter 16

Sydney returned to the house and her list. But her mind couldn't focus. Her body felt heavy and dragged down to the point that her bones ached. *Why is this all-consuming feeling of dread continuing? Enough all ready. It's about Jax and the fire. I'll deal with it. Go away.* Once again her intuitive power took over. *Wrong!* She couldn't shake the feeling that the worst hadn't happened yet. *Okay, so things happen in threes. Bring it on.*

She got back to work on her list. The next thing she needed to do was find a cook. *I don't know any. Who will? Jessie maybe.* But she was at work at the hospital in Oliver. *Jessie's mother?* Sydney looked up the phone number and gave Nancy Farrow a call.

"Hello?"

"Hi, Mrs. Farrow. It's Sydney Grey. How are you?"

"I'm well, dear. I hear you're pretty busy setting up the farmhouse. It must be getting close."

"It is and I'm really looking forward to having it done. Did you hear about the fire crossing into Canada?"

"I have and it's scary."

"It certainly is. The reason I'm calling is to ask if you know of a cook I might hire short-term. Someone who does camp-style cooking. The Fire Centre is leasing my place to set up because the Community Hall is now a refuge for evacuees. I need someone to cook meals for about four to seven people."

"Hmmm… You know there is a widow, Beatrice Gurka. She recently retired from full-time work and does part-time catering. I'll bet she'd love the work. When she was younger, she and her husband catered logging camps in the Okanagan."

"She sounds perfect."

"Hang on while I get her number for you. She isn't listed."

Sydney heard Mrs. Farrow put the phone down. When she returned and gave her the number, Sydney thanked her. A few minutes later, she'd booked an interview with Mrs. Gurka for one o'clock. *Another thing off the list.*

An hour later, the Fire Protection Officer was back with a contract.

"Wow that was quick." She invited him into the kitchen, made fresh coffee and sat down to read the paper. "This is more than generous and covers it all." She signed the contract and its copy, smiled and held out her hand. "We have a deal, Mr. Summit."

"Not until you call me Gord."

"Gord it is."

Gord reached into his briefcase and handed her a cheque and a brown envelope. "Here's some money in advance. I'm sure you need some operating capital to get set-up quickly."

Sydney raised her eyebrows. "Thank you."

"We aren't going anywhere for awhile and we want you to be happy."

She picked up the envelope. "What's in this?"

"That's a temporary inspection approval and a business license. The town says you can settle up with them later."

She rose and got Gord a coffee. "Were you planning on sleeping here tonight?"

"If the truck arrives from Kamloops with our cots and blankets. Don't worry about feeding us today."

"I have a lady coming shortly who might work out as a cook. I'll let you know."

Gord gulped down his coffee. "Okay. I'm off. We'll be back this afternoon to set up upstairs. Oh, there will be two helicopters working the east side of the fire. They'll be using the Osoyoos lakes to fill their buckets. A third one will be spot checking the north side on his own. We'd like him to refill in your lake. He can come and go without worrying about the other guys. He's fuelling up in Osoyoos and should be here shortly for his first fill."

Sydney felt overwhelmed. She knew the activity level was about to hit mega proportions. "Uh...I'd better get Brian and the boys to switch hats. No more project work for now. They're going shopping for me for a washing machine and dryer for the residence laundry and a whole list of other things."

"Then I'm out of your hair."

She walked Gord to the door and followed him outside.

"I'm glad we found this place. It will really make things central for us." Gord paused, appearing to study her face. "And don't stress about any of it. It'll all come together. We'll help you out. Believe me, we've done this too many times than we'd like to remember."

"Thank you. See you later."

Sydney headed around the side of the house to fill Brian in on the latest news. Brian called the men together and gave them their orders to cease work. They put away their tools and cleared up their work area in case the Fire Centre needed the space. Then they headed to the residence to make it occupancy-ready.

Sydney returned to the house to regroup. Mrs. Gurka arrived and Sydney filled her in on what was needed.

"So what are you asking of me? You want me to assist you in the kitchen? Do you want me to stay over or only be here for dinners?

Sydney was horrified. "Heavens no, Beatrice. I'm a lousy cook. I need a take-charge person to run the whole thing. The kitchen is yours, along with the buying of the supplies, the meal planning, and the cooking. I want someone to take it off my hands and run the show with no interference from me. I could be your assistant though, if you need one. I'll help with the cleanup and such."

The woman's head went back along with her shoulders and she grinned from ear to ear. "In that case, I'm your woman…and call me Bea. When do need me to start?"

Sydney looked pained. "Yesterday?"

'Here's what I'd like. If you have a room for me, I'll move right in today. These guys keep weird hours. Sometimes they'll skip meals and want mug-up and snacks at all hours."

Sydney let out a sigh. "Let me think. I have a room but… " She leaned on her elbow and placed a hand over her mouth. "Okay, forget that for the moment." She grabbed a piece of paper and wrote down a figure. "I'm thinking a flat rate contract that includes the cost of supplies. This amount is for one week to be extended as needed." She slid the paper over to Bea.

The woman's eyes shot open. "Holy cow, woman. That's a lot of money."

"The government is paying for all of this. They've been more than generous to me and you deserve the same."

"Done."

"I don't have any cash on me, and I can't leave here. I'll give you a cheque to cover the first week. You can cash it in town today and pick up some groceries. By the way, you get paid for a full week at a time regardless of when the job ends."

"I'll be back in a few hours, in time to make a dinner for those who'll be here and that includes you by the way. You can feed off of this too."

Sydney laughed. "I'm looking forward to some home-cooked meals."

Bea looked around the kitchen. "And I'm looking forward to working in this beautiful state-of-the-art kitchen. Do you mind if I look around in the drawers and such? I may want to bring some of my favourite pots and utensils with me."

"Absolutely. Look away. I'm so glad I found you Bea. You've lifted a lot of stress off of my shoulders."

Bea patted her arm as she wandered around, lost to her own thoughts of pots and equipment.

Sydney settled on the couch with her feet up to enjoy a few minutes of peace. Probably her last for awhile. Bea had left to run her errands and any minute she expected the fire administrators to arrive. Her thoughts went to the Rhyder crew. She snickered. *Poor Brian.* When they came to pick up her shopping list, she'd added a single bed, a dresser and a lamp for Bea. Again, she told Brian she didn't care what it was as long as they were clean and looked nice. The spare bedroom was still empty and something held her back from giving Bea her Nan's bedroom. She also gave him the spare building keys and asked him to make some copies. She was asking a lot but if they split the jobs up between them, they'd get it all done that afternoon. Once they'd left, she'd gone out to the residence and placed the sheets, pillows and spare towels in the cupboards in the laundry room. She made sure there were piles of towels and soap in the shower rooms as well. She placed some linen, blankets and a pillow in the closet of the spare bedroom for Bea.

She'd had all of ten minutes to rest when she heard the trucks arrive and she went to the door to greet them. Gord told her the cots were on their way and would arrive that evening. Sydney took him out to the residence to show him where the linens were stored in the residence and that the showers were ready for use.

She also told them she'd hired a cook and dinner would be served.

Gord grinned. "See I told you, it would all work out. Look what you've accomplished since we left."

Sydney stood back to let the first of the Fire Crew head up the stairs with boxes. Two of the public works crew came in carrying two eight foot tables. She led them to the dining room and they opened one table. One of the men turned to her.

"We'll set this on up against the wall just in case you need another one. And we'll leave a pile of chairs in the corner over there." He pointed to the corner by the French doors.

"That's wonderful. Thank you."

As the organized chaos unfolded her cell phone rang. Sydney ran to the kitchen and stared at it on the counter. The call display read *Interior Health.* Her gut tightened with fearful dread. She knew. *This is it! The third incident that will change my world. This is the bad one!*

Sydney reached for the phone and put it slowly to her ear. "Hello?"

"Is this Sydney Grey?"

"Yes it is." The next words hit her skull like a jack hammer in an echo chamber.

"This is the Kelowna General Hospital. I'm afraid your grandmother, Elizabeth Grey has had an accident."

Chapter 17

Sydney sat in the waiting room while Jessie went to get them some coffee. Her Nan was in surgery. She'd tripped on the stairs and broken her ankle. Having Jess with her was a godsend. When the hospital called, they told her it would be a few hours before they could get her into surgery to reset the bone. They had her on morphine and she was resting comfortably.

Jessie returned with the coffee.

"Thank you. I'm so grateful I caught you as you got home from work. It means a lot having you here with me. I just spoke to Brian. Everyone's settled in, Bea's bedroom is all set up and she made them all a wonderful dinner of lasagne, Caesar salad and garlic bread. Tomorrow the fire crew arrive with their tents."

"I told you they'd be fine. The Fire Centre guys have been through this over and over. They know what to do. And Bea sounds like a find."

"She sure is. I had Brian copy new house keys and residence keys. He gave one to Bea and one to Gord and another to Kathleen, the Fire Information Officer. They're on their own until we get back." Sydney leaned back and put her head against the wall. "Damn, Jess. It's been one hell of a day."

"That it has. All we have to do now is get your Nan out of here and back to the farm."

"She's going to protest but there's no way around it. I can't stay here with all those people living at my place. And Nan can't stay alone initially."

"I'm scheduled off work for a week. I asked for it when the fire status changed. I'll be able to help you with your Nan. After all I am a nurse."

Sydney turned her head towards Jessie. "You really are a good friend, Jess. I owe you."

Jessie frowned at her. "I'll take the compliment but friends don't owe each other. A true friend is there when it counts."

She reached out for Jessie's hand and squeezed it tight. "I hate having her live so far from me. The first time I'm off on my own and boom, she's in trouble."

"Stop it. You're feeling guilty and that's ridiculous. Your grandmother isn't an old senior you abandoned to take care of herself. She's in her early sixties, working, has friends and a life of her own. You know she can take care of herself. This is an accident that any of us could have had. And you came when she needed you."

Sydney smiled. "You're right. Nan would tell me the same thing."

"So why is Brian handling everything for you? Where's Jax?"

"Jax? Apparently, he's on business here in Kelowna for his father." The day had been too chaotic for her to give Jax a lot of thought. It wasn't that she was upset he was gone indefinitely. She wasn't possessive. Business is business. It was that he hadn't let her know himself. After last night she thought their relationship had moved on to a new level. From everything they'd talked about, she'd believed him when he said that he wanted to keep seeing her. And they had a coffee date this morning. All he had to do was call her and let her know. And Brian said he wasn't coming back.

"Sydney?"

She came out of her muse and looked up to see Dr. Vaser walking towards her. She stood to face him.

"She's out of surgery and in recovery. She's awake. Everything's fine. We reset the bone and used screws to secure it in place. She has a cast on her ankle to just below the knee. They should have her out of recovery and into a room in thirty minutes. You can visit her then. We'll keep her overnight and if all is well, release her tomorrow."

"What happens after that?"

"The first two weeks, total rest with the foot up in bed or in a chair. She won't be able to walk on it for about four weeks. That means crutches. But no crutches for the first two weeks until her pain meds are cut back. She'll need a wheel chair. After that we will give her a walking cast and physio. It will take at least three months to heal properly if she follows my orders."

"Thank you, Doctor." Sydney said.

"Does she have someone to stay with her for the first month?"

"I'm taking her back to the farm house in Stoney Creek. Jessie here is a nurse and we'll take care of her."

Dr. Vaser smiled and nodded at Jessie. "That's good. She'll need to come back in two weeks so we can check the incision and healing, then two weeks after that for the walking cast or boot. The nurse will come and get you when she's moved upstairs. See you in the morning."

"Thank you again." Sydney sat down with Jessie. "You and I can stay at Nan's tonight. We'll pack her things and bring them with us when we pick her up. I don't want her near the house. She'll fight us on everything and want to stay at home."

The nurse came shortly after and gave them her room number. Sydney couldn't believe how pale her Nan looked when they entered the room. She was in a private room. The nurse said she was lucky. It was all they had and they decided she could use a good night's sleep, so it was hers.

"Nan?" she said, softly.

Her grandmother opened her eyes. Her mouth curled into a smile. "Hi, honey."

Sydney took her Nan's hand. "You certainly gave us all a scare. But you're going to be fine."

"I was carrying laundry upstairs and something was hanging down. I stepped on it and it stopped me short. Down I went. Doctor says I broke my ankle."

"Yes you did. The surgery went well. All you need to do now is laze around, be pampered and let it heal."

"Doc says I can probably go home tomorrow. Will you go by and feed Caesar?"

"Jessie and I will stay at your place tonight, Nan. Don't worry about your cat."

Her grandmother patted her hand. "You're such a good girl."

Sydney smiled. Her grandmother was so drugged up, she was talking to her like she was a kid. "Nan, I'm going to go and let you sleep. We'll be back in the morning, okay?"

"Okay." Her Nan's eyes closed and she was asleep immediately.

Sydney kissed her on the cheek and they left.

The next day, Sydney carried two suitcases out to her car. She found the cat carrier in the garage, gave it a wash and put a towel in the bottom, along with his favourite toy. Caesar was skittish. He knew like most animals that something was amiss. When she picked him up and carried him into the kitchen, Sydney kept his attention focused on her face so he wouldn't see the carrier set up on the counter with the door open. She walked up to it rubbing his ears and speaking in soft tones. She grabbed the back of his neck with one hand and slipped her other hand under his back end. She pushed him into the carrier backwards before he knew what was happening. He let out a howl but by that time the door was closed and locked. Caesar protested with a series of loud meows. Sensing it was futile, he settled down on the towel and went to sleep.

When they got to the hospital, her mother had been discharged. The doctor gave her Nan final instructions and the nurse handed Sydney a prescription for pain meds, bathing instructions, and a sheet of paper listing medical equipment to be picked up at the Red Cross cupboard in Oliver on their way through.

Sydney broke the news to her Nan that she was coming home with her.

"Oh no, I'm not. I want to be in my own house," she said, defiantly.

"That's not possible. I can't stay in Kelowna right now and you can't stay home alone."

"I have my friends and neighbours, they'll help me."

"They'd have to live with you for the first month. You're on bed rest for at least two weeks."

"Then I'll hire a live-in nurse."

Jessie moved forward and sat down beside Elizabeth. "Do you really want to have a stranger live in the house with you when you have me and Sydney? I'm a nurse and I'd love to take care of you."

Elizabeth Grey softened a little. "That's very sweet of you. But there's a lot to do to leave my place for a month."

"It's all done, Mrs. Grey. Sydney took care of it all this morning."

Elizabeth looked suspiciously at her granddaughter. "What did you take care of?"

"Well let's see. I packed two suitcases of clothes and toiletries, brought your own pillow and favorite blanket. Packed your personal papers; mortgage, insurance, banking, etc. and packed up your lap top. I turned off the water, put your phone on vacation rate, set the light timer for night time, cancelled your newspaper, turned off the air conditioning, and let your neighbours know so they'll keep an eye on the house. On the way here, I stopped at the Post Office and got your mail temporarily transferred to my mailing address. And Jessie is following us back to the farm in your car. It'll be safe at the farm. Did I miss anything?"

Her grandmother tried to hide a smile. "Smarty pants. I don't like that you did all that without consulting me. And I don't like being told what to do."

Sydney smiled. "You were in a drugged state. How could I talk to you first?"

Her Nan sighed. "How come you're so smart."

"You, of course."

Elizabeth giggled and slapped her arm. "In that case, I forgive you. I've been dying to see what you've been doing with the farm anyway. So let's go. What are we waiting for?"

The nurse went for a wheelchair and they all headed to the elevator. "Wait," her grandmother yelled out.

Startled, Sydney turned and looked at her grandmother who appeared to be in a state of shock. She kneeled down beside the wheelchair. "What is it? What's wrong?"

Elizabeth looked from Sydney to Jessie. "Caesar. What did you do with my Caesar?"

Sydney and Jessie laughed. "Caesar is fine, Nan. He's in his carry case in my car. He's going to love life on the farm. There's a lot of fat mice who are in for a shock."

Chapter 18

The drive down was easy enough. Her Nan slept for the first half of the trip. Sydney gave her another pain pill when they reached Oliver and her grandmother was quite comfortable the rest of the way. While Jessie went into the hospital in Oliver to get a wheelchair, a pair of crutches, a shower stool, and a medical seat riser with arms for the toilet, Sydney filled her in on the fire and what was happening at the farmhouse.

"What will happen if they evacuate Stoney Creek?"

"They'll move the Fire Centre elsewhere and we'll pack up and move back to your house in Kelowna. They won't need the farm anymore."

Elizabeth looked aghast. "Oh dear. I hope you don't lose it to fire."

Sydney thought about what Jax had said to calm her fears about the same thing. *Was it only two days ago?* Her heart sank. "That's not going to happen. And if it does, we'll rebuild."

It was dinner time when they arrived at the farm. As soon as Sydney drove into the yard, she realized one thing none of them had thought of. *How am I going to get Nan into the house? There's no wheelchair access and she isn't allowed on crutches yet.*

She parked in front of the steps. "Hang on, Nan. I'll be right back."

Sydney went into the house and to her surprise there was a full table of people eating in the dining room. They didn't notice her at first. The noise level as they laughed and ate reminded her of being in a rowdy pub. "Hi," she said. The table of diners stopped talking and stared at her.

They began asking her questions at once. She heard someone say: "Sydney. Welcome home. How's your Nan." It was Brian. *Why was he here?*

"She's as well as can be expected. But I need a little help. We have to get her up onto the porch from the car. I have a wheelchair."

Gord, the Fire Protection Officer stood. "Brian and I can handle this. Come on, son."

They followed Sydney outside. Jessie had arrived and was setting up the wheelchair near the car door. "Hello, Mrs. Grey, I'm Gord and this is Brian. We're going to get you into this wheelchair and inside." Gord was a tall, well-built man and certainly in top shape. 'I'm just going to swivel you sideways towards the door. Aren't you just an itty bitty thing. If you want to slip your arms around my neck, I'll lift you right up and into the chair." He did it so fast, Elizabeth was settled in the wheelchair with her leg set up on the support before she knew it. He wheeled her over to the porch and turned her backwards to the stairs.

"Okay. Brian you grab that side and I'll get this one. Hang on, Mrs. Grey, we're going to lift you right up in the air and over these stairs to the porch."

Sydney followed behind just to make sure she made it safely.

Her grandmother raised her eyebrows to Sydney, and a sly smile spread across her face. She nodded her head towards Gord. "I like this one."

Sydney was shocked. *Is she flirting?* Never in her entire life had she heard her Nan flirt with a man.

Gord laughed as they deposited Elizabeth on the porch. "That's good to know since we're going to be sharing some space for awhile."

"Well isn't this going to be fun and call me Elizabeth."

He turned the chair around and wheeled her into the house, the two of them chatting like magpies.

Sydney and Jessie exchanged looks. "It must be the drugs, Jess." The two of them laughed. She turned to Brian."Thank you so much for everything you've done. But why are you still here?"

"Jax asked me to stay over until you returned."

Her heart raced. "Jax? Is he back?"

"No. I called him to report on the project and fill him in on what was happening here. When I told him about your Nan's accident, he asked me to stay and help out. I'm the only one here who knows the workings of the place with you gone. He wanted to be sure the residence was worthy of guests and there were no glitches with the showers, etc."

"That was very kind of him."

"He was also concerned about the final inspection not being done and I explained all of that to him. Now you're back and everything seems fine, I'll be heading out."

"I interrupted your dinner. Please finish eating before you go."

Brian laughed. "I'd love to. Bea is a wonderful cook. I'm sure there's more than enough for you and Jessie."

Jessie groaned. "I'm starving. But let's get your Nan settled in bed first."

When they joined her Nan inside, she was gushing about the renovations. "Oh Sydney, it's so beautiful. I had no idea it would look like this. The wood floors, the staircase—gorgeous work."

"Isn't it? Let's get you to bed, Nan. You must be exhausted."

"I am tired, but not yet, I want to see the house. At least this level."

Jessie pushed the wheelchair and Sydney walked beside her grandmother, showing her the things Jax had done. When they reached the kitchen, she was speechless. "Uh…wow. I would have loved a kitchen like this when we lived here.

Bea came bustling into the kitchen carrying empty plates. "Hi, Lizzie, welcome home!"

"Bea? Is that you?"

"You bet it is. How're you feeling, dear?"

"At the moment, a little stoned. I'm sure the pain will settle in again eventually."

Sydney interjected. "You two know each other?"

"Of course we do. We were rival pie makers at the Annual Fall Fair. Bea beat me every time. I never could best her apple pie."

"That is until that final year, when Pam stole my recipe and gave it to Chelsea."

The two women laughed and shared a moment of nostalgia.

Sydney stared at Bea. "You must be Pam's mom. My mother's best friend."

"That's right."

Sydney looked at her grandmother who was staring at her strangely. *Oops.* Her Nan didn't know about the journals. *I'm not supposed to know about Pam.* She sprung towards the laundry room. "Come on Jess bring her majesty along. Let's continue the tour." She prattled on to distract her grandmother until they made it to the master bedroom.

"I debated putting you in my room because it's bigger and has the en suite. Then I realized we couldn't get the wheelchair in that bathroom anyway. So I think you're better off in your own room with us wheeling you to the master bathroom."

"This is a lovely room—for you. I don't know about these purples and oranges. Show me my room."

Jessie and Sydney laughed and they wheeled her out into the hallway. They stopped at the bathroom. Gord had already emptied the two vehicles and installed the chair riser."

"Now there's a good man," Elizabeth said.

"Mrs. Grey, why don't I get you on the seat since we're right here. It's been a long drive. Then we'll get you into bed." Jessie wheeled the chair into the bathroom.

Sydney continued down to the bedroom. She placed the suitcases out of the way and set up the kitty litter box in one corner and a food and water bowl for Caesar in another corner. Caesar was very annoyed, banging against the door to get out of his carrying case.

Jessie came in with Elizabeth, whose head went in every direction at once. Her hands flew up to her mouth. "Oh, Sydney... this is so me. You know me well. The warm colours and flowers. So much more restful than your room." Again they laughed.

"You like it then?"

"No, I love it. I never expected you to furnish it this fancy. Thank you so much for this."

Jessie placed her beside the armchair by the bay window and she and Sydney prepared the bed.

"Oh my, will you look at that." Elizabeth said.

They joined her at the window. The meadow beside the magnolia tree orchard was full of tents. There were men sitting around in groups and laying on the ground. Some were swimming in the lake.

"The fire crew," Sydney said.

Suddenly, a noise overhead became louder and louder. The men swimming in the lake got out in time for a helicopter carrying a bucket to appear. They watched as it flew lower until the bucket submerged. It hovered for awhile and rose up to pull the full bucket out of the lake.

The noise and amount of people on the farm gave Sydney pause. It felt like they were in a war zone. "I'm not so sure bringing you here was such a good idea. So much noise."

"Are you kidding? If I have to stay off my feet for two weeks, I'd go mad at home. Here at least I'll have some stimulation. I love it. And I love my room."

They got Elizabeth settled in bed.

"Comfy?" Sydney asked.

"Mmm...very."

"Are you hungry?"

"No. I think I need to nap for a bit. Maybe later."

Sydney kissed her. "I'm going to let Caesar out of his cage. He's all set up in here. We'll close the door so he can stay with you for the night. Tomorrow, we'll let him explore the house."

They let Caesar explore the room. He sniffed around the kitty litter and made his way to his food bowl. He took a couple of bites and moved on. Sydney picked him up and put him on the bed beside Elizabeth. Her Nan rubbed his ears and talked to him softly. "Hi, baby. I'm here. Come and see your mama." Caesar licked her hand and moved up close. He settled down and made sure his back leaned up against her hip.

When Sydney and Jessie left, her grandmother's eyes were closed. Caesar had a paw resting on her hand. He was purring and Nan was smiling. They closed the door behind them.

The two girls stared at each and Sydney's let out a long sigh. "Thanks, Jess."

Jessie opened her arms and the two embraced and held each other tight."You did good, granddaughter."

Settled in her bed that night, Sydney thought she'd be too pent up to sleep. But the stress of the past view days had left her exhausted. Once she closed her eyes, sleep took her immediately.

Her eyes shot open. She sensed a change in the room. The temperature had dropped and she felt chilled. The red digitalized numbers on the alarm clock read three fifteen in the morning. A sudden movement caught her attention peripherally and she turned her head. Filtered moonlight through the blinds highlighted a black figure standing at the bottom of the bed.

A gasp escaped her lips. "Uh…" Sydney bolted up in bed and stared at the darkened figure. Her heart pounded in her ears. She couldn't make out who it was. *One of the administrators or firefighters?*

"Who are you? What are you doing in my room?"

As soon as she spoke to the figure it dissipated into a shapeless mist. A moment later it had disappeared from her view.

Sydney stared into the darkness stunned. She switched the bedside lamp on, her eyes searching every corner of the room. *Nothing. What the hell was that?* She left the bed and entered the en suite. She washed her face and hands and stared at her image in the mirror. *It must have been a dream. What other explanation can there be?*

She returned to bed, wide awake. *No sleeping now.* She picked up her mother's third journal from the bedside table and started to read.

Chapter 19

An Unexpected life, 1995-96

September 02
Dear Self,
I can barely write this. But I must because I can't ignore it anymore. I'M PREGNANT! OMG...I can't believe I'm actually writing this. And you know what's worse? I don't know who the father is. I think my last period was the week before Chaz left. We made love twice that week. Then two weeks later, I was with Danny. Jesus...I don't even know his last name. I spotted blood in July and thought it was because I've been so emotional over Chaz. But my body is showing changes. I went to the Doctor yesterday and it's official. I'm due in April. I don't know what to do. Pam is the only one I told 'cause we're supposed to move to Kelowna in December and start schooling in January. How do I tell Mom? She'll be so disappointed in me. And Dad? He'll hate me even worse. Maybe he'll throw me out. I used protection so how did this happen????

September 05
Dear Self,
Mom is looking at me suspiciously. I threw up this morning. Morning sickness. I can't put it off any longer. I'll tell her when Dad goes to the barn.

September 06

Dear Self,

My parents know. But I wouldn't tell them who the father was (like I know). It was hard when my mother cried. She told Dad. He was so mad he walked out of the house and didn't come back all day. Remember how I said they never talk? Just co-exist? Talking is all they do now—about me. I guess it isn't really talking—they argue. Mom says I should have an abortion. It'll ruin my life to have a baby and it's not fair to the baby. Dad says that's a sin before God. He says I should have the baby and give it up for adoption. Mom told him he has no idea how painful it would be to carry a child for nine months and then give it up forever. Dad said it's God's penance for me. That I must pay for my sins. No one asks me what I want. I don't know what I want to do. They talk like it's their decision. I'm so scared, Self.

September 07

Dear Self,

I told Mom and Dad that I didn't know who the father was. I refused to tell them who I'd been with. I've heard nothing from Chaz since he left and to put this on him if he is the father) would ruin his life. I don't know how to contact Danny or even his last name. He wouldn't want anything to do with me or the baby anyway 'cause he's married and has kids. Dad's disgusted with me. They're still fighting about the plight of my baby.

September 13

Dear Self,

I'm so sick of their arguing. I told them that it's not their decision. It's mine. Legally, even though I'm underage, it is the pregnant mother's right to decide to have an abortion (if I choose to). It's legal in Canada. And if I choose to have the baby, I would never give it away. This is my baby and no one is raising it but me (if I keep it). I told them if I keep the baby it will have my last name. I'm so confused.

September 15

Dear Self,

This isn't the life I had planned for myself. I wanted to be free. Maybe I should have an abortion and I would have my freedom back. Pam and I have plans to leave. I would never give it away so abortion's the only alternative. Am I being selfish?

September 17

Dad came in my room last night. He said he doesn't care what the law says. This is his house, his rules, If I have an abortion, he'll kick me out. This is a Godly house and I'd be a sinner and he wouldn't tolerate me under his roof. If I have the baby and decide to keep it, he won't abide with Mom raising it for me. It's my responsibility and I must carry the burden of it. And he doesn't want to be reminded of my sins every time he looks at the baby So me and the baby would have to leave. My baby is not a sin! I cried myself to sleep.

September 20

Dear Self,

The doctor says I need to make a decision. If I'm having an abortion, it would be better now before I'm too far along. On the outside, I could be twelve weeks along if it's Chaz' baby.

September 23

Dear Self,

Omigod... morning sickness is so bad. Mom gives me crackers every morning. They really do help to settle my stomach. I wonder how long it lasts?

September 25

Dear Self,

My decision is made. No abortion. Not because Dad would hate me (he already does) or because it's a sin in God's eyes, but because a life is growing inside me. It's a part of me. How beautiful and wondrous is that? And I'm keeping it. I told Dad I'd like to stay until the baby is born and then we'll leave if that's what he wants. He never said a word. The hardest part was telling Pam. She's going to school in Kelowna without me.

October 03

Dear Self,

Guess what? No more morning sickness. Yay! But boy my boobs are sore and they are getting big. I wish I could share this with Chaz (if he's the father). It's hard doing this alone. I miss Chaz even though I'm still angry at him. But this baby is more important. It needs me, even if he doesn't. So there.

October 12

Dear Self,

Mom and Dad are back to their old selves. No conversation. Co-existing. At least it's peaceful. Thanksgiving was tough this year. We went to a community dinner at the hall. Everyone knows I'm pregnant. Mom held her head high and ignored the stares. She stayed by my side the whole time until I begged for some alone time with Pam. Me—I don't care what they think. Lots of them have skeletons in their closets, so to hell with them all. My Dad got away from us as soon as he could and sat with some of the men.

November 28

Dear Self,

The baby kicked today. How can I describe the feeling? I'm not showing much at all. Mom says I'm carrying in the back and that usually means a girl.

December 20

Dear Self,

I'm suddenly showing. I look fat. I'm buying a few things out of my tips every day. Some of Mom's friends have given me old baby things they had stored away. Still nothing from Chaz. I thought maybe with Christmas coming he might make contact. I have to put him behind me once and for all. My daughter is going to be my life and have my love.

January 15

Dear Self,

Christmas was quiet. Mom bought me a basinet for the baby with some bedding. Did I tell you it's a girl? They asked me if I wanted to know and I said yes. A girl! I can't believe I'm going to have a baby in three months. She moves a lot now. I wonder if she'll look like me? OMG... maybe she'll look like Chaz. I hope so. But then everyone would know he's the father (if he is). He's never contacted me over the holidays so I made the right decision to not contact him. I'll always love him but he hurt me. Still, I forgive him. I don't want to carry the burden of hate. I wish him well.

February 20
Dear Self,
I miss Pam. She calls once in awhile. But we are living different lives now and growing apart. We don't relate anymore. It's scary sometimes thinking that I'm all this baby has to meet her needs. She'll be totally dependent on me. Wow!

March 01
Dear Self,
I had to quit work at the cafe. The doctor has put me on bed rest for the duration of the pregnancy. My blood pressure is high and my iron is low. Apparently this is common with teenage mothers. Dad says it's all part of my penance. He's so negative.

March 10
Dear Self,
Mom and Dad had one hell of a fight last night. Dad was talking about after the baby comes and how he hopes I've made enquiries in Kelowna. There are resources to help me and the baby get settled there. He said he'd give me a month and then we had to leave. I have never heard my mother yell at him like that. She told him we were staying as long as we needed and wanted to. And he damn well better get used to it. I'm her only child and my baby her granddaughter and she wasn't going to let him take us away from her. And if he threw us out of the house, she'd be going with us and he could stay home and rot all alone here on the farm. She was a hellcat. Dad was so shocked. He stared at her with his mouth open

for the longest time. Mom never said a word, but glared at him in total defiance with her hands on her hips. In a quiet, defeated voice he said, "Okay, Mother. You win." I have so much respect for her now. Probably the first and only time she stood up to him in their marriage—and it was over me. Love you so much, Mom.

Chapter 20

Within a few days, a routine was established. Every morning, the CAO of the town, the Mayor and the RCMP Staff Sergeant drove to the farm for breakfast. After breakfast, a meeting was held upstairs with whoever was required in administration and staff that day. The numbers varied depending on the demands of the fire. Sydney was invited to the meetings to keep her abreast of who was coming and going and why. It helped her oversee the laundry and bedding needs in the residence and Bea plan her meals. By the end of the week, Stoney Creek was put on Evacuation Alert.

Gord could sense her panic at the news.

"Don't let it throw you. The alert gives everyone time to pack what they want to take with them, make arrangements for moving animals, and be ready to leave if and when the word comes. Once the RCMP tell you to leave, you usually have to go within thirty minutes to two hours. That's when you would panic if you weren't ready. It may not come to an evacuation but at least you're ready to go."

"I get it. My main concern of course is for my grandmother, not for myself."

"Don't you worry. Most of the time there are any number of people around here that would help you with her. It's rare that you're ever alone. But, I would make it my personal mission if an evacuation is called, to make sure I'm here. I should be anyway because this is our incident command centre"

"You've reassured me. Thank you."

Her grandmother found a routine as well. She always had breakfast and lunch in her room. Sometimes she rested in bed and other times moved to the lazy boy by the bay window where she read books, watched the activity of the helicopter reloading its bucket and the fire staff tenting out back. There were lots of visitors too. Women who remembered Elizabeth from the old days and still lived in Stoney Creek, came to see how she was doing. When dinner was served, Elizabeth would come out and set up in the living room with a TV tray. Sydney would join her there and sometimes Gord.

One night after her first week at the farm, Gord and Elizabeth were sitting in the living room finishing up their dinner.

Sydney sat at the table with Kathleen, the fire information officer. She studied her Nan. It appeared her grandmother and Gord had become friends. They certainly seemed to enjoy each other's company. Gord got up and took their empty plates to the kitchen. He came back and wheeled Elizabeth towards the French doors.

"We're going outside on the deck to have our coffee," Elizabeth said. "I don't know who decided to put in the French doors but it's a wonderful idea. It opens the house up to the lake and lets in so much more light."

Sydney thought of Jax and the day he suggested she put the doors in. His gift. It was also the first time he kissed her. She was sad and angry at the same time. Her anger was directed at herself as much as at Jax. But she wouldn't dwell on it. *It is what it is. One night of awesome sex. Move on.*

She watched her Nan and Gord outside. She couldn't hear what they were talking about, but saw the ease they shared with each other and the laughter. Nan looked happy. Warning bells went off. Perhaps it was because she herself was nursing a broken heart and she wanted to protect her grandmother. *And what do we know about Gord anyhow? Does he have a wife back in Kamloops?*

"What's the story with Gord?" Sydney asked.

Kathleen looked out the doors. "He's a great guy. I've worked with him for a number of years. He's dedicated and he cares."

"And what about his personal life?"

The other woman stared at her for a moment. "He's been divorced for years. I don't think his wife liked that his work took him away from home so much, especially since it was seasonal during the time of year when families usually go on holidays together. He has two grown sons and five grandchildren."

Sydney smiled at her. "I know it's none of my business. But he and Nan seem to have hit it off."

Kathleen smiled back. "And you're being protective."

She nodded. "You have to understand, growing up with my grandmother, she never had boyfriends or ever showed an interest in men. This is a first. I've never seen her flirt or laugh as much as she has this week. At first, I thought it was because she was so drugged up. I'm... surprised."

"I haven't seen Gord so taken by a woman since his marriage broke up. I wouldn't worry about her. If nothing else, he'll be a good friend."

Sydney laughed."Then let's leave them to it and let nature take its course."

Later that night, Sydney sat on the bed beside her grandmother. Elizabeth was propped up on pillows.

"How are you feeling? Is your ankle giving you much pain?" Sydney asked.

"The pain comes and goes. But I'll be glad when I can get a walking cast and move about. Relying on the wheelchair is a big pain."

"I notice you've cut back on the quantity of pills you're taking. Perhaps when you go back to see the doctor in a week, he'll let you walk with crutches. You're not as groggy as you were when you first got here."

"That would help until I get the walking cast or boot."

"You seem happy, Nan. I've never seen you laugh so much."

Elizabeth stared at her. "You mean with Gord."

Sydney started to protest but her grandmother cut her off.

"Don't play innocent, young lady. I saw you watching Gord and I. He's become a friend. And it's none of your business."

Sydney laughed. "I know. But come on, Nan. I've never seen you with a man ever."

Elizabeth softened. "You know, after your grandfather died, I was so happy being on my own. Raising you was such a joy for me and it was all I needed. But after you moved to the farm, I realized that I had cut myself off from a social life. Oh I went to bingo and had my neighbours over for tea. But my social life was restricted to that and my hair clients. I lived through their lives, their kids and grandkids, and their holidays."

Sydney felt bad. "I'm sorry you felt so lonely after I moved out."

"Don't be silly. It's perfectly natural for you to become independent and live your own life. And it was really the best thing that could have happened to me. I'm been doing a lot of thinking these past months. I was ready for a Gord to come into my life. Oh, I don't know if we'll be anything more than friends. It's all new for both of us. But we're comfortable with each other and make each other laugh. We've decided to take it slow and enjoy whatever it is. We want to see where it leads."

"Wow, that's a lot considering you've only known each other a week."

Elizabeth laughed. "When you get to our age, you realize life is too short to play games. You never know what tomorrow will bring."

'Well, I'm happy for you." Sydney reached out and took her Nan's hand. "You also seem to have settled into being back on the farm without looking stressed. Maybe it's the drugs."

Her Nan patted her hand. "If the farm looked the same as when I lived here, maybe the old memories would come back to haunt me. But this is a new home, a new start. And as you can see, I'm all about new starts right now."

"I'm surprised at how many visitors you've had."

"That surprised me too. I didn't know so many people cared. Coming back to the farmhouse has been a good thing," Elizabeth paused. "If you can understand this, it's given me some closure on the past."

"My grandfather was a hard man wasn't he?"

"Yes, he was hard to live with and controlling. His religious beliefs were a little over the top. It was his way or no way. But he was never physically abusive. He didn't drink. He worked hard and provided for his family."

"Did you love him?"

Elizabeth stared at the blankets for a moment. "I did in the beginning. We were both raised in families that believed women stayed home to look after the home and their family. That was a woman's job."

"Did you ever dream of something else for yourself?"

"I did. I dreamed of being a singer like Barbara Streisand."

"Really? That's cool."

"Not that I can sing mind you, but that was my dream."

They laughed. Sydney stood and went around the other side of the bed. She climbed on and sat cross-legged, facing Elizabeth.

"I've never told anyone that, let alone your grandfather. He never understood your mother. He thought she was wild and full of sin. I understood her because she was everything I wanted to be. She was a free spirit. You're a lot like her you know."

This was the first time her grandmother had ever talked about her mother openly. It was a turning point. Sydney wasn't sure how far she should push it, but since her Nan appeared to be comfortable with the conversation she continued.

"Did you ever try to find her as time passed and you heard nothing?"

"Yes. After your grandfather died and you and I moved to Kelowna. That was where she wanted to go for more schooling and I looked for her every time we went out. Once your grandfather's life insurance money arrived, I hired a private investigator. He never found anything. He said she either met with foul play or had changed her name so she wouldn't be found."

"What do you think happened?"

"I really don't know. She loved you and was really good with you. It just didn't make any sense that she'd leave without you. Especially since she fought about that with her father. He never wanted her to keep you when you were born. She did and he came to love you. When she told us she was thinking of moving to Kelowna to go back to school, he wanted her to leave you here with us. But she was adamant that you'd go together. Then one day she packed a suitcase and disappeared."

"Did she leave a note?"

"A typed note off her computer, printed on her printer. She said she was leaving to find herself and would come back for you later. She never even signed it. Just stamped it with this little wooden stamp she had...some woman in a yoga position."

"She hurt you. And you were angry for a lot of years," Sydney added.

"That's true. But my anger was more about her abandoning you and how that might hurt you."

Sydney weighed her words. "I suppose if I'd had more time with her, I might have suffered more. But I don't remember her at all. You were my mother and you were always there. I had a good childhood, Nan."

They sat in silence for a few minutes lost to their own thoughts.

"Did you ever contact her best friend, Pam? Had she heard from her?"

"I spoke to her once. There'd been no contact. By the time you and I moved to Kelowna, Pam was married and living somewhere else." Elizabeth looked at her with a puzzled expression. "How do you know about Pam and that Bea is her mother?"

Time to fess up. "When Jax remodelled the upstairs he found a locked wooden box under the floorboards in the bedroom closet. It contained four journals. My mother's journals."

Her grandmother sat up straighter. "Really?"

"I've read three of them, Nan. The first two are about her last years in school. The third one is about the year she was pregnant with me. I haven't read the last one yet."

They stared at one another in silence.

"Would you like to read them?" Sydney asked.

She watched her grandmother's face contort through a number of emotions. "Not yet. I think it's time for me to turn in."

Sydney sensed the change in her mood. "I understand. It took me a while too." She climbed off of the bed and came around the other Side. Once her grandmother was comfortably laying down, she kissed her on the forehead. "Good night. Love you."

She got halfway to the door when she barely heard her grandmother speak, her voice so soft. "Does she talk about me and her father?"

Sydney turned and quickly thought about the words she should say. " Yes she does. I'm afraid she thought her father didn't like her. But she had a lot of respect for you. She loved you very much."

Tears filled her Nan's eyes. She smiled. "Goodnight, dear. Love you."

Chapter 21

The next afternoon Arne Jensen came to visit Elizabeth. The Fire Centre people were upstairs working. Bea was in town buying groceries. Sydney wheeled her Nan into the living room and left the two of them with coffee while she headed to the residence to do laundry and clean the shower room.

"In spite of your broken ankle, you look well, Lizzie," Arne said.

"Thank you. You've aged well, I see. I guess the physical demands of farming keep you in good shape." Lizzie was actually surprised. She remembered Mary telling her that he couldn't boil water or even use the washing machine. Being on his own this long, she expected him to look dishevelled and thin. She stifled a smile. *Reverse chauvinism.* "I'm sorry about, Mary. She left us far too young. It must be lonely for you in that big farmhouse all on your own."

Arne cleared his throat. "It was in the beginning. But I had my dogs."

His dogs? So Mary has been replaced with his dogs? He always was a strange one. Elizabeth tried not to show her surprise. "Here." She pointed to the plate of cookies on the coffee table to change the subject. "Have one of Bea's delicious chocolate chip cookies. That woman is an amazing cook."

"Thank you." Arne took two. He took a bite of one, and spoke while he chewed. "Anyone's cooking is better than mine, I'm a terrible cook."

Humph...he doesn't look like he's suffered too much. Elizabeth watched the crumbs fly out of his mouth and hit the coffee table while he talked. *No manners that man.*

"Lot's going on around here. I'm surprised you came back to the farm with the Fire Evacuation Alert called for Stoney Creek.

"I arrived before that happened. I needed someone to help me for awhile. If it wasn't for the Fire Centre being set up here at the farm, Sydney would have stayed with me in Kelowna. But I'm glad I'm here. It's actually been exciting with all these people around. Bad circumstances I know but it's been rather fun.

"Better here than my place. I don't like this many people around."

"Mmm...you're a lot like my Frank was. A bit of a loner."

Arne stared at her for a moment. "You were a good friend to Mary. I know she never took to the isolation."

"No, she didn't."

"But you did. You even worked with Frank in the fields."

"Well, I came from a farming family, she didn't. And I had my daughter to keep me busy."

Arne choked on a piece of cookie and started to cough.

"Are you all right? Take a sip of your coffee."

"I'm fine."

Sydney came in the back door and joined them. She sat down on the couch and looked at Arne. "Have you packed the things you plan on taking with you if we get evacuated?"

"Nope. I'm not leaving the farm."

The two women looked shocked. "But we have to if the RCMP say we need to leave," Elizabeth said.

"I told the triage people they could set up my place with sprinklers, but I'm not leaving. If the evacuation comes I'm staying. They can't make me leave. If I leave the property, they can stop me from returning and if I resist they can arrest me because I'll be on public ground. As long as I stay on my property, there's nothing they can do. My place is well-stocked with food and water."

"Why would you do that?" Sydney asked. "You could be endangering your life."

Elizabeth interjected. "And the lives of the people who will have to look out for you."

"I've lived my whole life in that house. If fire comes, I'll fight for it and that's my choice."

Elizabeth could see that Arne was getting agitated. "Well, let's hope it doesn't come to that. I'd hate for you or any of us to lose our homes or our lives. Stay safe."

Arne smiled and relaxed. "So, are you planning on going back to Kelowna as soon as you're able?"

"I will. I must say though that with all the renos Sydney has done, the farm certainly holds a certain appeal."

He gave Sydney a blank stare. "She's so like Chelsea, isn't she? But prettier...and of course younger." Arne stood. "Well, I just wanted to pay my respects and make sure you ladies are all right. Time for me to go."

"Thank you for stopping in," Elizabeth said.

Sydney walked him to the door. Elizabeth heard her open the door.

"Bye now," Sydney said. The door closed and Sydney came back to sit on the couch.

Her Nan shook her head. "I never liked that man. He's coarse."

"I don't know him at all. He's always been polite to me and offers his help if needed. But still..." Sydney trailed off.

"The problem is Mary told me things about him. Your grandfather was controlling and demanding but Frank never laid a hand on me, your mother, or you. Mary had no one. I was the only one she could talk to. And she had bruises. Not that you could see. Mary told me once that he always hit her where she could hide it with her clothes. That's cruel and calculated."

"That's awful."

"Yes, she wasn't happy. Maybe if she'd had children but Arne was sterile from a bad case of mumps as a boy."

"Maybe that's what made him mean."

"Well, enough about him. Talking about your renos, I sure wish I could see what you did upstairs."

"You know, I did take some before and after pictures. I haven't unloaded my cell phone yet. Too much going on. At least you can get an idea of what we did up there."

"Wonderful." Elizabeth pushed the wheels of wheelchair backwards and swung it around to leave the living room. But she cut it short and whacked her ankle against the coffee table. "God Dammit." Her face contorted in pain.

"Ouch. Let me help you." Sydney straightened out the wheelchair, making sure to clear the table. "Are you all right."

" Yes, thanks. That was stupid. Could you wheel me into my room? I feel a nap coming on."

Sydney went to her bedroom and sat down at her laptop. She hooked her cell phone to the computer and started the picture download to a new file. She stared out the window while the pictures were processing. Life had been so busy the past few months. She'd met so many wonderful people. And she loved having her grandmother here. Once the fire was under control and everyone left, she'd be alone. Somehow the prospect of that wasn't as exciting as it seemed when she first came to the farm. *But it's called growing up. Maybe once I get the business up and running, I'll feel more at ease and settle into a routine.*

She looked at the laptop. The download was complete. The pictures were awesome. Sydney had almost forgotten what the farm house looked like before they started the renos. The studio pictures came up finally. *What?* She stared at two of the pictures that had part of the mirrored wall in them. They were taken from different angles but each one carried a reflection in the mirror in the same spot—a silhouette of a man. He was dark, his features indiscernible. It sent chills up her spine.

Sydney checked pictures she had taken of the exact spot directly, not through the mirror. There was nothing there. The timer showed the pictures were taken seconds apart. And yet the silhouette appeared in the mirrored pictures. She studied the silhouette again. *OMG… it looks just like the one I saw in my bedroom the night Nan arrived.*

It all came together in that one moment; the doors banging shut, the cold rooms, dark silhouettes, the girl with the pink hair. Chills went down her spine.

Is the farm haunted? And if yes, by who?

Chapter 22

Sydney drove down the main street of Stoney Creek. It had been two weeks since her Nan's accident. They had returned to Kelowna yesterday to see her Nan's doctor. The ankle was healing but not as fast as the doctor liked. The break has been a bad one. He suggested she stay off of it for a few more weeks and come back for a walking cast. He allowed that she could walk with crutches as long as no weight was put on the foot.

The smoke in the valley came and went. They had good days and bad days. Today was a good one. People were out and about. Glancing ahead to the left, she gasped. *There he is.* He'd just exited the post office and started down the stairs. Her heart pounded. *My stalker!* She pulled into an empty parking stall and watched him cross the street. The familiar black RV was on the road moments later. She was driving her Nan's car today, having taken it in for an oil change. She put on her sunglasses and pulled her ball cap down low. *Okay, sucker. It's your turn to be stalked.*

She followed at a safe distance behind, hoping not to attract his attention. He made a left turn and headed towards the north end of town. Sydney followed suit but allowed a couple of cars to stay between them. A few minutes later they left the town. He made a right hand turn towards the river. The area was unfamiliar to her. New subdivisions were sprouting up along the river and before long, the stranger turned into one of them. As she approached the turn, a wood carved sign identified this one as Riverside Estates. She barely caught the tail end of the SUV disappear up a driveway at the end of the street. She drove slowly down the road, turned around and parked on the opposite side. The vehicle was parked in front of the garage, with the man nowhere to be seen. *Wow, corner lot, about an acre of property, right on the banks of the river. Whoever he is, he's done well.*

Sydney noted that the SUV was a newer model Hyundai Santa Fe. She couldn't make out the licence number. The backend of the vehicle was covered with dirt. Sydney looked for house numbers but couldn't find any. A glance around the street told her these houses were still in a state of being built. Some were occupied, others were still for sale. A cedar hedge hid the front of the house from view. Maybe the numbers were there but she wasn't about to go snooping. Sydney drove slowly along the road, noting the visible addresses of other occupants. She wrote them down and headed back to town.

The post office had a reverse address index. Sydney found a copy and searched for Cherry Point Road. It wasn't there.

One of the attendants at the counter was free. "Excuse me," Sydney said. "I'm looking for a road in one of the new subdivisions north of town. It's not listed in the book."

"Which subdivision?"

"Riverside Estates, Cherry Point Road."

"No, it missed this year's book. What's the house number?"

Sydney shook her head. "I don't know. The house isn't marked."

"Do you know the owner's name?"

"No," Sydney said in despair.

The clerk frowned and shrugged. "The only thing I can suggest is going to the Realty company that's handling that subdivision. They might be able to help you."

"Thank you."

Sydney sat in her car and thought it through. She couldn't think of a reason why she'd be making enquiries of the realtor about a house that is already occupied. The realtor would be suspicious. She could go to the police with what she knew so far about this guy. But they might think she's stalking him. *Okay, this requires some help and I know just who I need.*

Twenty minutes later, Sydney was headed back to the subdivision with a reluctant Jessie sitting beside her. "I think you should report it to the police and let them check this guy out."

"I don't think I have enough for them to take me seriously, Jess. We'll knock on the door and you can see if you recognize him. If you don't, we'll see how he reacts to me being at his door. I'm just going to confront him and find out why he's stalking me. If he's really creepy, we'll take off and go straight to the police."

Soon they were parked back at the house on Cherry Point Road. The Santa Fe was no longer parked in the driveway.

"He must have gone out again," Jessie said.

Sydney opened her door. "Or moved it into the garage. Come on, we'll stick to our plan. If someone else answers the door, we'll make up a name of someone we thought lived at this house."

"I'm not comfortable with this."

"So you've said a dozen times. I really need you to be here with me. I can't go in alone and I'm tired of wondering about this guy." It was a plea as much as a statement.

"Okay."

The two women crossed the road and walked up the driveway. There was no way to see into the garage. Sydney walked straight up to the door and rang the bell. They waited. She rang again. And they waited some more.

Jessie turned towards the driveway. "Let's go. No one's home."

Sydney looked in the opposite direction, along a path in front of the house. She grabbed Jessie by the hand and pulled her along the path.

"What are you doing?" Jessie asked.

"Look." Sydney stepped up to a set of French doors and peered inside. "It looks like an office." She turned the handle on the door and gave it a little push. The door swung open. "Come on."

"Sid—stop. This is breaking and entering."

Sydney turned towards Jessie. "We're not breaking in. The door is open. I just want to find a piece of mail or paper that has his name on it. We'll be in and out in no time."

"If we get caught, it's a crime. We could go to jail…not to mention have a criminal record."

Sydney stepped behind Jessie. "Don't over think it, Jess." She gave her a shove through the open doorway. "Go."

While Jessie stood frozen to the spot. Sydney looked over the desk. There was nothing there to identify their guy. She pulled on the drawers but the desk was locked. She peeked under things on the desk to see if a key was hidden but no such luck. "Nothing. Let's go search the hallway or maybe a kitchen junk drawer. There has to be some mail laying around somewhere."

The two women snuck into the hallway. There was a table by the door with some papers on it. Sydney rifled through the papers to no avail. Frustrated she turned to find the kitchen. "This house is way too clean and tidy." Halfway past the staircase to the upstairs, a voice boomed at them.

"What are you two doing here?"

Jessie let out a squeal and Sydney froze. She turned her head and looked up. Standing mid-way was a naked man, save for the towel wrapped around his waist. His wet hair hung down over his face. She couldn't move and then something clicked. All she could spit out was: "Jax?"

"Jesus, Jax. You scared the shit out of us," Jessie said.

"And you me." His eyes scanned the front door. "The dead bolt's locked. How'd you get in here?"

Jessie shrugged. "We knocked and no one answered. We didn't think anyone was home. Whose home is this?"

"You haven't told me how you got in here." Jax addressed Jessie, ignoring Sydney, which was fine with her. She was speechless.

"Well, the French doors were open," Jessie giggled and threw her hands up. "And here we are."

Jax looked confused and angry. "So you don't know who lives here. Didn't know I was here. But you walked right in? That's a crime you know."

"Yeah, I told Sydney that but she was determined." Jessie looked at Sydney who still appeared to be shell shocked. "So why are *you* here in the middle of the day naked.?"

"I'm allowed to be here and I was taking a shower."

Sydney suddenly came to life. So many thoughts and emotions jumbled together in her head and the words poured out with no sense of order or control. "Hiding from me. That's what he's doing here. I thought you were working for Daddy in Penticton? Hmmm..." She marched over to the stairs. "So what *are* you doing here in this house? Is there some little piece hiding upstairs in one of the bedrooms? Does she know you'll just drop her tomorrow and disappear?"

Jessie spoke first. "Sydney—what the..."

Jax face reddened and Sydney took that as a sign of guilt. She was on a roll and the words kept coming. "Or are you having an affair with the wife of the creep who owns this house. A little tete-a-tete while he's away stalking me."

Now Jessie looked speechless.

Jax looked completely crushed. "Stalker? What are you talking about?"

Before Sydney could continue her rant, a noise on the outside stoop caught their attention. Sydney turned to see the mail slot slam shut and letters fall to the floor. Time stood still for what was seconds but seemed like an eternity. Sydney raced across the floor and picked up an envelope to read the name.

No.

She lashed out at Jax. "Your *father* owns this house?"

Jessie came over and read the envelope. Her eyes popped. "I didn't know your Dad lived out here."

"Yes, this is my father's house. But if you didn't know that, why are you here?"

"Because I followed the man here who's been stalking me for two months. Your *father*."

"That's ridiculous. My father isn't a stalker," Jax retorted. "What's going on Sydney?"

Sydney dropped the letter that was labelled *Wesley Rhyder* back on the floor with the other mail, but not before another envelope caught her eye. She picked it up and stared. This one had his full name typed in bold print.

"Omigod…" *It's not possible. Is it?* All the anger and emotions she'd felt were gone. One look at Jax and her eyes popped. *What did this mean?* "Did you know?"

Jax looked pained. "Know what? I…I'm not sure we're on the same page here. Look you need to talk to my father. I can't talk to you right now."

Jessie looked from one to the other. "What is going on with you two? Someone want to clue me in here?"

"I have to get out of here." Sydney headed towards the office and then back to the door.

She twisted the dead bolt knob the wrong way and tried to pull the door open. She did this repeatedly. She spun around in a panic. "Would someone please open this goddamn door?"

Jax stood in a zombie state, his eyes fixated on the floor. Jessie rushed over and opened the door.

Sydney raced through the doorway, stopped and turned back to Jax. "When your father gets home, tell him he better get his ass out to the farmhouse. I'll expect him before the day ends."

Chapter 23

Sydney couldn't drive. She threw her keys to Jessie and climbed into the passenger seat.

Jessie waited until they were on the road before she spoke. "Are you okay?"

"Do I look okay?" Sydney shouted. She glanced at Jessie. "I'm sorry. Oh, Jess, I don't even know where to start. This is such a big mess."

"Well, start at the beginning."

"The beginning?" she asked.

"Yah. What started this big mess?"

Sydney thought about that. "What started it was me sleeping with Jax."

Jessie's head spun sideways. "You slept with Jax? When?"

"A couple of weeks ago. The night the fire jumped the border."

"And you never told me?"

"I was going to. It was magical, Jess…the best sex I've ever experienced…not that I'm that experienced…I…"

"You're rambling, Syd. So why didn't you tell me?"

"He led me to believe it meant something. That I wasn't just another one of his girls. But the next day he was gone out of town and he never called. I heard about it from Brian. Then the fire happened and Nan's accident. It all got so muddled. Today is the first time I've seen or talked to him since that night. Something changed after we slept together. You saw him. He was hostile and evasive."

"Well we had just broken into his father's house."

"It's more than that, Jess. He told me to talk to his father."

"And what was all that about?"

Sydney put one hand over her mouth. "Oh God, this is where it really gets complicated."

"Try me. I've got a few brain cells."

Sydney gave her friend a half-smile. "In my mother's journals, she refers to everyone by initial. Like Jess would be J, except for a boy she nicknamed Chaz, and so if her parents read her diary they wouldn't know who anyone was."

Jess snickered. "Typical teenage thinking."

" She loved Chaz. They went to Grad together and she slept with him that night. And a few more times after that until he moved to go to university." Sydney paused to get her thoughts.

"And?"

"A few weeks later, heartbroken, she partied with a carnival worker who was married. She got drunk and slept with him once. One of them is my father. She didn't know which one."

"I'm so sorry, Jess. But what's that got to do with Wesley Rhyder?"

"Wesley Rhyder's middle name is Charles. Chaz is a nickname for Charles."

"So your mother slept with Jax' father?"

"Based on Jax behavior, I'm thinking so. Do you get it now?"

"So if he is Chaz, he *could* be your father."

"Jess? Think a little harder."

Jessie was silent.

"Are you hearing me? Do you not get it?

"I get it. You and Jax could be half brother and sister," Jess said, softly.

"A half brother and sister who slept together."

Jessie almost drove off the road. She pulled over and stared at Sydney."Oh Syd..."

Sydney burst into tears and Jessie held her while she cried.

"This really is messed up." Jessie said. "But maybe he's not Chaz."

Sydney blew her nose and put her head back on the head rest. "Jax was upset. He couldn't talk to me. I think maybe Wesley is Chaz. Somehow he found out we were together and he told Jax."

"Your grandmother should know."

Sydney turned towards Jessie. "Why would she know who Chaz is?"

"She may not know him as Chaz but she knows who your mother went to Grad with."

"Of course. I'm so emotional I'm not thinking. But I don't want to bring her into this yet. I'm going to wait until I talk to Wesley Rhyder. Why didn't he tell me? I don't get it."

Jessie started to pull back onto the road and stopped. "Maybe that's why he's been watching you. If your mother didn't know who your father is, he's not sure either."

"All I know is that it's time I find out. No more secrets."

They drove home to the farmhouse each lost in thought. Jessie pulled into the driveway. As they got out of the car, they felt raindrops. They looked south and saw black clouds coming in.

"That's good news at least. We haven't seen rain for two months," Jessie said.

They went into the house. Bea came out of the kitchen to greet them.

"It's sure quiet in here. Where is everyone?" Sydney asked.

"They're all in Osoyoos. Big meeting there. Big rains are coming apparently. It's already raining in Washington State. I could have told them that last night. My arthritic bones have been aching since then."

"You can tell if it's going to rain by your bones?" Sydney asked.

"Absolutely. Don't need any weather stations or meteorologists to read computer screens."

Sydney gave Bea a hug. "You are so funny, Bea."

"And sometimes you just have to look out the window. This could be the break they need to get that fire under control.," Jessie said.

Bea nodded. "We can only hope. Are you in for awhile? I'd like to run into town on some errands. Didn't want to leave your Nan home alone."

"By all means go. Where is my grandmother?"

"Lizzie's napping."

Sydney touched Bea's arm. "Thank you for sticking around."

"Not a problem. There's sandwiches and a salad in the refrigerator if you girls are hungry. And some fresh coffee. I'll be back to make dinner for the four of us if you're staying Jessie."

"I'll be here," Jessie said.

The girls went into the kitchen and made up a plate of food and sat at the island. They ate in silence.

"I'm so glad it's quiet around here if Wesley Rhyder shows up," Sydney said. She'd no sooner said the words when the doorbell rang. Sydney froze.

"Do you want me to give you some privacy?" Jessie asked.

"No…I need your support."

Jessie put their plates and cups into the sink and followed Sydney into the living room. She sat down while Sydney went to the door.

As soon as she saw him, Sydney recognized Mr. Rhyder as the man she thought was stalking her. "Mr. Rhyder, please come in."

He followed her into the living room.

"I believe you know Jessie."

"I do. Hello."

Jessie nodded at him. "Mr. Rhyder."

"Jess will be joining us. She's here to support me and she's discreet."

He looked a little unsure but sat down on the edge of the couch. "I want to apologize to you. Jax told me that you thought I was stalking you. It certainly wasn't my intention to scare you. Selfishly, I've looked at this whole thing from my own perspective without considering your side of this."

Sydney sat down opposite him. "And what is your perspective, Mr. Rhyder."

He took in a deep breath. "I knew your mother. We went to school together. In fact, I was in love with her." He paused, looking pained. "Umm…your mother and I, we were… " He faltered.

"You're Chaz, aren't you?" Sydney asked.

His eyebrows shot up. "How'd you know that? To my knowledge, no one knew she called me that."

"Jax found her journals hidden in the floor when he started renos upstairs in her bedroom. Let me help you out here. I know you and my mother were lovers. I know you left after high school ended with your family. And I know you broke her heart."

"She wrote that?" Mr. Rhyder asked quietly.

"She did. I didn't know who Chaz was until today. She loved you and waited for you to write to her. You never did."

"Oh but I did write her. And please call me Wes," he protested. "I wrote her once a week for two months. She never responded to any of my letters so I stopped writing. I tried to call her a couple of times, but she was at work."

"Really?"

"Yes. I don't understand."

He looked so bewildered that Sydney was inclined to believe him. *But what happened to the letters?*

"So why were you—for lack of a better word—stalking me?"

"The first night I saw you when you ran into me in the restaurant, I was stunned. You look so much like your mother that for a minute I thought you were her. Of course that sounds ridiculous because she would be my age now. I couldn't stop wondering who you were and why you were here in Stoney Creek. So I stayed and watched you. Then I found out you were Elizabeth's granddaughter and I knew you were Chelsea's daughter."

"And what about all the other times? Why didn't you come to me and talk to me right away?"

"And say what? I wanted to approach you but I had no idea, and still don't, what you were told about your mother and your father. When I finally decided to talk to you, every time I drove out to the cabin or here, you were either surrounded by people or turned in for the night."

Sydney was angry. "In lieu of the mess this has turned into, I'd suggest that you didn't try hard enough. It's been two months."

"You're right and I guess all the times it didn't work out to talk with you gave me a good excuse to procrastinate for awhile and I'm sorry about that."

Sydney sighed. "Well, everything I know about my parents comes from my mother's journals. My grandmother couldn't bring herself to talk about it. Growing up, my Nan carried a lot of anger towards her daughter and a lot of pain. The subject was taboo."

"Can I ask you to share what you've learned from Chelsea's writings?"

"Of course. My mother wrote that she was sad when you left and not hearing from you broke her heart. She made a mistake a few weeks after you left when she and her best friend, Pam partied with some carnival workers. She slept with one of them. He told her later that he was married. She carried the guilt of not knowing which one of you was the father."

"I don't understand why she didn't try to find out. If it was me, I would have stood by her."

"But she never heard from you. She… "

"But I… "

Sydney held up her hand. "I know. You say you wrote her letters but obviously she never got them. She wrote that if I was Danny's baby, he wouldn't want anything to do with her because he already had a family. And she thought you'd moved on and she didn't want to ruin your life."

Wes' eyes filled with tears. "She couldn't have been more wrong. When I heard she was pregnant, the story was that she'd been sleeping around. I called to ask her face to face if you were mine and her father answered. He told me the baby wasn't mine and that she wanted nothing to do with me. He was very rude and blamed me for messing her up. He also said that she wasn't going to keep the baby and that he never wanted me to call again."

Sydney gave him a hard stare. "And you believed him? You must have known how controlling he was of Chelsea and my grandmother."

"Of course I knew. So I wrote one more letter to her. In the end, I believed him because she never answered the dozen letters I wrote to her."

A realization hit Sydney. "Nan told me that he was a creature of daily habits. One was picking up the mail at the rural boxes. He must have held the letters back from her."

"It's the only explanation isn't it?" Wes said.

A voice spoke from the hallway "And it's the right one."

Wes, Jessie and Sydney stared in the direction of the voice. Elizabeth stood balanced on her crutches in the entranceway.

Chapter 24

Elizabeth made her way into the living room, and sat down beside Sydney. "Hello, Wes. My goodness, you still look the same as you did eighteen years ago. Just a little grayer at the sides."

Wes gave a weak smile. "Mrs. Grey. I was sorry to hear about your accident."

"Thank you. But if I may be philosophical for a moment. Sometimes things happen for a reason. I'm beginning to think that this accident was providential. As was Sydney choosing to move back to Stoney Creek."

"What do you mean, Nan?" Sydney asked.

"That if it weren't for everything that's happened the past few months, none of us would be sitting here together today. And I truly believe it's time."

Sydney held her Nan's hand. "How much of our conversation did you hear?"

"All of it. The doorbell woke me up. I wasn't going to push myself into the conversation until Wes mentioned the letters."

For a moment, they all looked at each other. Wes took the lead. "Mrs. Grey, can I ask you what you know about Mr. Grey intercepting my letters to Chelsea?

"Call me Elizabeth. I do believe my husband hid the letters from her. If I'd known at the time, I would have raised the roof. Whether he agreed with your relationship or not, it wasn't his call. She was eighteen. What he did contributed to her unhappiness and as a mother that's unforgiveable."

"If you didn't know at the time, why do you think he stopped delivery."

"After Chelsea's father died, I chose to move to Kelowna with Sydney. I leased out the farm to a family who wanted to work it. I went into the equipment building to pack up Frank's tools and take them with us. I found the letters stashed in his tool box. I have them in Kelowna. I knew what he'd done. I did read them. That was the first I knew about how intimate your relationship had been. Chelsea told us she'd had more than one partner and couldn't identify who the father was. But she wouldn't say with whom. She gave Sydney the Grey name at birth."

Wes looked upset. "So she never knew that I did love her and hadn't forgotten about her."

"I thought about returning them to you with a letter of explanation but I'd heard you were married and had a child of your own. At the time, it seemed cruel to open up old wounds and upset your new family. Chelsea had disappeared and we still didn't know if you were Sydney's father." Elizabeth paused. She looked pained. "And, I'm afraid I was being selfish. What if you turned out to be Sydney's father? You might want to take her away from me and I couldn't bear losing her too. She was all I had left. I was wrong."

"I think perhaps all of us have made some decisions that in retrospect seem wrong. But retrospect doesn't reflect real life and circumstances at the time."

Emotion hung heavy in the room. No one appeared to know what to say next.

Jessie cleared her throat. "If I may interject here. I've sat quietly in the background listening to you all and realized something that doesn't quite fit in all of this."

"Go ahead, Jess," Sydney said.

"Sydney isn't just grappling with the idea that you might be her father, Wes. She and Jax may be half brother and sister. Jax is a year older than Sydney. How is that possible? You would have had to father him in your last year of high school while you were dating Chelsea."

Sydney froze. Her eyes grew big. "I've been so upset today, I never thought about that." She stared at Wes waiting for his answer.

Wes' red face showed his embarrassment. "That's because Jax isn't my biological son. I adopted him when he was two years old. My..."

"Omigod...so even if you are my father, Jax and I aren't related." Sydney let out a long breathe. "Thank God for that."

Elizabeth looked puzzled. Wes appeared stricken.

"That's not the whole story, I'm afraid. Jax never knew he was adopted. I saw you and Jax together that night outside the restaurant. When you held onto each other and kissed I knew I had to tell him the truth. I went to his house that night. He was devastated."

"So his leaving town was about you and him, not about me and him?" Sydney asked.

"Not entirely. I'm afraid there's more. Jax is my older sister's son. He's my blood nephew. I was in second year of university when my sister and her husband died in a plane crash. My parents were too old to take Jax in. I was seeing a girl at the time for ten months. She fell in love with Jax and we decided to get married and adopt him. We were a little too idealistic I think. The marriage didn't work. However, over time while we were together Jax called us Mommy and Daddy and we let it go. He was happy. I always intended to tell him but never guessed it would be under these circumstances."

Sydney was deflated. "So we could still be cousins?"

Wes grimaced. "I'm sorry, Sydney. I wish we had spoken sooner."

Elizabeth looked at Wes and then at Sydney. "Why are you so upset about being related to this Jax fellow."

Sydney looked at her grandmother. It was truth time. "Because Jax and I became close these past two months. Two weeks ago, the day before your accident, we were intimate." Tears filled her eyes. "Oh, Nan."

Elizabeth took her into her arms and stroked her hair. "I'm so sorry, Sydney. What a tangled web we've all weaved."

Sydney felt her grandmother's strength. She drew in her energy and sat up determined to stay strong."So, where do we go from here?"

Jessie took over again. "We need to do a paternity test to see if Wes is your father. I can help you both with that if you like."

Wes spoke first. "Absolutely. Sydney?"

"Of course."

"Blood type can rule out paternity or establish potential paternity. A baby has to have either his mother's blood type or his father's, or a combination of. Wes, what's your blood type?"

"I'm type O."

"Elizabeth, what was Chelsea's blood type?"

"She was A."

"Then Sydney's blood type has to be A or O."

Sydney looked sad. "I'm an O."

"So we can't rule Wes out as the father. However, it's not proof that he is either. It only means he could be. But understand that type O blood is the most common type of blood. Danny could be O as well."

"What do we do now?" Sydney asked.

"A DNA test. If you both want to come to the hospital tomorrow, I can do it for you. We have the kits. It's very simple. We swab the inside of your cheek. I'll forward it through the hospital to the DNA Specialists in Penticton. It'll take a couple of weeks for the results. The cost is a hundred and ninety-five dollars."

"I insist on paying for it," Wes said.

Sydney thanked him.

Elizabeth addressed Wes. "When I return to Kelowna for my walking cast, I can get the letters if you'd like to have them back."

"That's kind of you. Yes, I'd like to have them," Wes said. He studied Elizabeth a moment. "Can I ask if you ever heard from Chelsea? Do you know where she is?"

"No, we never did. I tried to find her when I moved to Kelowna but there was no trace. I knew she would leave one day but I never expected her to leave Sydney behind. I was blinded by my anger for years and believed she abandoned her. But now that I'm seeing things more clearly, I remember how she was as a mother and how much she loved Sydney. I'm beginning to think that she met with foul play."

Wes looked at Sydney. "Is there nothing in her journals that might suggest why she left like she did?"

"I've only read the first three. The first two were all about school and typical teenage angst. The third journal ended with her about to give birth to me. I'm about to start the final journal which I'll do tonight. We'll see."

Wes nodded. "I'd best get going. I think we're all a little overwhelmed at the moment. How about I pick you up in the morning and we'll go to the hospital together?" Wes looked at Sydney expectantly.

"All right."

He turned to Elizabeth. "We'll talk again, I'm sure." Elizabeth shook his hand. Impulsively, she reached up and pulled him into a hug.

Sydney followed him to the door. "I'm sorry we broke into your house today."

Wes smiled for the first time. "That's okay. You not only look like Chelsea, you're very much like her in personality. Like you, she was impulsive. And I sense strength in you. She had that too."

"Thank you. See you in the morning."

Sydney closed the door and walked back into the living room and leaned down and gave her grandmother a kiss. "I'm so glad you're here, Nan."

Chapter 25

Me and Sydney, 1996-97

April 10

Dear Self,

I, Chelsea Grey, am a MOTHER! That's right, dear Self. And you'll never guess when she was born. April 1st. On my birthday. My water broke March 31st and I was in labour for twelve hours. OMG...I thought I'd die. It was so painful. But you know what? When I saw that tiny little bundle in my arms, all that was forgotten. She's tiny, only five pounds, fourteen ounces. But she's healthy and proportioned. It's quite normal for a teenage mom to have a small baby. And she was two weeks early. That's normal for us teenage moms too. She's so beautiful, wisps of fine blonde hair and fair creamy skin. Her eyes are dark with a glint of grey. But they can change. The doctor says they'll probably be blue like mine. This past week was tough 'cause she wasn't getting enough milk. But I seem to have come into my milk and she's getting on a routine. Just in time 'cause the doctor almost put her on formula but all is well.

Sydney reread the entry, over and over again. All the doubts her mother may have experienced during the pregnancy disappeared once she was born. Chelsea loved her as soon as she saw her. *She loved me.* It was a bittersweet moment for Sydney, knowing her mother loved her at the moment of her birth but not knowing why she'd left her one year later, so many years ago.

April 20

Dear Self,

Loving my mom. Dad's been grumpy 'cause I can't help him prepare the fields for the first hay. Mom told him to hire someone to help 'cause I'm too busy with the baby right now. It's exhausting, trying to nap when Sydney naps and get laundry done etc. Sydney really is a good sleeper though. Mom helps when Dad's out in the fields. He's so adamant that I do everything on my own. I didn't expect that babies would need twenty-four seven care and it's an eye-opener. But I'm so glad I didn't have an abortion. As for giving her away, we won't even go there—never, never.

May 15

Dear Self,

Sydney loves her baths and is smiling now. I love bath time and I love her so much. She's gaining weight and the doctor is happy with her health. On a personal note, I'm getting into yoga and meditation. I never get out of the house and I need to get back in shape. The mobile library book bus stops by every two weeks. I'm reading a book called 'Be Here Now' by Ram Dass. It's about the principles of Yoga and how one man transforms his life, as well as, about our spiritual side.

June 30

Dear Self,

I don't have much time to write in my journal. I spend my free time doing yoga, reading and meditating. Dad thinks the Ram Dass book is garbage. He's says meditating is self-centered, egotistical and allows me to be lazy. He says all I have to do is pray on Sundays and get the same benefits. He told me we were going to begin Sunday lessons again and I rebelled. I said I was an adult now and old enough to make my own choices. I told him I was spiritual not religious and that the higher power I believe in is loving and not full of hate and punishment. He got angry and started the same old 'my house, my rules' bullshit. One look from mom and he shut up. Mom is coming into her own. So sad it took so long. Do you think I should tell him I'm reading about soul travel? Boy would he freak out at that one. He'd probably call me the devil or a witch.

July 15

Dear Self,

Dad allowed that Mom could look after Sydney so I could work with him in the fields with the first haying of the season. It felt good to be out in the fresh air and soak up the sun. It was the first time I actually enjoyed the work. Look what I found in a craft store? A yoga stamp! I use it on everything. Isn't it cool?

Sydney stared at the symbol. She'd seen it many times. Yoga was her business after all. *This must be the stamp Nan said she used on the letter she left the day she disappeared. How strange that I gravitated towards Yoga and meditation, and my mother practiced it as well.*

August 22

Dear Self,

Sydney is almost six months old. And guess what? Her eyes are full blue. She sits up and rolls over. She's trying to crawl. Such a happy baby, always smiling and laughing. Even Dad looks at her differently now. Before now, he acted like she didn't exist. Mom made him hold her the other day. Can you believe it was the first time? Sydney reached up and touched his cheeks and giggled. His whole body relaxed and he actually smiled back.

October 13

Dear Self,

Been so busy. Helped Dad with the second haying and I'm working part-time at the cafe again. Sydney is crawling all over the place now. We've had to kid proof the house. She's the love of my life. She's on soft foods and a night bottle, So I'm getting full night sleeps from her last bottle about ten until six in the morning. My life finally is in a regular routine. I'm really into meditating and love my yoga exercises. I feel at peace. First time in so long. Sometimes I wonder about Chaz and if he's happy. He's in my past now and I must look forward. And I love my music. Cindi is still my fav and Madonna. But there's some new ones now I like too, Gwen Stefani, Melissa Ethridge. And of course, two Canadians with a different style, Sarah McLachlan and Diana Krall. Dad likes Diana Krall, only because she sings some of the Jazz greats he knows.

January 2

Dear Self,

Christmas was quiet as always. Just the four of us. Dad said grace at dinner. He asked that we pray for a few minutes. I gave him that. Christmas is a time for family and giving thanks. Mom has been teaching me to cook. I actually enjoy it. Imagine. Me? We had some of my parent's friends and their families over for New Year's Day dinner yesterday. Mom and I cooked for two days and we had a smorgasbord of cabbage rolls, cheese and onion perogies, cooked ham, salads and baked desert goodies. We rarely have people over and it was so much fun. Asshole came. He still creeps me out. Always watching me. I'd say something but lately I've been thinking a lot about my life and Sydney's. I'm checking out some things in Kelowna. If I leave, I won't have to worry about Asshole.

February 8

Dear Self,

WALKING! Ten months old and Sydney is walking. She's early. Only a few steps and down she goes. But she gets that stubborn, defiant look on her face that Mom says comes from me, and up she gets and is off again. So cute. I've been in contact with Social Services. They have a program for single teenage moms who want to go back to school. New classes for Lab Technician training start June 1st. There's a daycare at the school for Sydney. They'll help set me up in an apartment and I can collect social service cheques until I graduate and get a job. Pam is still in Kelowna too. She met someone at school and they're living together. Time to talk to Mom and Dad about it.

February 20

Dear Self,

Why is my Dad such a jerk? We've been fighting for a week now about my moving to Kelowna. He thinks I should stay here where I have family and friends. I told him I didn't want to spend my life working as a waitress. Nothing wrong with being a waitress. They work hard and all but I have other dreams. I want to be able to earn decent money and take care of my daughter. I reminded him that he wanted me to take responsibility for my life and Sydney and that's what I'm trying to do. A few days later, he said he was pleased that I'd been thinking about my future and Sydney's but that if I want to go to school, I should leave Sydney here with them. Once I'm done and have a job, then I could take her. I explained to him how the program works and that without Sydney I wouldn't qualify for their program which is only for single teenage moms.

February 25

Dear Self,

Dad won't budge. Nor will I. I have three days to let Social Services know if I'm enrolling for June 1st. He doesn't like that strangers will look after Sydney while I'm in school. I explained that the daycare is in the school so I can see her on breaks and the people are vetted and qualified. Mom is sad to see me leave but she says it's my decision.

Sydney put the book down and turned off the lamp. She wanted to read more but couldn't keep her eyes open. *I don't get it. She loved me. She really did. Why did she leave me? And what happened to her?*

Chapter 26

Sydney stared out the window of the black SUV—the one she thought for months belonged to a pervert. She glanced at Wes' profile and out the window again. So far their conversation had been stilted. They'd talked about the weather, the renos at the farm, the fire…but nothing on a personal level. It had been raining hard since last night. A good sign for the fire fighters.

Finally, Wes started to talk. "I wonder sometimes if things would have been different if I'd just come back to see Chelsea face to face, instead of waiting for her to contact me. But so much was against me back then. My parents, classes at university…" he trailed off.

"Wasn't it you who said yesterday that hindsight is a wonderful thing but it has nothing to do with reality?"

Wes smiled. "It was. Not in those exact words but the same meaning."

"Can I ask you something?"

"Sure."

Sydney swivelled towards Wes. "If you'd connected with my mother, and it turned out that the baby wasn't yours, would you still have wanted her in your life—with me?"

Wes took a moment to answer. "If it were today, absolutely. Back then? I'm sure I would have wanted to. But the pressure from your grandfather and my parents would have been enormous. Who knows what would have happened."

"That's honest. You know, even if you and my mother stayed together with me, with your sister's passing and Jax thrown into the mix, you both may have buckled under the pressure and gone the way of you and your ex-wife.

Wes gave her a quick glance and smiled. "How come you're so smart?"

Sydney laughed. "I'm just saying, things may not have worked out happily ever after that way either. And my point is, I don't remember my mother so although I know I missed out on having a mother like other kids, Nan was a very stable and positive influence in my life. I love her to bits and she's like my mom. My childhood was a happy one."

"I'm happy to hear that. Nowadays with divorces and single-parenting there is no norm. Being happy is what counts."

"That's right. So let's forget the 'shoulda woulda coulda' thing. It is what it is. What's important is where we go from here."

Wes was silent for a moment. "You definitely have your mother's strength."

"Thank-you."

"So how are you coping. I mean with the whole Jax thing?"

Sydney felt like she'd been punched in the stomach. She stiffened. "Could we just not go there right now? I understand why Jax disappeared after you talked to him that night. Until I know if we're cousins, I just can't process it. I can talk about anything but not that."

"Of course. Jax is in the same mindset as you. I'm sorry I brought it up. But his disappearing after that night was to get away from me as well. He's harbouring a lot of anger against me for not telling him sooner about his adoption. And he blames me for the pain you're going through as well. Going to Kelowna for awhile was a good escape."

Sydney stared at his profile once again. All three of them were suffering. "I guess time will resolve some of this for us all." She needed to change the subject. "What brought you back to Stoney Creek?"

"Well, my marriage broke up and I had full custody of Jax. I didn't want to raise him in the city. I had a great job with an architectural firm, good money, future prospects within the executive, but I decided to move back here and open my own company. Small town life seemed better than the chaos of meeting the demands of a large firm and being a single father. Here I could spend more time with Jax."

"Does Jax ever see your ex-wife?"

"Yes. He always thought she was his mother and she loved him as one. She's remarried and has two girls of her own but they've always included Jax."

Sydney kicked off her shoes and put her feet up against the dash. "How'd your parents take the move back? I bet they didn't like it."

Wes frowned. "No they didn't. Back in those days they didn't like anything I did from falling in love with Chelsea to adopting Jax, and getting married. What made you think they wouldn't approve of my moving back to Stoney Creek."

"My mother mentioned in her journals that they were controlling like my grandfather. And that my grandfather thought your parents were 'hoity toity'."

Wes roared with laughter. "Chelsea was right. They were and still are but they've come to accept my choices."

"She also said that they had great plans for you and she wasn't good enough for them."

"I don't think it was that she wasn't good enough. They felt the timing was wrong for us. It was your grandfather that tried to put those thoughts into Chelsea's head because he didn't like my family. I think he was the one who felt not good enough and he was trying to protect her."

"I suppose you're right but he was a hard man. I guess all parents think they know what's best for their kids. The trick is letting them find out for themselves, make their own mistakes."

Wes gave her a surprised look. "Thank you. That's something I needed to hear right about now. Without realizing it, you just helped me with a big business decision I've been grappling with."

Sydney smiled. "Glad to be of help."

They pulled into the hospital parking lot in Oliver and went searching for Jessie. Once they were done with the swabs, Wes drove Sydney back to Stoney Creek. He pulled into the Rattlesnake Grill and parked. "How about I buy us lunch before I take you home?"

Sydney pursed her lips. "I'm sorry. Can we go somewhere else? This is…our place, mine and Jax."

Wes looked stricken. "Oh dear, sorry again. Absolutely." He pulled out of the lot and headed to the main street. They entered a small cafe. "They have great lunch specials here. Nothing fancy but good food."

They ordered their food and while they waited, Sydney looked around the cafe. A sly smile spread across her face. "And this was your place."

Wes raised his eyebrows. "My place."

"Yours and my mother's. She used to work here."

"Uh…yah! You're right. When we were in high school, we'd come here with our friends at lunch for French fries and coke. And after winter skating we'd come for cocoa to warm up."

Lunch was an easy banter and Sydney was surprised how at ease they'd become with each other. An hour passed and they headed to the farm.

Wes pulled into the driveway and leaned across her to open the door. "So…I guess now we wait. I just want to say that for a lot of reasons I hope I'm not your father. But on the other hand, if I am, I'll be so proud to call you my daughter. You're a fine young woman."

"Thank you, and in spite of the fact that for a couple of months I thought you were a pervert, I think you're a good man. I can see why my mother loved you." They shared smiles and she got out of the vehicle.

Elizabeth and Gord were sitting at the dining room table finishing their lunch when Sydney walked into the house.

"How'd it go, sweetheart," Elizabeth asked, patting the chair beside her. "Are you hungry/"

"Fine. We had lunch on the way back in town." She turned to Gord. "All this rain must be having some impact on the fire, I hope."

"We're expecting more rain tonight but sadly, being an arid area it will probably create mudslides rather than curb the fire. What we need is for the wind to die down. At least the helicopters and bombers got a day off. We'll reassess tomorrow. The fire fighters are coming back pretty wet and dirty so they've been keeping the laundry room going full tilt."

"I should get the towels and sheets then from the residence and bring them over here," Sydney said.

Bea entered the dining room with three cups of coffee. "Already done. I did them this morning. You sit down and have a coffee with your Nan."

"Oh Bea, you sweetheart, as if you don't have enough to do. I could have done them this afternoon."

"You've got enough on your plate right now. Come on—sit."

"When this is all over, I'm going to miss you."

"No you won't. And I'll tell you why. Because when you get that business of yours up and running and have those yoga retreats, no one is going to want to eat your cooking. You'll be hiring me to come in and do it for you."

Sydney's mouth dropped open while everyone else laughed. "Aren't you the presumptuous one—and oh so right."

Chapter 27

Gord stood at the wall with a pointer and tapped on the map. "Here you can see the new fire line."

Sydney sat back in her chair and observed the table. They had a full house today because they had reached the turning point they were waiting for. It was a big day with big news. They'd just come up from downstairs after Bea had bustled around the dining room serving a smorgasbord of breakfast foods and pots of coffee.

"The winds died down and that gave them the time they needed. The fire is seventy-five percent controlled on both sides of the border. The Evacuation Alert will be called off for Stoney Creek. About seventy-five percent of the Osoyoos evacuees can return home. And it'll no longer be considered an interface fire."

The Mayor spoke up. "When do you think they can go home?"

"Probably late this morning, once the spotter planes and ground crew have verified the call. We should have word here at the centre in a couple of hours. The few still not allowed back home will be sheltered in Osoyoos. I'd like to get the Stoney Creek Hall cleared and set up for a community meeting tonight."

"What can we do to help?" the Chief Administrative Officer of the town asked.

"The staff here will make up the flyers about the meeting tonight. We'd like to get them out to businesses, up at the school so the kids can take them home to their parents after school, and drop some off at the post office, etc. If you could lend us some staff to help distribute them and get it up on your website, we'd appreciate it."

"Done."

"Sydney, we'll move out of this floor this afternoon and back into the Community Hall. That way residents can pop in and ask questions over the next few days. But myself, one of the office staff and Kathleen will stay on in the residence until we're done with the fire. If all goes well, we'll probably be here until the end of the week. And please, please don't send Bea home until we leave." Everyone laughed.

The CAO spoke up. "We'll contact our janitorial staff and see if they can clean the hall when everyone is out. Sydney, we'll send someone out with public works to pick up the furniture here and clean this room for you.

Gord added to the Mayor's words. " Most of the fire fighters will be sent home. We'll keep a mop-up crew in the meadow. One helicopter will handle hot spots and will fill up his buckets in Osoyoos. It's going to get a little quieter around here."

Sydney excused herself from the meeting. She'd learned all that she needed to know. The rest was procedural and didn't involve her. When she returned downstairs, her Nan was sitting in the living room with Bea having coffee. She let them both know what was happening and headed over to the residence to do the laundry.

An hour later, Gord joined her in the residence. "We just got the word. I'm heading to the hall to make arrangements for the evacuees to get home and move the others to Osoyoos. The office staff are working upstairs printing the flyers. One will bring them into town and the other one will stay behind and pack up the centre. We'll see you for lunch."

Sydney finished up her chores in the residence and went back to the farmhouse to find Brian waiting for her. "Hey you. How's it going?"

"Good. I came by to see if you were free to come with me to look at a dining room table. Jax found it at an estate sale and thinks it's what you're looking for. The family is holding it for you."

Hearing Jax' name gave her a start. "Umm...yah! Did you want to go now?"

"You bet. We'll go in my truck and if you want it we can bring it back with us."

They headed towards Stoney Creek. "It's just south of town."

"It was nice of Jax to think of me. I hope I like it."

The house was huge. The dining room faced the back gardens and had floor to ceiling windows. The table itself was set for six people with leaf ends dropped down at either end. If you lifted one leaf it added three more seats. Both ends raised seated twelve people. The table itself was natural pine beetle planks stained with a clear matte finish. The blue streaks in the wood added to its beauty.

The pine beetle that destroys the pine trees carry a blue fungus in their mouth that helps break down the tree's defenses. Sydney ran her hand over the table. "Wow, this table is incredible. I love that the wood was left natural so the blue streaks standout. Having the leafs drop at the end is ingenious." The legs and supports were squared off and painted a navy blue. The wooden chairs were also navy blue with a pine beetle wood seat. "How many chairs do you have?"

"Twelve chairs."

"Awesome. Let's make a deal."

Twenty minutes later, they were headed back to the ranch with her purchase in hand.

"There's a public works truck behind us. Bet they're following us to your place to pick up tables and chairs," Brian said.

"It'll be strangely quiet when they're all gone."

Brian snickered. "Just you and your grandmother...and the ghosts."

Sydney's head jerked sideways. Brian was smiling. "Excuse me?"

Brian turned red. "Didn't you hear about that/"

Sydney stared at his profile. "About what?"

"Gee, I would've thought with all the teasing going on, you'd have heard. When we first started the renos, one of the guys swore he saw a girl standing in the magnolia grove. Then last week, one of the fire fighters couldn't sleep. It was pre-dawn and he walked over to look at the lake. He glanced at the house and saw a man standing in the window of one of the bedrooms—your Nan's room."

Sydney felt a sense of shock, remembering the dark silhouette she'd seen standing over her own bed.

"Did he describe him?"

"He was tall and thin, wearing bibbed jeans and round, horn-rimmed glasses. He didn't recognize the man and thought he might be someone visiting your family. When the figure saw him staring at him, he disappeared. Didn't back away or step out of sight…just evaporated into thin air. It really freaked him out and the guys really razzed him over it."

She was stunned. And now she knew exactly who the man was. *Or I should say, who the spirit is—my grandfather.*

When they pulled into the driveway, the public works truck followed them in. Two men got out and walked up to Brian's pick-up. "You finally found your table," one said. "Good timing. We can take back the table and chairs inside and help you set this one up."

Sydney clapped her hands. "Thanks, guys."

Before they entered the house, Gord drove into the yard.

In a matter of minutes, the dining room table was in place. Bea had a huge pot of stew heating on the stove and sandwiches wrapped in the fridge. Sydney invited Brian and the public works guys for lunch. Bea and Elizabeth had already eaten so the table was set for six of them.

Bea placed the plates of sandwiches on the table and brought out steaming bowls of stew.

"No crackers today. They all went soft from the dampness from the rain."

"There's plenty of food here. We don't need them," Sydney said.

Elizabeth sat in the living room, admiring the set. "It looks so natural and with the stone wall, it warms up the room. It's a great choice."

"What sold me on it was the leafs dropping at the ends. I didn't want a huge table sitting in here when it wasn't needed. And the extra chairs can be stored in the mud room," Sydney added. She looked at her lunch guests. "Go ahead and eat everyone. Let's christen my new table."

Over lunch, Gord filled them in on what was happening in town. "All the evacuees are on their way home or headed to the hall in Osoyoos. My staff are setting up now for tonight's meeting."

An hour later, Gord went upstairs and helped his staffer finish packing. All the boxes were loaded onto his truck and they were gone. The public works boys loaded up all the tables and chairs to take back to the town yard. Another vehicle arrived.

Sydney opened the door to two women carrying cleaning supplies. She smiled. "Come on in. It's like grand central station around here today." They introduced themselves as the janitorial staff. One carried a floor steamer and a box of cleaning aids, while the other carried in a polisher. Sydney showed them the way upstairs and left them to their work. It didn't take long for the women to be done and ready to go. "Wow, you're fast. Thank-you so much, ladies."

Bea slipped out the door with the two women. "I'm off to town too. I'll be back inside of two hours."

"Hang on, Bea." Sydney went to her bedroom and returned. "Here's your cheque for this week in full."

"Thanks, hon. See you later."

Sydney went in search of her Nan and found her sitting in her easy chair in the bedroom. She had a book in her lap, but was staring out the window.

"Just the two of us, Nan. The house is so quiet and tranquil."

Elizabeth laughed. "A rare occurrence since I've been here. I'm watching the fire fighters pack up. Looks like half of them are leaving."

Sydney sat in the bay window on the bench Jax had built. 'I'm looking forward to getting back to normal and having the work finished around here. It will be nice to have the place to ourselves." She looked at her Nan. "At least until you go back to Kelowna."

The two women stared at each other in silence.

"We have probably three more weeks anyway," Elizabeth said.

"Have you thought about staying? You certainly seem content here."

Her Nan stared out the window at the lake. "I will admit that I'm more comfortable here than I thought I would be. You've turned the old farmhouse into a cosy country home. But…I do have to return to Kelowna at some point. It's time for you to fly on your own."

"I know. I'm excited to get started with the business and that will keep me more than busy."

"You won't have to drag me down here though. I'll come often. After all, this is *my* room."

Sydney giggled. "Yes it is. No one else gets to sleep in here. The spare room will be a guest bedroom for other people that visit."

"Can I bring some things from home to put in here. Like my own paintings and knick knacks? And that beautiful crochet blanket you bought me for my birthday to throw over this chair?"

"Of course, whatever you want."

Elizabeth reached out and squeezed her granddaughter's hand. "I'm very proud of you, you know."

They exchanged warm smiles. "Thank you."

Sydney stood and stretched. "I haven't had a good workout for weeks. They've finished cleaning the studio. I think I'll go upstairs and do some yoga stretches and meditation." Sydney paused. "Can I ask you a question?"

"Shoot."

"My mother writes in the last journal about her study and practice of yoga and meditation. Didn't you think it odd that I chose to study the same thing and make a career out of it?"

"Yes. I was shocked when you first mentioned it. But we weren't talking about your mother back then…my fault. It was another reminder to me of how much you are like her."

"It struck me when I read about it in the journal that maybe it was genetic memory."

"Except you were born before Chelsea became immersed in its practice. Perhaps it's more a sensory experience. You were only a baby but she often ran through her routines in front of you. You'd giggle at some of the contortionist positions she put her body through."

Sydney looked pensive. "You might have something there. Well…I'm off."

"Before you do, I've been thinking. Could I have Chelsea's journals? I'm ready to read them now."

Sydney looked surprised but felt pleased. "I'm half-way through the final one. I'll get you the first three."

Sydney went to her bedroom to retrieve the journals. It was hard to believe the one hundred percent turnaround her grandmother had reached regarding her mother. They talked quite easily about Chelsea now and when she had questions, Elizabeth was prepared to answer. *They say you can't go home again. But that's exactly what her Nan needed to do.*

Chapter 28

Sydney climbed the stairs to the studio. *Wow. You'd never think anyone was ever up here.* True to his word, Gord had come through. The walls were untouched and the floors steamed and polished. *It looks brand new. And it is.* She smiled. Sydney walked around the whole studio a couple of times, swinging her arms and warming up her legs. She mused about her classes. Sydney wanted to teach all levels; beginners, intermediate, advanced, and gentle classes for those with physical restrictions. Her courses would incorporate mind, body, and spirit though the combination of exercise, philosophy, breathing, diet and meditation. Her meditations would include Earthing practices in season.

She opened a cupboard and took out a mat, a bolster and a pillow. From another cupboard, she retrieved a CD player. For her yoga workout, she loaded *The Great Mystery* album by Desert Dwellers. Sydney started with stretching exercises, followed by intermediate yoga, leading her into advanced positions. She held each position for two to three minutes each, the required time to challenge her flexibility. Once she passed her point of ease and her breathing control lessened, Sydney changed positions. The total routine took an hour to complete.

She reloaded the CD player with *Yellow Brick Cinema,* relaxation music for meditation and sat on the mat in the lotus position. With her legs folded and crossed, she placed her hands on her knees, her thumb and forefinger enclosed in a circle. Sydney concentrated on her breathing exercises, letting the music flow through her body. She felt the warmth and protection of the healing light of the white universal energy moving from her toes. through her legs to reach her torso, pushing the bad energy above it. She concentrated on this warmth, erasing all other thoughts from her mind. It ascended into her chest and shoulders, pushing some of the bad energy down her arms, into her hands, passing out of her body through the tips of her fingers. Her muscles relaxed. The warmth travelled up her neck and into her head until all the tension flowed out of the top of her head. The muscles in her forehead relaxed, followed by her cheeks, until her chin relaxed and her teeth unclenched, leaving her lips slightly parted. Her exercise was complete and she felt devoid of all stress.

The vibration of the tantric music pulsated through the floor and into her body. She felt one with the room. Her breathing was deep and relaxed. Her physical body felt light, her mind clear. Sydney lost herself to the music until it ended. She stayed in position, not wanting to move. The CD reloaded and started over. This suspended state was so appealing, she didn't want to break its euphoric spell.

And then two things happened.

The distinct odour of magnolias filled the room. The sweet pungent aroma with a touch of vanilla filled her nostrils and she inhaled the all too familiar scent deep into her lungs. Next, she heard a voice talking to her.

A voice? Is that what it is.

Not a talking out loud type of voice but one that spoke to her in her mind. Softly and pleadingly, the 'voice' whispered: *Be careful. Please be careful.* These words were followed by the sound of sobs. They weren't heavy or loud, but echoed in her head as if they'd travelled from a place of great distance to reach the inner recess of her mind.

Sydney opened her eyes. She was facing the mirrored wall and she stayed in the lotus position as her body reoriented to its physical state. She stared into the mirror and let her eyes travel the room through the mirror's reflection.

Wonderment, incredibility—but mostly fear—froze her stare to one spot in the mirror.

About five feet behind her right shoulder, stood a young woman. The same girl she'd seen in the tree. She stood motionless, barefoot in torn blue jeans, a white t-shirt, and that head of long pale pink hair. *My imaginary friend.* She could still hear the faint resonance of sobs in her mind's eye. The girls face was wet from tears spilling out of her blue eyes.

Sydney unlocked her lotus position and spun around on the mat. The room behind her was empty. She twisted back and looked into the mirror. No one. Standing up, she shook her legs and arms, regaining her physical balance. She walked to the window and stared out into the fields across the road.

The woman gave me a warning. Why was she crying? Where did she come from? And be careful of what?

For all the unanswered questions, there was one thing Sydney felt sure of.

This girl is not and never was an imaginary friend but a spirit. Who is she?

The end of the week brought a finish to the wildfire—at least on the Canadian side. The last of the mop-up crew went home. And the Fire Centre people returned to Kamloops the day before, except for Gord. He was leaving tomorrow. He and Elizabeth loaded their cell phones with each other's contact information. Gord insisted on taking her out for dinner that night. It was Canada Day, July 1st, Canada's celebration for federation. But Stoney Creek and Osoyoos had cancelled their celebrations for that year because of the wildfire.

Elizabeth was managing at a snail's pace on her crutches but at least she was mobile. Gord took her to a Greek restaurant in Osoyoos overlooking the lake. It was a warm night and they watched the swimmers jumping off the raft and little kids digging in the sand.

"I'd forgotten how peaceful it is at the south end of the Okanagan. Kelowna has beautiful beaches too, but a lot more traffic these days," Elizabeth said.

"I've enjoyed living in Kamloops. It's been good to me financially and career wise, but my retirement comes up soon. I've always loved the Okanagan." He looked at Elizabeth. "You know, Lizzie…perhaps I'll move closer this way." He took a hold of her hand.

Elizabeth smiled. "When's your date?"

"My birthday is in February. I'd like to leave before the fire season starts up next year. I may put the house up for sale when I get back in case it takes a while. I need to downsize anyway and could go into an apartment until I leave."

Elizabeth thought about his words. "I'd love to see you closer. If we intend to see each other exclusively, it's a two-hour commute back and forth. But I don't want you to uproot yourself because of me. This is all new for both of us and I'm not ready for anything too permanent, you know that. I mean, if it doesn't work with us, you might come to regret such a big change in your life."

"Well, first of all, We have about eight or nine months before I'd move. We'll know by then how we stand together. I planned on downsizing when I retired anyway. If we don't work out, I could buy into a townhouse or condo in Kamloops. But my kids are scattered from Kamloops to Kelowna to Vernon. So my preference after retirement is to be somewhere in the Okanagan area rather than the Thompson River locale anyway."

"Then I'm looking forward to having you closer." Elizabeth squeezed his hand back.

Gord sat back in his chair as the waiter brought their plates of beef souvlaki, rice, and Greek salad. "I have a feeling that Sydney would like you to stay on here and not return to Kelowna."

"I think you're right. But I'm two years away from retirement. I can't see giving up my business at this stage. My financial planning is tied to these last couple of years. Besides, she needs to get her business set up and be independent."

"Umm…this meat is so tender." Gord finished chewing and swallowed the spicy morsel. "Wasn't that why she came to Stoney Creek in the first place?"

"That was her plan but with everything that's happened, I think she's clinging to me because she's feeling insecure. Once I return home, she'll find her way."

"When do you think you'll head home?"

Elizabeth sipped her red wine. "I was going to leave when I get my walking cast, but it's been so chaotic with all the wildfire people at the farmhouse. Maybe I'll stay a couple of weeks longer if only to enjoy the tranquility."

Gord laughed. "And to make sure Sydney is alright?"

"You see right through me."

"You've been a good mother and grandmother to her. I don't mean to pry. But she seems a little stressed out this week. Is everything all right?"

Elizabeth weighed his question. She wasn't used to sharing her private business with anyone. *This is new and awkward. But if Gord and I are to have a relationship, we need to trust each other and be each other's confident.* She found herself relaxing as she filled Gord in on the story about her daughter and Wes Rhyder. She hesitated initially when she told him about Sydney and Jax because that was Sydney's personal business not hers. But she continued and before long he knew it all.

"Jesus. No wonder she wants you to stay. She needs your support right now. I think you should stay on for awhile. You're collecting medical insurance and if you're hair clients can wait, it's necessary."

"I've had most of them for years, they're being very supportive. And if I lose a few, I can find new ones."

"Then stay. Maybe even longer if that's what it takes. It's summer and my busy season. I'm going to busy with other wildfires for a few months anyway, so our time together will be sparse. You still need her help too. Once you start physio, you can't drive yourself."

Elizabeth chortled.

"What?"

"I'm not used to having someone look out for me. It's been a long time since a man told me what I should do."

Gord put his fork down and reached across the table. He linked his fingers in with hers. "You listen up. I'm not telling you what to do. I'm only suggesting what I'd do. The choice is up to you."

"Thank you. Bad choice of words on my part—old programming. If I really thought you'd tell me what to do, I'd send you packing."

They laughed. "I bet you would."

They finished their meal and left the restaurant. Instead of heading north to Stoney Creek, Gord turned south and drove towards the US border. They turned east onto the Crowsnest Highway and climbed up to Anarchist Lookout which sits about fifteen hundred feet above Osoyoos.

They parked and got out of the vehicle. "I haven't been here since I was kid," Elizabeth said.

"It's been a lot of years for me as well."

They found a big rock to sit on and watched the sun set to the west. Eventually, the sky started to darken and the night air cooled.

"Feel the breeze? I love the night breezes. Without them, the desert temperatures would be unbearable," Elizabeth said.

"It's funny how visitors are surprised that some areas in Canada have deserts. They think we're all about cold and snow."

Elizabeth chuckled. "Our geography is quite diverse.

They watched the lights come on in the town. They sparkled like stars against the blackness.

Gord stood and helped Elizabeth to stand and handed her the crutches. When they reached the car, he opened her door and placed the crutches in the back seat. He turned back to Elizabeth who was holding onto the door waiting for him to help her lower her body into the car. Before he did, Gord took her into his arms and held her tight against his chest. He lowered his head to hers and found her mouth. Their kiss was short and sweet; a test to see if their feelings matched. He pulled back and looked into her eyes. Elizabeth smiled and their lips came together a little more needy this time. Elizabeth gave in to the sensation and felt a warmth envelope her.

As they drove down the mountain, she savoured the moment. They had shared a few quick kisses in recent weeks but this was their first passionate kiss that cemented their mutual feelings. Elizabeth smiled to herself as she watched the lights below. *How romantic is this? Young people think they've cornered the market on romance. Who says you can't have fun and romance after sixty?*

Chapter 29

Brian called her from Rhyder Contracting to say the men would be back mid-week to continue their work on the property. Bea had been paid out for the remainder of the week and insisted on staying with her and Elizabeth. Sydney was grateful. She'd been helping Bea in the kitchen with some of the meals and had picked up some great cooking tips. But she intended on learning more. Of course, her Nan was a great cook. But balancing on crutches while cooking was not an option. By the time Bea left, Sydney figured she could handle the cooking adequately.

The cell phone in Sydney's pocket vibrated. She pulled it out and looked at the screen. "Hi, Jess. What's up?"

"Hi. I hate to tell you this. But I got a call from the lab about your DNA specimen."

Sydney heart started to pound. "Already? It's been barely a week."

"Sorry, I don't have a result. Unfortunately, your sample was compromised and it's contaminated. I need you to come in and do another swab."

Sydney let out a deep breath. "I can do that. When do you want me in?"

"Can you come today? We have a batch going to the lab late this afternoon. I'd like to include yours."

"On my way. See you soon."

She sought out her Nan to tell her where she was going.

"Can I come with? It's a beautiful day for a drive and it's way too quiet around here."

"Of course."

Twenty minutes later they were heading to the hospital in Oliver.

"They better not mess this one up. Now we have to wait even longer for the results," Sydney said.

"What a shame. It'll be over soon, hon and you'll have your answer. Have you talked with Jax at all?"

"No. We're avoiding each other. What's there to say until we know if we're related? And if it turns out we're cousins, it'll be embarrassing for both of us. And we thought we had something special."

"I wish I could make it easier for you. But I can't. Sometimes I feel like such a failure as a mother and grandmother." Elizabeth stared out the side window.

Sydney was shocked. "Oh Nan, why would you say that? You're a great grandmother. And Chelsea wrote well of you in her journals as her mother."

Elizabeth grunted. "I never really knew my daughter until I started reading the books. I mean I recognized that she was stronger and freer in her thinking than I was. I admired her character and personality traits. But I really didn't know or understand the angst she felt about her father. She always stood up to him, sometimes in anger and sometimes with humour. I thought she'd found a way to cope with his ways. I was wrong and she suffered because of it."

"Don't sell yourself short. Teenagers and their parents have always had tenuous relationships and trouble relating to each other. I think that last year after my mother gave birth to me, she understood you better and she loved you very much." Sydney glanced at her grandmother and saw a tear slide down her cheek. "You're a good person, Nan. You did your best and that's what counts."

"Thank you, hon. I just wish I'd stood up to your grandfather sooner than I did."

"It's called maturity."

Elizabeth laughed. “There you go, being the smart one again. You’re way more mature than I was at your age.”

“That’s because you grew up in a sheltered life and Papa continued to shelter you. I on the other hand was exposed to more of life. Television, videos, and the internet have exposed kids to more than in your day growing up on the farm.”

A car darted out of a driveway right in front of her. She hit the brakes to avoid hitting it. “What an idiot. Can I ask you something?”

“Sure.”

“Do you believe in God?”

Sydney could feel the silent stare her grandmother gave her.

“If that’s what you want to call it. I do believe in a higher power. We certainly aren’t in control, are we?”

“How come you never sent me to church when we moved to Kelowna?”

“I went to church with Frank and Chelsea because he demanded it. And back in those days, Stoney Creek was scarcely populated. The only social life was the church socials. I enjoyed them. But I always believed if God is everywhere and sees everything, then he’s in my garden. So when I’m on my knees digging around, I can pray and he’ll hear me.”

“Makes sense.”

“I also believe that you only need to follow one rule to be a good person—the Golden Rule. Do unto others as you would have them do unto you. To me that sums up everything written in the Bible, Quran, Torah, and Buddhist Tripitaka.”

Sydney nodded. ‘I remember you talking to me about the Golden Rule as a child.”

“When Frank decided the church became too liberal, we had Sunday morning prayer meetings at home. Poor Chelsea had to read the verses and tell him what she thought they meant. Then he’d discuss it.”

“Umm…I remember hiding in the magnolia tree and hearing him call me in for my lessons. I was too young to read but I remember him reading the scriptures to me. I didn’t understand them at all but some of it scared me. I'd stay hidden until I heard that certain tone in his voice and knew if I pushed it any further, he'd be really mad and take away privileges."

"And that's why I didn't send you to church in Kelowna. He scared the hell out of you and your mother with his fire and brimstone impression of the bible. I believed that going to church should be a choice and one that is desired and enjoyed. So I decided to teach you the golden rule and let you figure the rest out when you became an adult."

They reached the hospital and went inside. They found Jessie and Sydney submitted another swab.

"I'm so sorry, Syd. The waiting on this must be awful," Jessie said.

"It's not your fault. I'm fine." Sydney gave Jessie a hug. "Why don't you join us for dinner tonight? It's just us and Bea now that everyone else has gone home."

"I'll be there."

"See you at six."

They moved at a crawl through the hospital with Elizabeth using crutches and holding her right leg in the air. Sydney would have put her in a wheelchair, but her Nan insisted on being independent. Sydney glanced around as they slowly moved through the entranceway. Sitting in a chair in the waiting area, she spotted Arne, their neighbour. He'd already noticed them and they locked eyes. There was no ignoring him. He stood and walked towards them.

'Good afternoon, ladies. Everything all right?"

"Yes, Arne. Just came in for a test," Elizabeth said. "How about you?"

"Same here. I'm waiting on an x-ray on my back. Twisted it lifting hay bales."

Elizabeth kept walking. "You take care of that. Back pain can be the worst."

"Good day, ladies." Arne looked at Sydney who hadn't spoken a word. He looked her up and down, nodded and smiled. "Sydney."

Sydney nodded back. "Take care," she said, following her grandmother to the electronic doors. *Why do some men think it's okay to undress you with their eyes and then expect you to be flattered?* By the time they reached their vehicle, Sydney felt disgusted with the man. She helped her Nan settle in the passenger seat and walked around to the driver's side. She noted that Arne's truck was parked right beside them. There wasn't much space between them. When she reached her door, she glanced into the passenger window of his vehicle. What she saw stopped her in her tracks. She moved closer and stared through the glass. There were a pile of books on the front seat from the Okanagan Regional Library, Oliver Branch. The pile had slid sideways and scattered around the seat. One book in particular caught her eye. A book on Yoga. *Arne?*

She got into her own vehicle and tried to visualize the prospect of her old neighbour sitting on a mat in position. A giggle escaped her mouth.

"What's so funny?"

"Arne's truck is parked next to us. There's some library books on the seat. One is on Yoga."

"Now that is funny," Elizabeth said, with a laugh.

"Do you really think he's into Yoga?"

Her grandmother shrugged. "Who knows. He does have a back problem and Yoga is a gentle and effective exercise."

Sydney shook her head, backed out of her spot. Once back on the highway home she forgot about Arne.

They spent a pleasant evening with Jessie and Bea. Sydney insisted that for the duration of her time with them, Bea was not to consider herself on contract. She was part of the family, one of them. Sydney told her she intended to work with her in kitchen and pick her brain. Come meal time, she was to sit with them, eat and socialize. Cleanup would be done together. Jessie and Sydney let Elizabeth and Bea do most of the talking as they shared their childhood and younger years in Stoney Creek. It was a fun evening full of laughter. All too soon, Jessie had to leave and it was bedtime.

Sydney settled under the covers, propped up with pillows. Once again she picked up the last journal and continued reading.

February 26

Dear Self,

I did it. I enrolled. I haven't said anything to Mom and Dad. If I confide in Mom she'll

tell him at some point and I'm done arguing with him. I feel bad not telling her. I have about ten weeks before we leave and I don't want any more of Dad's wrath. I can't wait to start my new life. Let them think that I've caved in to Dad's wishes.

March 10

Dear Self,

Social Services found me a furnished basement suite a couple of blocks from the school. I can get in mid-May, two weeks before classes start. They'll give me some money to buy furniture for Sydney from the Salvation Army. I'm only taking the umbrella stroller, Sydney's favourite toys, and her clothes. I'll have one suitcase and a backpack with my laptop. COUNTDOWN HAS STARTED!

March 23

Dear Self,

Mom asked me today if I was still planning to go to school. I lied. I know Self, I lied to my mother. I told her I couldn't get into the June 1st class and would probably take the next one in December. I feel terrible lying to Mom. Hopefully, one day she'll understand. Dad grunted and let it go 'cause that's so far off.

April 1

Dear Self,

Today is my birthday and Sydney's. Mom made us a combined birthday cake and she bought me a yoga mat. It was from both Mom and Dad but I know she was the one who ordered it in. They bought Sydney a teddy bear that is as big as her. She loves it. Imagine—my Sydney is one years old. She's walking or I should say running now and getting into everything. She's such a cutie. I love her to bits.

Sydney's eyes closed and she shook her head to stay awake. She wanted to read more. In a dozy state she read the next entry. *What?* She stopped and started over. When she finished, she bolted straight up in bed and read it again. Her head spun and her body went cold. *Holy shit!*

April 4

Dear Self,

Guess What? I watched a biography about Cyndi Lauper last night on television. She was dressed so cool. I'd never find her style of dress in Stoney Creek (snicker)…probably not in Kelowna either. Her clothes don't fit in with small farming towns haha. But what I really loved was her hair. Dyed pink! Can you believe it? So cool. Now that I could do. And…you know me, self…YES I DID. I dyed my hair pink like Cyndi's. Mon and Dad are out. Don't know what they'll think. Oops…too late.

Chapter 30

Jax picked up his cell. "Hi Jess. How's it going?"

"Hey Jax. Not calling too late, am I?"

"Nah. I'm cleaning up my place trying to make myself sleepy."

"Oh, so you're back at your own house are you?"

"Yah. I needed some space from my Dad. And once Syd knew I was back in town, there was no need to hide out."

"How are you coping, my friend?" Jessie asked.

He slumped into an armchair and put his feet up on the coffee table. "I'm angry, really angry. How's Syd doing?"

"I think she's over the anger part. She understands why you disappeared like you did. She let your Dad off the hook and told him hindsight isn't reality and you all have to move forward."

Jax thought about that for a moment. "She's probably right but Dad left it way too long to tell me about my past. And he should have gone to Sydney sooner about his suspicions that he might be her father."

"I can't speak for your Dad on that, but he did tell Sydney that he had no idea what she'd been told about her past and he was afraid to push himself on her and upset her life. I think it was a valid point."

"I guess it was."

"Look, I wanted to let you know that the lab contaminated Sydney's specimen. She came in today and did another test. So it's going to be a little longer before you all find out. I left a message for your Dad."

"Damn. Poor Sydney. This has to be really hard on her."

"It's hard on all of you."

The doorbell rang and Jax went to see who it was. "Someone's at my door. I'd better go. Thanks for calling, Jess."

"Not a problem. We'll talk soon."

Jax opened the door to see his father standing there, looking a little unsure.

"I just got back from Kelowna and saw your lights were on. Can I come in?" Wes asked.

"Sure." Jax led them back into the living room. "Do you want a beer?"

"Yes, thank you." Wes sat down on the couch.

Jax returned from the kitchen and handed Wes a bottle. He returned to the armchair. "How did things go in Kelowna?"

"Fine. It's all coming together well." Wes paused to take a swig of beer.

"I was talking to Jess. She told me about Sydney having to redo the swab."

Wes shook his head in disgust. "As if she isn't stressed enough. I heard the fire is over and all the firefighters left."

Jax said, "Yes. Brian and crew will be back out to the farm tomorrow to restart the project."

"That's…that's good. I'm sorry you had to leave the work, son. I know what that project means to you."

Jax shrugged. "I could use a few days off. I'm getting the house in order."

"You're still angry with me. We never got to talk it out the night I told you. Then when you came back to work the fire line with the bulldozer, I never saw you. Can we talk about it now?"

He studied his father's face. Jax could see how tired and stressed he looked. This whole thing was weighing on him too. "I couldn't talk about it when you first told me that I was your nephew, not your son. I think I would have handled it better if Sydney and I hadn't happened. The whole incest thing was too much…thinking at first that we might be brother and sister and then maybe cousins, I was way overwhelmed."

"I'm so sorry that I hurt you. My reasoning sounds like excuses and rehashing how badly I handled it all isn't going to make it any better for either of us. But you have to know that adopted or not, you're my son and you always will be." Wes took a couple of more swigs to relax and smooth his nervousness. "I love you, son."

Jax relaxed a little. "I know you do. You were a good father to me. I know being a great Dad is more than blood. And hey, we are still blood." He watched some of the tension leave his father's face. "I was talking to Jess about some of this. She helped me see things a little more in perspective. I think maybe I can let my anger go now, Dad. I love you too."

The two men sat in silence for a few minutes. Wes spoke first."Thank you. Are you…" Wes paused. "Are you up to talking a little business?"

"Sure."

Wes opened a zippered briefcase he'd carried in under his arm. He pulled out a file and handed it to Jax.

"What's this?"

"Open it and see." Wes said.

Jax read the papers inside the folder. His eyebrows rose and he looked back at his Dad. "What does this mean?"

"It means that Rhyder Developments is moving into Commercial projects and that's not a direction you should be following. I've offered the head of the Stoney Creek Division to Josh Peterson. He's a good man and more than qualified."

"Yes, I agree. He's a good choice. But this?" Jax held up the papers.

"I couldn't just cut you loose to start all over again and struggle. You've earned your way in this company and I want to help you. My lawyers have drawn up a subsidiary company, Jax Rhyder Construction, Residential Remodelling and Renovations. It's yours and you can have your crew if they want to stay with you."

Jax was speechless. "But you said Rhyder Developments couldn't carry both commercial and residential."

"The lawyers found a way. And when you're established, we can look at separating you from Rhyder Developments. It will be your company to run as you see fit."

"I don't know what to say."

"You can thank Sydney. She's the one who opened my eyes to letting you travel your own path."

Jax' face clouded over and he put the papers down.

Wes saw the change in his demeanor. "Jesus. I'm sorry. I shouldn't have mentioned Sydney."

"No, it's okay. It's just…" Jax took a deep breath. "You don't know what this means to me. Of course, I'd love to have my own company. But can I think about this?"

Wes looked confused. "I don't understand. I thought you'd be excited about this."

"Oh Dad, believe me, I am. But if it turns out that Sid and I are related, it'll be hard to hang around here you know? I'll need some time to sort this out and so will she."

Wes sighed. "Of course. I get that. Sit on it until this whole mess is sorted. When your mind is clearer you'll know what to do."

"Thanks, Dad."

Chapter 31

Sydney got out of bed and walked to the bay window. She sat on the built-in seat and stared out into the night. A partial moon shone down on the lake affording enough light to see the magnolia grove. She stared at the trees, digesting what this latest post in her mother's diary had divulged. She now knew without any uncertainty that who she thought as a child was an imaginary friend, and who she'd come to know as a spirit these past weeks, was now her mother, Chelsea Grey. The weight of it compressed on her chest. If her mother's spirit was here along with Sydney's grandfather's spirit, it meant she was dead. A chill ran through her body. The knowledge of it opened up a new set of questions to which Sydney had no answers. *Why are you here at the farmhouse? How did you die? What are you trying to tell me?*

A door opened in the hallway. Sydney heard the steady movement of her Nan's crutches on the wood flooring. Elizabeth went into the bathroom and a few minutes later, emerged to continue through the house. A rustling in kitchen cupboards caught Sydney's attention and she went to join her grandmother.

"Hi, Nan. Can't sleep?"

"I'm starving. I can never sleep when I'm hungry. Bea has some leftover chicken and potato salad in the fridge. Want some?"

"Not for me, thanks. I'll grab some trail mix out of the pantry." Sydney opened the door, finding what she craved right away. "You sit down, I'll get your food for you." She got a plate and some utensils, retrieved the foodstuffs out of the refrigerator, and placed them on the island. "How about a glass of lemonade?"

"Yes, please," Elizabeth said.

Sydney poured them both a glass and returned to the island. She sat on a stool across from her Nan. She watched her grandmother eat while nibbling on raisins, nuts and dried fruit.

"Why aren't you sleeping?" Elizabeth asked.

"I was reading the last journal. I'm almost finished. I heard you get up and decided to join you." Sydney hadn't told her about the paranormal things that had been happening on the farm. She didn't want to upset her. But the time had come for them to consider what may be some hard truths. "Nan…my mother wrote that she'd dyed her hair pink like Cyndi Lauper. Do you remember that?"

Elizabeth snickered and nodded while chewing on a chicken leg. "Yes. It was different but it did suit her. She was crazy about the woman's music. We didn't know the singer, but the two of them appeared to have similar personality traits. Free spirits. Your grandfather, of course, freaked out."

Sydney decided to jump right in with both feet. "When I was in Kelowna back in May, I asked you about my imaginary friend. Since I've been back at the farm, I've seen her on more than one occasion."

Elizabeth put her fork down and wiped her hands on a napkin. She stared at her granddaughter. "You've seen your childhood imaginary friend here? Recently?"

"I have. And she isn't imaginary, Nan. She's a spirit. You told me I called her Candy. Do you know why?"

Elizabeth nodded no, without taking her eyes off of Sydney's face.

Sydney sucked in air and spoke in barely a whisper. "Because her hair was long and reminded me of cotton candy…pink cotton candy."

The two women looked deep into each other's eyes in silence. Elizabeth raised a hand to cover her mouth. Sydney reached out and took her other hand.

"Did my mother still have pink hair the day she disappeared?"

Her Nan cleared her throat. "Yes, she did. Would you go to my room and bring me my purse, please?"

She brought back Elizabeth's purse and put it on the counter.

Her Nan took out her wallet and pulled out a picture. She handed it to her granddaughter.

Sydney stared at the picture. "Omigod...that's her." She couldn't take her eyes off the picture. "I don't think she ran off at all, Nan. Something happened to her. Her spirit is trapped here between two realms. I saw her in the studio the other day and she was crying. She begged me to be careful."

Elizabeth clutched her hand tighter. "Careful of what?"

"I don't know. She disappeared without telling me. Something in my gut says that whatever befell her, it happened here. She never left the farm that day." Her grandmother's eyes filled with tears. "Are you okay?"

Elizabeth spoke in a whisper. "I've known deep down that something happened to Chelsea. A mother knows. But it was easier to believe she ran away from us. Easier to be angry with her all these years than allow myself to accept she was gone forever."

"Oh, Nan, there's other things going on too."

"What kinds of things?"

"A man standing over my bed at night when I'm sleeping. One of the firefighters saw a young woman in the magnolia grove and another saw a man at dawn standing in the window of your bedroom. His description matched Papa." Sydney watched her grandmother carefully, scanning her facial expression.

Elizabeth straightened up and put her shoulders back. "There have been dreams. Your grandfather visits me in them. Sometimes he sits and cries...other times, he says he's sorry. The last one, he asked me to 'help her'."

"It's like they're both trying to warn us of something," Sydney said.

"Oh, Sydney. Not me but you. Papa wants me to look out for you and if Chelsea is coming to you, she's warning you of danger."

Sydney drew in a deep breath. "It certainly seems like that."

"How close are you to finishing the journal?"

"A matter of pages. Why?" Sydney asked.

"Go and get it. Let's finish it together. There might be something else in there to clue us in to what happened to Chelsea."

Sydney cleaned up the counter.

Elizabeth grasped her crutches. "Come to my bedroom."

When Sydney joined her grandmother, Elizabeth was settled in bed, propped up with pillows. She patted the other side of the bed. "Join me, like when you were a kid."

Sydney climbed in the bed beside her Nan. She opened the journal and began to read, starting back a few entries to when she decided to enrol in the classes for June 1st of that year and up to the part where Sydney discovered her mother had pink hair.

Her grandmother cried softly. Sydney reached over for a Kleenex and pushed it into her hand. "I never suspected. She should have trusted me. I wouldn't have told her father. There's something very wrong when a daughter can't trust her mother."

"Are you all right?"

Her Nan gave her a thin smile. "Yes, I'm fine. Please, continue."

April 6

Dear Self,

We knew it was coming. Didn't we, Self? Mom just smiled at my pink hair. Dad did a total flip out. He said if God wanted me to have pink hair, I'd have been born with it. My defense was that lots of girls dye their hair. It's fun. He said only those entertainment people without morals dye their hair weird colours. And since I'll never be an entertainer, no will give me a job and they'll probably fire me at the cafe. Nope. They all like it. Well—not some of the customers but my charming personality wins them over—haha.

April 11

Dear Self,

I've been sorting through my stuff, deciding what I'm taking. Keeping my laundry and Sydney's up. I told Mom I'm cleaning out all my childhood stuff and old clothes to make more room. Then I packed things I'd want to keep and get at a later date and put them in the closet. Be proud of me, I am. My room has NEVER been this tidy.

April 25

Dear Self,

I haven't told Pam we're coming 'cause I want to surprise her. Another reason is that I'm afraid she'll make a mistake and mention it to her mom. I haven't even told anyone at the cafe I'm going. I'm off work for a couple of days before we go. Another thing I feel bad about, 'cause they've been good to me there. Can't risk Dad hearing it from someone. I could tell them and he can't stop me, but life will be hell. And what if Dad follows me to the bus station and embarrasses me in front of people. No... better this way.

May 10

Dear Self,

Asshole tried talking to me today. He said Dad told him I was thinking of leaving later this year. Gave me a start because I almost thought he knew I'm leaving in five days. He said I should stay here with the people who love me, not just Mom and Dad, but people like him who have known me all my life. I almost laughed at him. He loves me? More like

lusts after me. I always catch him looking at my boobs or I turn around and know he's been staring at my butt. Okay... most guys do that, I know. I never minded when Chaz did that (laughing). But, Self, Asshole's looks are so creepy and he makes me feel dirty. So glad I won't be seeing him anymore.

May 13

Dear Self,

TWO MORE DAYS…DUH DUH DA DUH! (that's a drum roll). Mom and Dad are leaving early on the 15th. They're going to Vernon for the day to pick up some farm equipment parts. We're leaving while they're gone. Sorry Mom (tears).

May 14
Dear Self,
I haven't packed anything yet. I'm so afraid Mom or Dad will see something out of place. Honestly, I'm so nervous that if she starts asking questions, I know I couldn't lie to her and it will be an ugly scene. And you, Self, are going back into my hidey hole with my other journals until tomorrow. So next time I write to you Self, I'll be in my own apartment with Sydney. I have all morning to pack our things. Then, I'll call the cafe and tell them we're leaving. Taking a taxi to the bus station. One more sleep… SO EXCITED! Got to go and finish the five page letter I've been writing to Mom all week. I'll leave it on the kitchen table when we go. I'm trying to explain to her why I did it his way. I didn't want to put her in the position of lying to Dad. It would make things bad between them. I thanked her for being here for me and all that she's done for Sydney. And how sorry I am for all the trouble I caused her and Dad. And that I'll call her tomorrow night so she won't worry when I'm settled in my own home. (happy) See you in Kelowna, Self.

Sydney put the journal down and turned to her Nan. She had a lot of questions but right now, they needed each other. She slipped into her Nan's arms and laid her head on her shoulder. The two women clung to each other.

Elizabeth spoke first. "You were right. Chelsea never left here that day."

Sydney sat up. Her grandmother was stoic. She stared straight ahead without blinking.

"That's what I'm thinking," Sydney said, quietly.

Elizabeth turned to her. "There are a lot of things that don't add up. First, right up to the night before, Chelsea was planning to leave with you. What happened the next morning to make her change her mind and leave you with Arne's wife, Mary? Second, she planned on calling the cafe to say she wouldn't be back. The cafe never heard from her. They called the day after Chelsea disappeared to ask why she hadn't shown up for work. And third, she never left me a five page letter saying all that. Why would she lie about it in her journal?"

"But you told me she did leave a letter."

"Yes, a half-page typewritten letter printed off of her printer. All she said was that she was leaving to find a better life for herself and you, but she agreed with Dad that Sydney was better off here at the farm with me until she was settled. She asked us to look after you and she'd be in touch. That's it. And she never signed it but used a stamp she was always playing with."

Sydney picked up the journal and found the page where Chelsea mentioned finding a Yoga symbol and had stamped the entry. "Is this the stamp she put on the letter?"

Elizabeth looked and nodded. "That's it. I've finished the other three journals. Leave me this one. I'm going to go back to the beginning of the last journal and read it through to the end. You go back to bed and we'll talk some more tomorrow."

"All right, goodnight." Sydney kissed her grandmother and returned to her own bed. Her bed was comfortable and warm, but sleep wasn't forthcoming. She turned on the electric fire place display for ambiance and comfort, but not the heater fan. Propped up by pillows, Sydney watched the flames casting shadows around the room as she analyzed her mother's entries. It was dawn before she finally fell asleep.

Chapter 32

By the time Sydney woke up, Nan and Bea had eaten breakfast. Bea had left a plate of bacon and scrambled eggs in the fridge for her with a fruit cup. She heated the plate in the microwave and poured a coffee from the thermos.

As she sat at the island eating, she heard her Nan come through the French doors from the backyard. Elizabeth came into the kitchen. "She's awake."

"Good morning. I had a hard time falling asleep. How about you?"

Her Nan sat at the island with a bottle of water. "Very little sleep, I'm afraid. Listen. I've called Staff Sergeant Reynolds. I told him we have some new information and I want him to re-open the case on Chelsea. He should be here any minute. Bea's gone to town. I didn't tell her about the spirits, but I did tell her about the journals. She'll be discreet.

"I've always believed in spirits, but I never expected my beliefs would be tested...and by my own relatives."

Elizabeth shifted on the stool. "You know I don't think we should tell the RCMP about our spirits. If they think we're basing our evidence on a haunted farmhouse, we won't be taken seriously. I'm thinking we should let the journals contradict their file."

Sydney popped the last of the fruit into her mouth. "Umm...I agree with you." She took her dishes to the sink and looked out the window. "Oh, my goodness, it must be Wednesday. I forgot Brian and the guys were coming back today." She watched them unload their tools and materials.

"I think I heard tires crunching in the driveway. It must be the Staff Sergeant."

Sydney turned from the window. "I'll let him in. Meet us in the living room."

A few minutes later, introductions were made and the three of them were seated. Elizabeth asked the officer if he was familiar with the case.

"Yes. I read the file before I came. To reiterate, the file states that you and your husband were away for the day and your daughter left a note stating she was leaving to get established elsewhere. She asked you and your husband to take care of Sydney until she was settled and working. She asked your neighbour Mary to watch your granddaughter until you returned home and left carrying a suitcase. Follow-up at the time confirmed that Chelsea never caught the bus out of town. It was assumed she must have hitch-hiked or someone she knew picked her up and gave her a ride. No one saw her on the road or saw her in town that day. Is that the report as you remember it?"

"Yes, it is," Elizabeth said.

"There was a follow-up note added that you'd received a call from Social Services in Kelowna. And that Chelsea and Sydney missed an appointment with them that day. They were holding an apartment for her and she was signed up to start school two weeks later. Is that correct?"

"Yes. I told them about her note to us and they said that sometimes young mother's get scared when the time comes for them to be out on their own and their behavior could be unpredictable. She assured me that Chelsea would be in touch at some point."

"The detachment did follow up with the Kelowna detachment. They investigated and came up with nothing new. It was concluded that since she was of legal age and there was nothing to suggest foul play, there was nothing more to be done. Right or wrong, she could leave if she wanted to."

"That's right. But I believe she did meet with foul play and I don't think she even left town," Elizabeth said.

"You mentioned on the phone that you had some new evidence, some journals."

"Four journals were found when the renovations began on the farmhouse. They belong to Chelsea. Sydney and I have both read them. It's the last journal that raises some questions about her disappearance. They're in that bag on the table."

"May I look?"

"Absolutely. You'll want to take them with you. But for now all you need to do is read the last few entries."

The officer read the last page. "Why don't you tell me how you think these entries change things."

"Right up to the night before she was planning to leave, Chelsea was excited. She couldn't wait to take her daughter and leave while we were gone. Something happened the next day to change her mind. At the time, I gave merit to the Social Worker that she may have panicked at the last minute. But that wasn't her nature. She was a free spirit and adventurous. And these entries contradict that assumption and there are other discrepancies."

"And what are they?"

"Chelsea said she wrote me a five page letter. You read that entry. All we found was a half-page typed note, no signature, just a stamp. She said she was going to call the cafe and let them know she wouldn't be back. She was very conscientious when it came to work and courteous. She never called them. Nor did she contact the Social Worker to say she changed her mind. That's not Chelsea."

"Okay. Anything else?"

"Yes. Chelsea was a good mother and whenever she left Sydney with Mary she'd pack everything but the kitchen sink in Sydney's diaper bag, even if she was only gone an hour. Mary and I used to laugh about it. I remembered this morning that Mary told me that the bag had one bottle, one diaper and one change of clothes stuffed in it like she was in a hurry to leave. Chelsea says in the journal she had all morning to pack. One diaper wouldn't carry her through the day until I got home. And she always packed Sydney's favourite teddy. Sydney wouldn't go down to nap without it. It wasn't in the diaper bag.".

Sydney had remained quiet and listened to her grandmother talk. She had a question of her own. "How did Mary get me and the diaper bag. Did Chelsea call her or did she take me across the road to the farm?"

"No. Arne came over to see your grandfather. He said Chelsea asked him if he and Mary could babysit you until we got home. She told him a sick friend had asked her to help her for a few days. He said she handed him the diaper bag and you, and walked out the door with one suitcase."

Sydney felt that old familiar rock sitting in her gut. She turned to the officer. "My mother wrote that she was taking one suitcase and one backpack for herself. Arne said she only had one suitcase. And she wrote about taking a taxi to the bus station. Why would she leave with one case and walk down the road? And she left her journals behind that she planned on taking with her. Is he the only witness?"

"He is," the Staff Sergeant said.

"Something isn't right. I don't like him and I don't trust him. He's creepy."

The officer returned the journal to the plastic bag."Has he done something to make you feel that way?"

"No. It's his demeanor and how he looks at me."

"So what happens now?" Elizabeth asked.

"You said on the phone that you hired an investigator to try to find Chelsea after you moved to Kelowna; and he found no trace. And you've never heard from her over the years?"

"No, nothing."

"We'll go over the journals, do some more enquiries. We'll need to talk to Mr. Jensen again. In the meantime, don't tell him about our conversation or the journals." Staff Sergeant Reynolds stood. He gave them his RCMP business card with a file number written on the back. "If you think of anything else, please call me. I'll be in touch, ladies."

Sydney saw him to the door and rejoined her Nan. "What do you think? Will they re-open the case?"

"I haven't a clue. They're trained to mask their reactions and to never reveal what they're thinking."

Brian walked around the whole barn studying the structure and stopped at the barn doors.

"Good afternoon, Brian."

He spun around and saw Arne standing behind him. "Hi, Mr. Jensen. How are you?"

"I'll be a lot better when the first cut of haying is finished. How's your Dad?"

"Fine, sir. He's away on holiday right now. I think he's finally eased into retirement and enjoying it."

"Humph... don't see the point of that. I've always believed that idle hands are the Devil's workshop."

Brian stared at the man. *Asshole.*

"So what are you eyeing the barn for?"

"We need to fix the door hardware. Then the whole exterior is up for a paint job. Some of the guys are finishing the residence interior. The rest of us thought we'd start painting the exteriors. But we'll do the barn last, so we're not in your way of hauling hay bales."

"I should be finished haying in a couple of days. Then it's all yours."

"You've got it. We have some deck building to do as well on the house." Brian turned to head back to the residence.

Arne cleared his throat. "So what was the RCMP doing here this morning? The ladies are all right I hope."

The foreman turned back to the farmer. "I'm not sure. I overheard Bea and Elizabeth talking about her daughter earlier. You know, the one that disappeared when Sydney was a baby?"

"Ya, I remember."

"Elizabeth mentioned something about journals. I didn't get the whole conversation."

Arne's eyebrows shot up. "Journals?"

"I think so. When we were renovating inside the house, Jax found a wooden box in the floor boards. There was something locked inside it. He gave it to Sydney. Maybe it was the journals."

Arne stared at the house. "So the old farmhouse has some secrets, eh?"

Brian realized they were gossiping about something they really knew nothing about. "I guess so. I'm not really sure what it was about." He turned and started to walk away to end the conversation. "Gotta get back to work. See ya."

"Yup, later."

Brian headed around the farmhouse and up onto the veranda. He knocked on the door and waited. Sydney opened the door and gave him a big smile.

"Welcome back. Come in."

The foreman stepped into the hall and took his boots off and followed her into the living room.

"Hi, Elizabeth."

"Hi Brian. Back at it, eh"

"I won't sit in my work clothes. I wanted you to know that two of the boys are working in the residence. Two more are going to finish the deck at the back and I'll be working on the front steps. It'll be a little noisy for a couple of days."

Sydney laughed. "Not a problem. It's been so quiet since the fire crew left. A little noise will help us to adapt."

" For safety reasons, I'd like to ask you to come and go through the mud room."

"We can do that," Sydney said.

"I saw Reynolds here this morning. Is everything all right?"

Elizabeth passed a hand through the air. "Just a little old family business. No worries."

"Good." It wasn't his business. As long as the women were okay, he wouldn't pry.

"How about you? I saw you talking to Arne. You looked a little upset," Sydney said.

Brian turned red. "He's an asshole, pardon my French. He asked me about my Dad and I said he was enjoying retirement. You know what he said? Idle hands were the Devil's workshop."

Elizabeth laughed. "He's old time religious. Not as fanatical as my Frank was, mind you. Don't pay him any never mind."

The foreman wasn't about to tell them the rest of his conversation with Arne. "I'd best get to work. Just wanted to update you on our work schedule."

Sydney walked him out. "Thanks, Brian."

The man rejoined his crew and discussed their plans for the next few days. Once the men got started on the rear deck, he drove his pick-p to the front steps, unloaded his materials and tools, and got to work. His thoughts turned to Jax. *Something's up there. Why isn't he here working with us? This project was his baby.* Jax told him he was taking some time off and that he, Brian knew what he was doing. *This has something to do with Sydney. I know it. Jax hasn't been out to the farm since before the fire. Too bad. They make such a cute couple.*

Chapter 33

A few days later, Elizabeth and Sydney sat on the newly extended and stained deck off the dining room, watching the workmen paint the residence. Brian was out front of the farmhouse applying the finishing coat to the porch and stairs.

They were supposed to be in Kelowna getting Elizabeth a walking cast but the doctor had an emergency. The office asked them to come in at the beginning of next week.

Elizabeth took a sip of her lemonade. "I love that brick colour you chose for the exterior walls. You know me, pastels are my thing. But the contrast with the black roof is rich, even if it is a little bold."

"That's why I chose white for the trim, to tone it all down a little," Sydney said. "By next week, they should be done."

"Then it's just you and me. Monday, I get my walking cast."

"There'll be no stopping you then."

Elizabeth laughed. "I can't wait to drive again. I'm not used to relying on other people to take me places."

Sydney smiled. "Well, I'm not ready to let you go home yet."

"And I'm not ready to leave. I'm looking forward to enjoying some peace and quiet with you when the workmen leave."

The two women sat in silence while enjoying the soft breeze that cooled the heat of the day. Sydney stared at the Magnolia grove. "Isn't it funny that my mother and I both hid in the grove, climbed the same tree, and sat on the same branch."

"It is, isn't it?"

"You know, whenever she was present inside the house, the room smelled of magnolias."

"The bond between mother and daughter is a strong one, even in spirit. I had a strange dream last night. Again, your grandfather was visiting me. He was very calm this time and gave me a message for you."

Sydney looked at her Nan. "For me? What was it?"

"He spoke very slowly with deliberate phrasing. He said, *'Tell Sydney to use the keys'*. It was strange because he smiled at me with a very tender and affectionate look. And we both know that wasn't Frank's way. He got up and walked to the door, turned and said, *'The keys—use them'*. I woke up at that point."

Sydney shook her head, feeling frustrated. "What good are a couple of spirits when everything they say confuses us more than before? What keys? What are they trying to tell us, Nan?"

Elizabeth laughed. "Sorry, it struck me funny. Most people would be freaked having spirits around and you're complaining about their inability to communicate. I think that maybe it's you and me with the problem, hon. You know when you were a kid and we did puzzles? We pulled out all the flat edges and created the frame of the puzzle. We just haven't filled in the centre yet. Perhaps it will all make sense soon."

"I'm sure glad we're talking about all of this. Having a haunted farm scared me. If word gets out, my business might never get off the ground."

"Well, spirits hang around for a reason. We know who ours are and it's up to us to figure out the mystery."

" I've been reading on the internet about spirits who don't pass over but stay suspended between the earthly realm and the spirit realm."

"What have you learned/"

Sydney sipped her lemonade. "There are a lot of reasons why one doesn't move forward. Sometimes, if they were bad people in physical form, they're afraid to enter the spirit realm. They think they will have to answer to a higher power for their misdeeds. Other ones, who died violently or suddenly, haven't yet discovered that they are dead and are locked in-between two parallels. And then others, stay behind deliberately to look out over loved ones—to protect them."

Elizabeth shifted in her chair to change the angle of her cast. "It seems the latter is the case for Frank and…" She trailed off, pushed her chin out and continued, "…and Chelsea."

Sydney reached out to pat her arm. "It must be hard for you to say those words after all the years of wondering about my mother."

"It is. But as I said before, I've always known deep down that something happened to her. I just wasn't ready to accept it and say it out loud. Now I am and I want to know the truth."

"In my research, I read some interesting things. Greek philosophers called these souls 'walkers'. They believed they were mediators or messengers that walked between the realm of the living and the realm of the dead."

"Walkers. I like that term. If the Staff Sergeant wont re-open Chelsea's file, we'll tell them about our walkers. We can quote Greek philosophy; let them know that we know what we're talking about." Elizabeth nodded her head in defiance. "Tell me more."

Sydney smiled at her Nan. "I read a book about a man who died and came back to visit his sister. He told her that we go through a number of transitions when we pass to the afterlife. First, our physical body dies, releasing our soul into the universe. The soul may visit with other family members who have passed before them. They see them in their earthly, physical form so that they recognize them. This can be very comforting to a new soul. This transition phase is where the soul sees the life it lived on the earthly plane and comes to terms with their transgressions, good or bad. There's no time frame attached to this transition. Time doesn't exist."

"Fascinating. And this is supposed to be a true story?"

"It is. Do you want some more lemonade?"

"Yes, thanks."

Sydney took their glasses into the house for refills and returned.

Elizabeth took one of her crutches and rested it on the edge of her seat under her thigh. She lifted her leg onto the crutch and stretched it out. "That feels better." She took her glass from Sydney and took a big gulp. "Mmm... delish. Tell me more, hon."

"According to the story, this soul transition is where a soul has three choices, either it reincarnates back into the earthly plane or stays there as a walker. The last choice, if the soul is ready, is to transition from a soul into a spirit. A spirit returns to the clan that it originated from. Apparently, there are different clans. The soul finds their clan and rejoins them as a Light Being. It's a bit of a simplification but that's the gist of it."

"So what you're saying, if we believe the story, is that Frank and Chelsea aren't spirits yet, but still souls, 'walkers' if you will." Elizabeth summed up.

"That's right. And if we were smart enough to figure out what they're trying to tell us, they can transition to their clans."

They sat in silence, until Elizabeth dozed in her chair. Sydney tried to put the messages all together and make some sense of it all.

"Good afternoon, ladies."

Sydney turned with a start to see Staff Sergeant Reynolds stepping up onto the deck. "Hello."

Elizabeth woke up at the sound of their voices. "Staff Sergeant," she nodded.

"I wanted to let you know that after reading your daughter's journals, we've decided to re-open her case."

"Oh thank you so much," Elizabeth said.

"We'll talk to those who gave us statements at the time. And we'll contact old friends to see if any of them heard from her over the years. One thing we noticed, is that Chelsea referred to people in the journal by initials, not by name. When you read the journals, did you recognize any of the people she wrote about?"

"Her best friend, Pam but she mentioned her by name. She's Bea's daughter. And Chaz is Wesley Rhyder."

The Staff Sergeant wrote the names down. "Did you keep any of your daughter's belongings after she left?"

"Yes. I have a box stored at home in Kelowna. What are you looking for?"

"Anything and everything. You never know what may end up being a clue. Specifically, did Chelsea have a year book from her graduation year?"

"Yes, it's in the box."

"Good. We'd like to have access to the box if we could."

Sydney interjected here. "We're going to the hospital in Kelowna on Monday to get Nan a walking cast. We could stop at home and pick it up."

"Thank you."

The sound of a tractor coming from the north field drew their attention. Arne drove the tractor up beside the barn. He got down and saw the three of them watching him. He gave a wave and sauntered over. "Staff Sergeant, ladies. Beautiful day, isn't it?

Sydney was silent, Elizabeth nodded to him. "Hello, Arne."

"Good afternoon, Mr. Jensen," Staff Sergeant Reynolds said. "The detachment is re-opening the case of the disappearance of Chelsea Grey, Elizabeth's daughter."

Arne's expression was stoic. "Really?"

"Yes, sir. We're interviewing all the people we spoke with at the time. I was wondering if you would mind coming into the station this afternoon to review your statement?"

"Can you wait a couple of days?" Arne turned to Elizabeth. "No disrespect intended, Lizzie. My helper and I will be done with the haying tonight and tomorrow we'll get the baling finished. Dan's making a delivery on Sunday."

"None taken, Arne. We've waited this long, a couple of days won't matter," Elizabeth said.

The Staff Sergeant nodded. "Can you come in Saturday afternoon?"

Arne addressed the officer. "Yup. May I ask why after all this time, you're looking into Chelsea's case?"

The Staff Sergeant smiled. "We like to pull cold cases and have another look when we get the time. Chelsea's case came up on the docket this time around."

Arne nodded. "See you Saturday, Staff Sergeant." They watched him walk back to the barn, close the doors and lock them.

The officer cleared his throat. "One more thing. One day next week, after the Rhyder crew are done here, we'd like to bring in a couple of dogs from Head Office."

"Dogs?" Sydney asked, confused.

Elizabeth took hold of Sydney's hand. "Cadaver dogs, dear."

The Staff Sergeant looked sympathetic. "We're in agreement that the journal suggests something may have happened to Chelsea the day she was planning to leave. We'd like to have the dogs search the whole farm."

Elizabeth frowned. "But Arne saw her walk off down the road. She could be anywhere."

"Mr. Jensen saw her leave the house and head to the road. He never actually saw her on the road. If the dogs don't detect anything; we'll bring in a diver to search the lake. It's a process of elimination and at the very least we'll know that she's not on the property."

Sydney felt a lump form in her throat. "Can they find something after twenty years?"

"A good dog can. And these two are the best we have.

"Let us know the day, we'll be here," Elizabeth said, quietly.

"You can drop that box off at the station, ladies. We'll keep in touch."

Alone again, the two women held hands.

"I can't believe it's really happening, " Sydney said.

She looked at her grandmother. They both had tears in their eyes.

Chapter 34

Staff Sergeant Reynolds led Arne Jensen into an interrogation room. He sat across a table and opened the Grey file. He pulled Arne's statement from twenty years previous.

"I know a lot of time has passed since the day Chelsea left but why don't you begin with what you do remember about that day, starting with going over to the Grey farm."

Arne sighed. "I'll try. It's been a lot of years. Frank and I had worked on the old baler I had in those days. I was having some problems with it. I'd pulled a broken part out of it and went over to see if Frank happened to have one sitting around. Most of our equipment was the same and we always gave each other a part if we had it, so we didn't have to wait for the order to come in. When it did arrive, we'd replace the part we'd borrowed."

"What time was it when you went over?"

The farmer shrugged. "I can't remember exactly, maybe midmorning."

"Please continue."

"Well, Chelsea answered the door. She said Frank and Lizzie had gone to Vernon for the day. She told me I could go back to the equipment building and look for the part if I wanted. I noticed a suitcase standing by the door and asked her if she was going on a trip. She said she had to help a friend who'd had an accident and asked if Mary could look after the baby 'til her parents came home later that day.

Later, Lizzie told Mary that Chelsea had left a note saying she wasn't coming back for awhile and wanted them to take care of Sydney. I guess she lied to me because she knew I'd try to talk her out of it."

"What happened next?"

"I said we'd be happy to watch Sydney and asked if she needed a ride anywhere, thinking she was taking a bus out of town. She said she was meeting a friend down the road."

"Did she say she was getting a ride to the bus depot?"

"Nope. She didn't say if she was taking a bus or getting a ride to where she was headed She seemed to have it all worked out so I minded my own business."

The officer studied his face and mannerisms each time he spoke. "Tell me about her demeanor."

Arne creased his brows. "What's that mean…demeanor?"

"Was she upset, nervous, in a hurry?"

"She was definitely in a hurry. Umm…maybe a little nervous. She got the baby and put her in a car seat and handed her over to me with one of those bags that you put baby things in. She kissed the baby on the cheek and left. That's the last time I saw her."

"How much time would you say passed from the time you arrived at the Grey farm to when you left to go home with Sydney/"

Arne whistled and shuffled in his seat. "I don't know after all this time, maybe thirty minutes. I strapped Sydney into the truck and drove around back. I spent some time looking for a part for the baler but never did find one. As I crossed the road to my driveway, I looked down the road towards town but she was nowhere to be seen. I figured she'd been picked up."

The officer picked up another statement. "This is your wife's statement. I'm sorry to hear of her passing, Mr. Jensen. How long since you lost her?"

"It's been fifteen years."

"It must have been a blow for you to not only lose your wife but someone to share the farm with."

Arne sneered. "Mary hated farm life. She tried but she wasn't much of a farmer's wife."

"What did Mary die of, sir?"

"Heart attack. Came as quite a shock 'cause she hadn't been sick a day in her life."

"How old was she/"

"Forty-five."

The Staff Sergeant changed the subject. "Mary told the officers that you were gone for over an hour that morning. Did you go anywhere else, other than the Grey farm?"

The farmer shrugged his shoulders. "No, I didn't. I guess I spent longer looking for that part than I remember. It was a long time ago."

"Yes, I'm sure it's not easy after all this time, sir. But your statement that you gave the day after Chelsea left was that you were only away for thirty minutes, as you just said."

Arne sat up straighter and stared hard at the officer. 'As I said, I may have spent longer in the equipment building. Time flies when you're looking for something. And Sydney had fallen asleep in her car seat, so I had all the time in the world."

"You said a few minutes ago that if you'd known Chelsea wasn't planning to return home, you'd have tried to talk her out of it. She was of legal age to leave home if she chose to. Why would you try to dissuade her?"

"Because I knew her parents would have worried about her and Sydney needed her. I would think that she should be home where she had family to help her. She was young and naive. Are we done here?"

"For now, Mr. Jensen. I'd like to thank you for coming by. And if you should think of anything that may be of help, please contact me." The Staff Sergeant handed him a card and saw him out of the room.

The officer joined his team. "His story was much the same as twenty years ago except his explanation about the discrepancy in time between Mary Jensen's statement and his own. Back then, he said Mary was wrong. She bowed to his version and said he was probably right. He insisted he'd only been gone for thirty minutes not over an hour.

But this time, to account for the difference of thirty minutes, he suggested he'd spent more time in the equipment building looking for that baler part than he remembered."

One of his men spoke up. "It's certainly not enough to prove anything. And Mary's gone. All we have is his word twenty years later against his own words back then. It just won't fly. What's next?"

"We'll see if the dogs turn up anything next week."

Chapter 35

Sydney wandered through the magnolia grove, inhaling the fragrance of the flowers. It was a quiet Sunday morning. The Rhyder crew had a day off and her Nan was down napping. Sydney smiled. Tomorrow they were going to Kelowna to get her grandmother's walking cast. She'd be able to walk on her leg for the first time with the use of crutches. It had been a long month for her Nan.

When she reached her tree, she climbed up onto the branch and scanned the meadows around the property. She had no doubt that she was in contact with her mother in the ethereal sense. She drew her knees up and leaned back against the bark. *Are you out there somewhere? I wish you could give us more clues.* She'd read that it was rare for spirits to talk directly to their loved ones. The energy fields they crossed from one realm to another was very exhausting for them. Visual contact was the normal form. In order for her mother and her Papa to talk to her grandmother and herself, a lot of energy and strong will were required. *The fact that you've both achieved what you have in coming before us accentuates your need to communicate.* Sydney felt absolute frustration. *Am I too stupid to put it all together? What are you trying to tell me?* She wondered if her grandfather and her mother were aware of each other's soul presence and were working together in their efforts to reach them. Her gaze focused on the lake. She shivered at the prospect that Chelsea's remains could be at the bottom of the lake. Until the lake was searched, the thought of swimming in it left her chilled.

A movement on the roof of the barn caught her peripheral vision and she focused on that. A chuckle escaped her lips. Caesar was perched on the edge of the roof. He laid down and let his head hang over the edge. He'd settled in quite happily on the farm and this was one of his favourite spots. His head moved back and forth as he studied the fields below. He'd wait patiently until he'd see movement. He'd disappear inside the loft and in a matter of seconds he'd be outside chasing mice in the long grass. He'd brought them a few gifts and dropped them at their feet since he'd perfected his hunting skills.

The sound of vehicles driving into the yard drew her attention to the front of the barn. Arne parked his pick-up by the side of the barn. The flat deck, driven by his helper pulled to the opposite side and turned around. Arne unlocked the barn doors and drove the front end loader out. He'd finished the baling yesterday. Today, he was using the front end loader in the fields to pick up the bales and transfer them to the flat deck. Arne got out of the truck and went back into the barn. When he returned, he spoke with Dan for a few minutes. Climbing into the loader, something fell onto the ground as he slammed the door shut. Sydney watched them both drive out to the north field. Dan unhitched the flat deck and came back with the cab and left the property. She could see him heading down the road to town. She turned back to the north field and watched Arne lift bales and place them on the flat deck. Normally, the flat deck would move along the rows ahead of the loader, not sit stationary. Without Dan's help it would take a lot longer to get the job done. *Probably sent Dan on an errand. He'll be back.*

Curious about the object she saw fall from the loader, Sydney climbed out of the tree and walked to the barn. She searched around in the dirt until she saw it. A set of keys. She picked them up and realized it was the same set Arne always wore on his belt. His truck keys were separate and this set never left his belt. The metal ring had worn through and broken the circle.

She looked towards the north field but on level ground it was impossible to see Arne. *He doesn't need the keys in the field. I'll hold them until he comes in.* Sydney walked around the front of the house and curled up on the new swing on the porch that replaced the old single one. This swing was also suspended from the roof joists but built for two people. As she rocked back and forth, she stared off in the distance. Her fingers ran absentmindedly over the ring of keys in her hand. Eventually, the contoured keys she was feeling caught her attention. There was a symmetric sameness to most of them. Sydney held them up and stared at them one by one. Apart from what looked like spare vehicle and house keys, the others were padlock keys. *Who needs that many padlocks? Arne has a few outbuildings and some sheds but this was ridiculous. Locks and keys. What's your story?*

Sydney started to sing a song by Rush called *'Locks and Keys'.*

Don't want to silence a desperate voice for the sake of security
No one wants to make a terrible choice on the price of being free
I don't want to face the killer instinct, face it in you or me
So we keep it under lock and key...

She stopped and stared at the keys. Her mind came alive. "Holy shit!" She jumped off the swing, ran into the entranceway and grabbed her car keys out of the bowl on the console table. Jumbled words and phrases filled her head. Sydney tried to sort them. She tore out of the yard in her car and across the road into Arne's driveway. You could just see the roofline of his farmhouse as it sat about half a kilometer from the road. She drove so fast a cloud of dust flew behind her.

Tell Sydney to use the keys... The keys... She looks a lot like her mother, except younger...I'm really into meditating now...I'm reading about soul travel... soul travel...Arne has a library book on Yoga in his truck...

Sydney pounded the steering wheel, yelling as she drove. "Shit, shit. I'm such a dummy."

I've been writing Mom a five page letter, I'll leave it on the table... She left a half page typewritten note...She always packed the diaper bag with everything except the kitchen sink... There was one diaper, one bottle, one change of clothes stuffed into the diaper bag... 'A' says he loves me... A is for Asshole... Know what he said about my father? He's such an asshole...

Sydney skidded to a stop at the farmhouse yelling into the air. "A is for Asshole, Asshole is for Arne. Shit."

She dove out of the car and ran up to the door. She tried the house keys until one worked and the lock turned. Sydney hadn't been in the house since she was a baby and had no idea of the layout. The hallway was dark so she turned on the light switch. All the draperies were closed over the windows. She found her way to the kitchen. There was a pot of stew simmering on the old gas stove on a low gas flame. Sydney searched all the rooms and made her way upstairs. None of the doors were locked. She returned to the kitchen and noted a curtain hanging over a door. She pulled it aside and found a padlocked door. With shaking hands, she tried the padlock keys until one snapped the lock open. With one hand, she pushed it ajar and saw a flight of stairs to a basement. Her hand hit the light switch and she raced down the stairs only to find another padlocked door at the bottom. She fumbled with the keys, once again the lock flew open. She found another light switch in the dank, dark room. There were storage shelves and boxes. Sydney noted three more doors. Two were not padlocked. Her heart pounded as she moved quickly to the last door with a heavy padlock. A struggle to find the right key for the final padlock, left her shaking like a leaf. She dropped the ring on the floor and had to start again. "Shit." Sydney started to panic. That deep gut feeling she had experienced her whole life when something major was about to happen, almost overwhelmed her. She knew this door was important and held the key to all the unanswered questions that had plagued her family for years. *Calm down. Take deep breaths. In and out, in and out.* Sydney gripped each key tightly as she tried the lock. Finally, the padlock released.

The seconds it took to open the door and step inside seemed an eternity. Sydney felt like she was moving in slow motion and what her eyes envisioned buckled her legs. Off balance, she slipped to her knees; her unblinking eyes frozen open. "Omigod…"

Sydney's words echoed faintly in her ears, as if she had spoken from a far distance.

Chapter 36

Arne put on the hearing protector earmuffs and fell into a rhythm of picking up the round hay bales with the balers and depositing them on the flat deck. He had to come back and forth to the stationary flat deck until Dan returned. His thoughts centered on the police interview he'd had in town yesterday. He thought he'd done well and smiled. He remembered every detail of that day. *But why investigate now? The RCMP said it was routine to pull cold cases. I don't believe it. Too coincidental that Brian mentioned some hidden journals. And no mistake that Chelsea's file got pulled after her mother and daughter came back to the farm after all these years. It's that daughter, Sydney. I bet if she'd never moved back to Stoney Creek, the case would have stayed cold.*

The whole Grey family were a big pain in the ass. Then there was his wife, Mary. Stupid woman. A sudden memory came back. He hadn't remembered everything yesterday at the police interview. Mary contradicted his time frame on that fateful day but it was a matter of his word against hers. She'd backed off and changed her statement when he'd pleaded that since he was the last one to see Chelsea he could be a suspect in her disappearance. "Goddamn," he blurted out. He realized his mistake in telling the Staff Sergeant yesterday that he probably spent more time searching for the baler part on the Grey farm, thus backing up her original statement. *So what? Mary's dead. They can't prove a thing. But it's all come too close to home. I'm going to have to make some plans.*

His thoughts returned to Mary and her death six months after Chelsea's disappearance. It had started with her and her damn interference in his private thoughts and actions. *It didn't have to happen but I guess it was an impossible situation.* Her suspicions and accusations became intolerable. He knew what he needed to do and he'd done it. Poor Mary had a fatal heart attack and his world became his own. Elation would describe the feeling. Freedom was another.

Three years later, Frank Grey came crashing into his world. *I'd become careless and complacent. Frank was my closest friend. He meant more to me than Mary. But he discovered my secret and that made him a threat. Frank had a heart condition so no one was surprised when he died of a heart attack. Lizzie had enough heartache and leased out the farm. Too bad she and Sydney hadn't stayed away.*

And then there was Chelsea, dear sweet Chelsea.

Arne made a turn to return to the flat deck for the umpteenth time. He was facing the back of the farmhouse. He heard a vehicle screech out of the driveway and looked beyond the house. He couldn't see a thing from out in the pasture, except plumes of dust rising in the air. The dust cloud was headed towards his place which meant whoever was causing it was in his driveway. *What now?* The farmer turned the loader around and headed towards the dirt road back to the barn and his pick-up. He bounced along the uneven ground as fast as he dared, afraid he'd bounce it over onto its side. *Bloody hell.*

Finally, he reached the barn and jumped down from the loader and ran to his truck. He backed up and spun it around. Arne drove around the side of the house to the end of the driveway. A number of vehicles were heading in both directions. *Goddamn.* He waited for the traffic to pass. *Sunday services are over. Damn church goers.* He tore across the road and into his driveway. *Good thing I saw that dust cloud. It's all gone now.* The drive to his farmhouse seemed endless. When he arrived, he saw Sydney's vehicle parked out front and her nowhere to be seen. His head spun to the front door. It was open. *What the hell?*

Arne turned off the truck, pulled the keys from the ignition and studied the ring. His door key was hanging with the rest. His hand went to his belt as he climbed from the cab. *Nothing*. He looked down at his belt. The ring was gone. *That bitch. She must have found them near the barn. But why did she break into his house? She couldn't know anything*. He ran towards the house, taking the stairs two at a time. He stopped inside the front door in the hallway to listen but heard nothing. Reaching the kitchen, the open basement door told him what he needed to know. Down the stairs he crept and across the storage room floor to the open doorway across the room.

In a flash, he was through the doorway and hovering over Sydney kneeling on the floor with her back to him. He grabbed her by the shoulders and pulled her to her feet. Screams of terror filled the room. Arne shook her like a rag doll. "You bitch. You had to come back and stick your nose into my business eh? Well, guess what? It'll be the last thing you'll ever do." He threw her across the room and Sydney fell hard against the cement wall. Her head hit a metal pipe running across the wall, knocking her out cold. She slumped into a heap on the floor.

Chapter 37

Elizabeth tossed and turned on her bed. Something was disturbing her in her sleep and she was being forced into consciousness. *What's going on?* Her eyes popped open and she became aware that her bed was shaking. Not a gentle vibration like those hotel beds where you put coins into a slot. This was a violent shaking that had her literally bouncing. *Holy shit!* She stared at the ceiling as the violent vibration tossed her around. *An earthquake?* Elizabeth searched the room. Her eyes zeroed in on a figure at the end of the bed. As soon as she saw him, the bed stopped shaking.

"Frank?"

Frank stood still with tears streaming down his face. He reached his hands out to her and his mouth moved like he was trying to talk to her. Elizabeth sat up and pulled her legs over the edge of the bed.

"Please, talk to me," she pleaded.

Frank pointed out the bedroom door. Elizabeth heard a vehicle screech out of the driveway. She grabbed her crutches and made her way down the hallway to the front window. Sydney's car was gone but she could see the dust rising from Arne's road to his farmhouse. *Was it Sydney?* She turned to see Frank standing beside her. His mouth started to move and this time she could hear a whisper of words. *Help her.* And he disappeared.

Before she could react, Elizabeth heard another vehicle racing in the yard. She looked out to see Arne hit his brakes at the end of the driveway. Traffic passed in front of the house and as he sped out of the driveway, the back tires spun, spewing rocks in every direction. *What is happening?* Once again dust clouds rose in his haste up his driveway. *What should I do. What can I do.* Intuitively, she knew Arne was chasing after Sydney. *She needs my help. That's what Frank is telling me.*

Elizabeth worked her way to the hallway. She picked up her cell phone and car keys. She reached the porch, stopped and threw down her crutches. "Bugger this!" she yelled out. *It'll take me all day to get there at this rate.* As soon as Elizabeth put weight on her foot, the pain shot through her ankle and up her leg. "Fuck!" But she kept going. *My granddaughter needs me.* She hobbled across the porch and reached the stairs. She leaned over the banister and hung on with both arms, hopping on one leg down each step, one at a time. Her car was parked around the far side of the house out of the way. "Dammit! Whose idea was that anyway?" The pain was excruciating but Elizabeth limped her way on the uneven ground, cursing every step. Once at her car, she collapsed into the driver's seat. Elizabeth lifted her hurting ankle onto the gas pedal, turned around in the driveway and followed suit into Arne's driveway. It felt good to drive like a bat out of hell after struggling to reach the car. Arne's house came into view and she could see Sydney's car parked by Arne's truck.

She struggled out of the car and started the arduous journey to the porch. That's when she noticed smoke coming out of the open door. *Oh no.* Elizabeth took the cell phone out of her pocket and punched emergency.

"911. What's your emergency?"

"This is Elizabeth Grey at 1266 Valley Road. There's a fire at Arne Jensen's farm across from me, 1260 Valley Road. We need the RCMP here as well."

"Is anyone hurt, Ms. Grey?"

"I don't know. I'm sorry I can't talk right now, I'll leave my phone open, please stay on the line with me."

"They're on the way, Ms Grey. Ms Grey?"

Elizabeth slipped the phone into her pocket. She'd reached the steps up to Arne's porch and needed both hands. After dragging herself up, she pushed on and through the doorway. The smoke was travelling along the ceiling above her head. Elizabeth lowered her body and limped on, ignoring the mind numbing pain. She found herself in the kitchen. This was the origin of the fire. The smoke was thicker here and Elizabeth coughed. Across the room, Arne had his back to her. He was struggling with Sydney. She could hear her muffled cries. He hadn't heard Elizabeth because he was loudly cursing the girl. She couldn't see her granddaughter who was dwarfed by Arne but he appeared to be choking her with his bare hands.

Oh no, no. I lost my daughter but I'm not going to lose my granddaughter. Frantically, her eyes searched for something to use as a weapon. She hobbled over to the sink and picked up a cast iron fry pan. With all the strength she could muster, Elizabeth literally ran across the floor. Where the strength came from she didn't know, but the adrenaline rush was huge. With all the aggression of a banty rooster and a war cry to match, she swung the heavy iron pan over her head. The force of her blow hit the Side of his head so hard that her body followed with it. She heard the crack on his skull, which split the skin and a back splatter of blood sprayed over her.

Arne went down with Sydney under him. They both hit the floor with Elizabeth landing on top of Arne's back. On her way down, she also heard the crack in her ankle as her leg slipped out from under her. She laid there in unbearable pain trying to get her breath before it registered that Sydney was lying at the bottom of the pile. Elizabeth tried to stand but collapsed, screaming out in pain and frustration. She pushed onto her side unaware of the odd angle of her foot where the plaster had cracked around her ankle, separating the foot cast from the lower leg plaster casing. She rolled onto her back and slid onto the floor moaning with the waves of torturous pain.

Sydney was struggling to push Arne off of her to no avail. Elizabeth could hear her granddaughter gasping for air, his dead weight pinning her chest to the floor, his shoulder across her face. Elizabeth pushed herself onto her stomach and looped one hand through Arne's belt. Once again her arm found strength and she pulled hard, letting out a high-pitched scream like a kick boxer. She managed to get him off of her chest, and left him laying across her thighs and legs. She'd read a story that screaming or grunting enhanced a kick boxer's power by ten percent and it certainly worked in her favour.

Elizabeth collapsed on the floor. She turned her head. The girl's chest heaved as she gasped in air. She was alive. Sirens wailed in the distance, getting closer and closer. Elizabeth wriggled up the floor, ignoring her pain. She found an arm and searched for a hand. The fingers grasped hers and held on tight. Elizabeth inched a little further up the floor past Arne's bulky body to try to see her granddaughter's face. The smoke had reached them at floor level and she started to cough. She wasn't quite in a position to see Sydney but had no more strength and her vision was blurry.

The sirens were outside now, the noise pounding in her head. Elizabeth pushed her chin forward and stretched her neck out as far as she could. *There you are.* Her eyes made contact with another set of eyes—intense blue eyes indicative to generations of the Grey family. Haunted eyes full of pain, and fear mixed with shock. Elizabeth tried to clear her vision and for a few seconds she did, seeing the girl's face clearly now.

A tortured cry that originated deep in Elizabeth's chest and took on the last of whatever energy her body possessed, came out of her throat and echoed throughout the house—a sound that can only be compared to that of a wounded animal.

Chapter 38

Sydney opened her eyes. Everything was white. The lights, the ceiling, the walls. She felt disoriented and dizzy. She moved her head and felt instant pain. She was in bed and that was white too. She was surrounded by equipment—beeping equipment. She looked around the room, even though her pounding head reminded her not to. Glass windows and door at the end of the bed exposed the nurse's station outside her room. *I'm in a hospital. Why?*

Slowly, her memory started to return. *Lost keys, Arne's house, padlocks, the basement, the padlocked room... then what?*

Sydney searched the bed and saw the push bell wrapped around the side bars on the bed. She grabbed it and pounded it. She kept pounding it in a panic, watching the nurse's station. One of them looked at a monitor and her head shot up to look into Sydney's room. She came running.

"Hi. You're awake."

"What happened?" Sydney asked.

The nurse smiled. "You've had a hard blow to the head. I'm just going to get the Doctor. You're going to be fine." She left the room.

Sydney felt confused. She tried to sort out the memories flooding to the surface.

The doctor came in a few minutes later. "Good to see you awake."

"What happened, Doctor?"

"Staff Sergeant Reynolds is here and will be able to answer all your questions shortly. Meanwhile, I'd like to look in your eyes and then I'd like to ask you some questions." He took a small portable light out of his pocket and examined her eyes. It hurt like hell. "What's your full name?"

"Sydney Madison Grey"

"Your birth date?"

"April 1st, 1996."

"And who's the Prime Minister of Canada/"

"Justin Trudeau."

"Where do you live?"

"On the farm in Stoney Creek."

"It seems your memory is intact. How's your head feel on a scale of one to ten, ten being the worst?"

Sydney put her hand up to her forehead and realized she had a bandage taped to one side.

"I've got a wicked headache—ten plus. My eyes hurt. Could we turn the fluorescent lights off, please?"

The nurse turned off the overhead lights and hit a lamp switch behind the bed.

"You have six stitches under that bandage. There shouldn't be any scarring." The doctor sat on the edge of the bed.

"My throat is sore. Why am I talking with such a rasp?"

"There was a fire at the farm house. You breathed in a lot of smoke. We'll keep you on oxygen overnight."

Sydney's eyes popped. "A fire?"

Staff Sergeant Reynolds appeared at the door.

"Aw, here's the Staff Sergeant now." The doctor stood. "You're suffering with a concussion. You need to rest."

"What day is it?"

"Sunday. You came in early this afternoon. It's nine o'clock in the evening now. The nurse will give you something for the pain. I'll check in with you before I leave tonight."

The doctor left and the Staff Sergeant pulled a chair over to the bed.

"Hi, Sydney. I'm happy to see you're awake. How are you feeling?"

"Like someone hit me over the head with a metal baseball bat."

"You hit your head pretty hard on a metal pipe. Same thing as a metal bat I'd say."

"The doctor mentioned a fire…I don't remember anything about that.

"You were unconscious when it started."

Sydney took in a deep breath and shut her eyes for a moment. The officer remained silent until she opened them again.

"Did everyone get out okay?"

"Everyone but Mr. Jensen."

Sydney thought hard trying to remember what happened after she unlocked the basement door. "He died in the fire?"

"No, there was an altercation upstairs in the kitchen. He died from a blow to the head."

Her body recoiled at the thought. "Omigod…" In that moment, it all came together. Sydney remembered unlocking the final door in the basement and stepping through the doorway. The vision of what she saw rushed back. She remembered sinking to her knees and the next moment Arne grabbing her from behind in a rage and throwing her across the room. *Did I imagine it?* Sydney spoke in a whisper. "Is she okay?"

"Yes, she's in recovery, they had to reset her ankle. I don't know how she pulled it off running on her broken ankle. Your Nan is a heroine."

Sydney frowned. "What? I was…Wait! She re-broke her ankle?"

"Sadly, yes. But the doctor said she came through the surgery fine."

"Dear God…are you sure she's okay?"

He nodded yes. "She's in recovery. As soon as she wakes up they'll move her to her room."

Sydney put her hands over her eyes. "I don't understand. What was she doing there? And how did she get to Arne's?"

"I'm not sure of the details yet. I haven't talked with her. All I know is she drove her car to Arne's. Saw the smoke and called 911. She reported the fire and called in an RCMP emergency at the same time."

The nurse came in and inserted a needle into her IV. "For pain, dear. You'll feel better soon." They both watched her work in silence.

"Thank you," Sydney said, as the nurse left the room. In a matter of seconds she began to feel the drug. "Mmm…I'm getting stoned already."

The Staff Sergeant leaned forward in his chair. "If you fall asleep, we'll continue in the morning. I don't want to stress you."

Sydney fought off the effect of the drugs. She had more questions. "Staff Sergeant, I'm glad my Nan's okay but I didn't know she was there. I wasn't asking about her… "

The officer looked chastised and cut in."Of course, you were downstairs in the basement unconscious. Sorry."

"Someone else was in the basement room with me. She never said a word, never moved. I think she was in shock like me." Her heart pounded. She spoke in barely a whisper, her raspy voice full of emotion. "She *was* there right?"

The officer smiled. "She was there."

"Where is she now?"

"Here in the hospital. The doctors are taking good care of her."

Sydney felt the full effects of the pain medication. She fought to maintain her thought process.

"You rescued her, you and your Nan." He paused. "Do you know who she is?"

Sydney's throat tightened. She could barely speak. "Yes—she's my mother."

"That's right, Sydney. Chelsea is alive and soon you'll all be together again."

She released a deep sigh. "I didn't imagine her. She's real."

Staff Sergeant Reynolds started to rise. "I think you need to sleep. I'll come back tomorrow."

"Please, before you go. Tell me what happened after I was unconscious."

" Chelsea tried to escape. She made it upstairs to the kitchen where they struggled. They fell into the stove. A pot of stew was knocked over and Mr. Jensen's shirt caught on fire."

"Yes, I saw the stew on the stove," Sydney interjected.

"He pulled off his shirt and threw it into the sink, but the curtains caught fire. It spread from there."

"What happened next?"

"While he was dealing with his shirt Chelsea made a run for the front door. Arne caught her at the door and pulled her back into the kitchen. She fought hard and he started to choke her."

"Oh no..."

"Your grandmother arrived at this point and charged across the kitchen floor and hit Arne with a cast iron frying pan. Elizabeth thought he was strangling you. That's when I arrived with the fire department."

Sydney had as many questions as the officer did. But the pain killer was working in full force and her mind couldn't focus. Her eyes closed and she'd almost drifted off when the Staff Sergeant spoke.

"I'm leaving now, Sydney. You need to sleep. I want you to know that you're all safe and I'll see you tomorrow. Good night."

She forced her eyes open and thanked him for coming to see her. "Good night." Sydney thought about her mother. The idea she was alive and someplace close to her was unbelievable. In her drugged state, it all felt surreal. *Maybe when I wake up it will all be a big dream.*

As if to prove her wrong, the nurse came in the room pushing a woman in a wheelchair. Mother and daughter stared at each other in silence. The nurse brought the chair to the opposite side of the bed and lowered the bed railing. "Chelsea insisted on seeing you when we told her you were awake."

Sydney couldn't believe she was actually looking at her mother. Chelsea was pale and a little on the skinny side. Her eyes, although haunted, were the signature blue of the Grey family women and the blonde hair left no doubt. "You're beautiful."

Chelsea's hand went up and she pulled at her long hair. She looked down and then up at Sydney, a little shy. "I look a fright, no make-up, and scraggly hair."

"Still, I think you're beautiful."

"You certainly are. I can't believe you're my baby girl." Her mother's eyes filled with tears. "You saved my life. And my mother saved both our lives."

"I don't know how she did what she did."

"I think she thought I was you. I'll never forget that look on her face when she realized who I was. She knew me right away. Her agonizing scream will haunt me forever. It was so full of pain."

Her mother grabbed a Kleenex from the bedside table, blew her nose and dabbed at her eyes.

Sydney couldn't talk. Her throat constricted and she knew if she spoke she'd cry.

Chelsea continued. "The moment you entered the room, I knew who you were. I couldn't believe it. Then Arne came rushing in. I thought he'd killed you." She paused. "But he was the one who died."

Chelsea wrung her hands and glanced all around the room. "He died instantly," she whispered. Her mother actually looked sad and a little lost.

That confused Sydney. It was all too much to handle and the drugs didn't help. She couldn't contain her emotions any longer and started to sob. Chelsea hesitated for a minute and slowly rose out of the wheelchair. She climbed onto the bed beside Sydney. The two women clung to each other and wept while Chelsea rocked her daughter in her arms for the first time in twenty years.

Neither one noticed the nurse quietly enter, close the curtains on the glass wall and slip out the door.

Chapter 39

The next morning the doctor came in to see Sydney. He decided to keep her in one more day. Her headache was still strong and he wanted to do an MRI. But she was ready to be moved out of ICU to a ward.

"How's my Nan?"

The doctor gave her a big smile. "She's awake this morning. Luckily, when the ankle snapped she didn't do any more damage than the previous break. She'll probably take a little longer to heal this time around, but rehab will get her up and walking again."

The nurse came for her with a wheel chair after breakfast. She wheeled her down the hall and into the elevator. They travelled up a couple of floors and started down a busy hallway.

"I'm going to miss the quiet of ICU and a private room," Chelsea said.

The nurse chuckled. "Oh, I think you'll like the ward better."

They travelled the full length of the hallway. Chelsea could see a police officer sitting outside the last room. She was surprised when the nurse wheeled her to that door.

"Police protection? From what?"

"From the media and looky loos, The three Grey women are the talk of the world. You're all over social media and television. It wasn't easy, but we did some shuffling to get you all together in one room." The nurse nodded to the officer, hit a button that opened the door and pushed Sydney through. "Here you are, ladies. All together, guard at your door." She wheeled Sydney towards one of the beds. It was a four bed ward.

"Please, can I see my Nan first?"

"Sure. If you're up to it, maybe we'll leave you in the chair. They'll be in to take you for that MRI soon."

The nurse pushed Sydney to one side of her Nan's bed. Chelsea was sitting on the bed holding Elizabeth's hand. Sydney smiled at her mother, then looked to her Nan. "Good morning. How're you feeling?"

"At the moment, I'm so high on pain meds, everything's fine. How are you doing, hon?"

"A few aches and bruises and one massive headache. The doctor is doing an MRI to be safe but I'll be able to leave tomorrow, I'm sure."

"I'm hoping they'll send me home tomorrow too," Elizabeth said. "I'm not sick and I can lay in my own bed and be a lot more comfortable."

They both looked at Chelsea. Sydney had no idea what was next for her mother. As if she'd read her mind, Chelsea blinked a couple of times and stared at the floor.

"They're waiting for my blood test results today and a psychologist to assess me to make sure I'm…" Chelsea hesitated. She gave a weak smile. "They want to be sure I'm stable."

Sydney was horrified. "Oh…" She didn't know what to say to that. After twenty years of confinement and abuse, she knew her mother would need counselling. *How could she be 'normal'? Can she heal from home or will she need to stay in a hospital?*

The door opened and a doctor came in with an empty wheelchair, followed by Staff Sergeant Reynolds.

"Good morning, ladies. I'm Doctor Sally Sauvé. I'm with the hospital's Mental Health Department. I'm here to talk with Chelsea. Is it all right if we go to my office, Ms. Grey?"

Chelsea became distant and her body tensed.

"We'll only be gone a short time. And you don't have to say anything you don't want to. Okay?"

Chelsea looked into the smiling face of Doctor Sauvé. She blinked a few times and relaxed. "Okay." She got into the wheelchair and they left the ward.

The Staff Sergeant sat in one of the chairs and pulled out a recorder. "Good morning. How are you both doing this morning?"

The women acknowledged him. Sydney said she was doing better and Elizabeth told him exactly what she'd said to Sydney when she'd asked.

"I'm going to need a statement from both of you. Shall we start with you, Sydney?"

"All right."

He opened his notebook, turned on the recorder and began. "Tell me in your own words, what took you to the Jensen farm yesterday morning and what happened as you remember it.

Sydney looked at her grandmother. She knew that what they had experienced wasn't a usual tale of mystery, family secrets, and murder on a physical plane. The positive outcome of their story would never have ended as it had without the involvement of a spiritual element. She looked back at the officer and weighed her words.

"There's no way to tell what happened and have it make sense without telling you everything. So get ready to hear some things that you aren't prepared for. You can decide what you think is relative in my statement." She looked at her grandmother and she nodded her approval.

She told him about seeing her grandfather's spirit and his words of warning. She spoke of Chelsea's visitations when she was a child and once she'd returned to the farm. She threw in the spiritual sightings by the fire crew to strengthen the validity. And she conveyed to him finding Arne's keys and instinctively knowing them to be the ones her Papa's spirit had mentioned. Sydney explained how she pulled all the information from Chelsea's journals, put that together with things Arne had said, and with those her Nan had told her. Thirty minutes later, she was done. The Staff Sergeant had listened until she was finished. His stoic expression had remained intact for the duration.

"And you drove over to Arne's without telling your Nan where you were going?"

"That's right. She was napping and I felt it was imperative to go right then and there while Arne was working the fields."

"You realize you committed a crime, a break and enter?"

Sydney blushed. "I guess I did. But at the time, I wasn't thinking straight."

The officer broke his impassive expression and half-smiled. "Sounds like a good defence. When you found your mother in the basement room, did you speak to her?"

"No. I knew it was her as soon as I saw her but I fell to my knees in shock. She looked terrified."

The officer wrote in his notepad. "How much time passed before Mr. Jensen came into the room."

"Not long. Maybe a couple of minutes. I didn't know he was there. But Chelsea saw him and she let out a horrific scream. But he was on top of me in seconds, pulling me to my feet. I remember flying across the room and that's it until I woke up here in the hospital."

The Staff Sergeant ended the interview and turned the recorder off. He turned to Elizabeth. "I suppose your statement is going to contain an ethereal element as well."

Elizabeth smiled. "I'm afraid so."

"Okay. Here we go." He turned on the recorder. "You were sleeping when Sydney went over to Arne's. Tell me when you woke up and what happened after that.

Elizabeth began with the bed shaking and her husband's spirit waiting for her to wake up. Sydney couldn't believe his facial expression remained unchanged with that piece of news but he sat and listened to her grandmother's tale and remained every bit the professional. When she finished, he again turned off the recorder. It was the first Sydney had heard her Nan's part of the story and it chilled her to the bone.

The officer looked from one to the other. "I have to say, you ladies were very lucky things turned out as they did. You both took very dangerous actions that could have gone very wrong. I wish you'd called the office and spoken to me."

Sydney spoke to that. "I thought of that but all we had to offer you were feelings, assumptions and visitations from spirits. Would that have been enough for you to get a search warrant to search Arne's farm?"

Before he could answer, the nurse came in and addressed the officer. "Dr. Sauvé sent me in to tell you that she's approved your request to interview Chelsea in her office. She would like to be present. I'll take you there if you're ready."

"Yes, we can go now. Ladies, when you get back to Stoney Creek, I'll bring your statements to the farm for signature. All of us at the detachment are truly pleased with the final outcome of this case and we're happy for your family. We'll be in touch."

"Thank you," Elizabeth said.

Sydney parroted her grandmother. "Yes, thank you."

They watched him leave. "My goodness, Nan, your story gave me the creeps. You were so brave."

"So were you. Hopefully, we can all go home and have some peace and quiet for a long time to come."

The attendant arrived to take Sydney down for her MRI. When she came back, her Nan was napping. Sydney got into her bed and fell asleep.

A few minutes later, Doctor Sauvé came in and woke them both up. "Sorry, ladies, but I need to talk to you before Chelsea returns. Staff Sergeant Reynolds is almost finished and the nurse will bring her back."

"Have you done your assessment, Doctor?" Elizabeth asked.

"Yes, I have. Chelsea is a very strong woman. Although, at the moment, she isn't aware of that. She's been through a traumatic experience that isn't going to be forgotten overnight, nor are the damaging effects going to disappear quickly. However, I do believe with counselling she can progress and eventually re-enter society. Having said that, it's all going to depend on her will to heal and tapping into her strength."

"Can she come home with us? Or does she need to be hospitalized?" Elizabeth asked.

"That's dependent on a few things. Chelsea is a very overwhelmed right now. She's going to have trouble trusting in people initially. First, I don't see any signs that she's in danger of self-harm. But that doesn't mean she won't slip backwards. Let's hope not. If she goes home, you both have to understand that she needs to be protected. She needs to rebuild her relationship with you both and that will take time. Of course, the three of you are excited to be back together but there will be issues for all of you. She'll be totally dependent on you. You'll be her life-line. Are you prepared for that?"

Elizabeth spoke first. "Of course. I've been given back my daughter and I'll do whatever it takes to help her through this."

Sydney almost panicked. "I don't know if I know how to help her. But I want to try."

Dr. Sauvé reached out and patted her arm. "Don't stress about that. That's where I come in. All you have to do is show her patience and understanding. Before I make my decision, I need you both to realize that Chelsea is going to suffer a sense of loss. To the rest of us, Arne Jensen was a very bad man who abused her terribly and people will think she should be shouting from the rooftops that he's dead and she has her freedom. But, that's not where she's at right now. Eventually, yes and that's our goal."

Sydney frowned. "You mean she's going to miss Arne and grieve his death?"

"Yes. What you need to understand is that Chelsea has never experienced life as an adult. She was kidnapped at nineteen from her parents' home. She's thirty-eight years old, and yet, has no idea what that independence means. She's scared to death. Her mental and emotional growth stopped at age nineteen."

Elizabeth interjected. "So you're saying that Arne became like a parent to her?"

"In a sense. If she resisted him, he showed her pain. She lost her sense of power and was made to feel worthless. If she behaved and gave him what he wanted, he'd reward her by holding back the abuse. Over time, she became dependent on him for her needs. It's normal for her to be fearful of losing him and grieve. He wasn't only her abuser. He was her provider and protector. Can you understand that?"

Elizabeth nodded yes.

"I get it," Sydney said. It tore her apart that her mother had suffered so. All she wanted was to see her get better.

"I asked Chelsea what she wanted to do. She'd like to go home to the farm. If you take her home, she needs to feel safe and secure. No media, no visitors to see her until she decides she's ready. Initially, she'll reject people. Expect her to be timid and cautious of men. She's going to carry the fear of the possibility that it could happen to her again. Eventually, she'll get over that. There may be days when she'll avoid both of you. I'd like to have her come once a week for counselling. I visit the Oliver Hospital on Wednesdays. We'll set it up there so she doesn't have to travel to Kelowna. I'd also like to have family counselling sessions every two weeks. That way I can address any concerns you both may have that will arise. If you both agree to this, then I'll discharge her and she can go home with you."

Elizabeth started to cry. "She needs to be with her family. Of course."

Sydney squeezed her Nan's hand and turned to the Doctor. "You can count on us. We want her with us."

Chapter 40

The nurse opened the ward door and Jessie came in. "I leave you two alone for a few days and look at you. You just can't stay out of trouble." Sydney stood and the two friends embraced. Jessie went to Elizabeth, bent down and kissed her. She turned to Elizabeth's daughter. "And you must be Chelsea. It's so nice to meet you.

"Hello." Chelsea appeared shy and a little flustered.

"Jessie is my closest friend in Stoney Creek. She's a nurse.

The doctors discharged all three women that morning. They were to return to the farm together and all stay there indefinitely. Weekly appointments were booked with Doctor Sauvé in Oliver and Sydney agreed to drive her mother in for the sessions.

Jessie addressed the women. "And today, I'm here as your chauffeur. I borrowed a van with tinted windows to drive you all home to Stoney Creek."

Chelsea frowned. "Tinted windows?"

Sydney turned to her mother. "They're tinted to filter sunlight in the summer, but also you can see out of them, but people can't see inside."

Two nurses made sure all three women had wheelchairs.

Jessie addressed the women. "Here's the plan. I'll push Sydney, and these lovely nurses will push you two ladies. We're taking the service elevator to the basement and out through a garage. Hopefully, there's no press snooping around and we'll be on our way."

Sydney knew they were exiting the hospital through the morgue. And Arne Jensen was there. It felt creepy but no one said anything. Ten minutes later, they were driving away from the hospital.

"Looks like we're free and clear. Just one stop and Stoney Creek beckons." Jessie drove towards Elizabeth's house. She parked the van a block away and soon disappeared around a corner.

"What's she up to, Nan?"

"She's going to my house to get some things I need. I gave her a list."

"What if news people are there?" Chelsea asked.

"She's going to my neighbour's house. Jessie called her earlier. Barb's going to let her out the backdoor and she'll go through the bushes to my place. You can't see either backyard from the street.

"Very clever." Sydney said.

Two hours later they drove into Stoney Creek. Chelsea's head spun back and forth, as she checked out the streets. "It's grown so much. The cafe I worked at is still there." She stretched her head backwards as they passed by until it disappeared from view.

Jessie continued across town. "By the way, I called the town this morning and asked if public works could set up traffic barricades across the highway frontage of your place. Anyone who crosses without permission will be charged with trespassing." They pulled onto Valley Road and Jessie pulled over. She picked up her cell phone and hit a contact. "Hi, it's me. We're a couple of minutes away. What can we expect when we get there?"

The three women were silent, all their attention on Jessie.

"Gotcha. Have a couple of guys outside ready to move the barricades so I don't have to dally. Thanks." She turned to the women. "Okay. We've got a crowd of news people waiting on the main road. When we get there, remember Chelsea, they can't see in."

Elizabeth snorted. "Humph…they better stay back. We've been through too much to feel intimidated entering our own home."

Chelsea looked confused. "I still don't get how they found out so fast. Or why they're interested in me."

"When I show you social media on the computer, you'll understand. And you're a heroine for surviving your ordeal, that's why they're so interested in you."

A police cruiser pulled up beside them. Jessie opened her window. "Officer?"

"There's quite a crowd up ahead. I'm going to lead you in and make sure no one tries to follow us."

Jessie pulled back onto the road and followed the cruiser to the farm. "Holy shit."

The women gasped. There were far more people than they had imagined. All three stared at the Jensen property on their left and noted the police tape across the driveway.

Sydney shuddered and turned back to her driveway where Brian and another Rhyder crew member separated two barricades.

"Here we go, ladies," Jessie said.

People were flashing cameras and yelling out their names. Sydney looked at Chelsea. She looked terrified but never moved a muscle. It was only a matter of seconds before they were in the driveway and the barricades were back in place. The police cruiser stopped out front and watched the crowd. Jessie continued around the house to the back deck.

They entered the house through the mud room, Jessie pushing Elizabeth in a wheel chair. Sydney lead the way into the kitchen. "Oh my, what's going on?"

Bea was standing at the fridge loading food containers piled on a counter. "Everyone in town has been dropping off food since yesterday. I stayed overnight to prepare for your return. I've frozen a lot of it and put some in the fridge." She shut the fridge door and came over to Sydney, enveloping her in a bear hug. "You gave us all quite a scare, I'll tell you…" She leaned down and hugged Elizabeth next and nodded to Jessie. Then she turned to Chelsea. "Welcome home, Chelsea, I'm Bea Gurka, Pam's mom. Do you remember me?"

"Hi, Mrs. Gurka," Chelsea said before dropping her eyes to the floor.

Bea turned to Sydney. "If you'd like me to stay for a couple of days and take care of the house and cooking, I'd love to. And you won't be paying me for it either. I'm here as a friend."

"I'd appreciate that Bea." Sydney put her hand up to her bandaged head. "At least until this headache subsides."

"Good. I prepped the guest room for Chelsea. I'll sleep in the residence."

"I'll be staying in the residence for a few days too to help Elizabeth while you two get your rest." Jessie said.

Elizabeth thanked them both. "It means a lot to have your help. God knows I can't contribute anything. Sydney needs to rest and Chelsea…she needs to do whatever she wants to do."

"A hot shower would be nice," Chelsea said.

Jessie wheeled Elizabeth to her room and settled her in bed. She left the house to talk to the Rhyder crew.

Sydney studied her mother. "You need some clothes. You and I look to be about the same size. Come with me." She took her hand and led Chelsea to her bedroom.

"Wow. I like the colours in this room. The farmhouse looks so different," Chelsea hesitated, "in a good way, I mean."

"Thank you." Sydney flung the cupboard doors open. "Here. Choose whatever you want. Underwear and bras are in that dresser." She watched her mother look over her clothes. Most women she knew closer to forty would find her clothes too young in style. But Chelsea gushed about them and was quite happy with her choices. *But then if she stopped maturing at nineteen, my clothes would seem perfect to her.* She showed Chelsea to her own bedroom. She couldn't believe the changes Bea had made. During the fire, the room was bare bones but she'd replaced the cheap comforter and curtains in a matching set of turquoise and burgundy Santa Fe motif. The small dresser was replaced with a six-drawer dark cherry wood bureau and a tallboy in the corner. A lazy boy in burgundy sat on an oval rug. The room was cozy and inviting.

Sydney showed Chelsea the main bathroom. "There's shampoo on the ledge and deodorant in this drawer. Snoop around and use whatever you'd like. If you want to blow dry your hair, the dryer is in a basket in these cupboards under the sink." Sydney started out the door and turned around. " And there's a lock on the door if you want some privacy." After she closed the door behind her, she heard the lock fall in place. Sydney felt exhausted and returned to her room. She stretched out on her bed and promptly fell asleep.

Elizabeth was propped up with pillows, reading a book when Chelsea poked her head into the room.

"Can I come in?"

"Of course." Elizabeth put her book down. "How was your shower?"

Chelsea smiled. "I stayed in there for ages. That was my first shower in twenty years. Arne had an old claw foot bathtub." Chelsea sat on the far side of the bed. "The best part was locking the door. Unless I was locked in the basement room, he never left me alone in the house. He'd sit on the toilet when I bathed. I hated it."

"I'm so sorry this happened to you. It breaks my heart to think that we were across the road the whole time that I thought you'd run away. It's hard to forgive myself.

"Don't think about it, Mom. It's not your fault."

Elizabeth sighed. "Where's Sydney?"

"She's asleep. I just checked on her."

"Oh good, she needs to rest."

Chelsea looked towards the window. "I noticed the vehicles out back belong to Rhyder Contracting. Do they have anything to do with the Rhyder family that used to live here. Wes?"

Elizabeth squirmed uncomfortably and studied her daughter's face. "Yes. Jax Rhyder is running the project. Jax is Wes Rhyder's son."

"Really? Is he the blond boy out there around Sydney's age?"

"I don't know. I've never met him. When the fire happened, they suspended work around here to set up the Fire Centre."

"So Wes returned to Stoney Creek then? I'm surprised."

There was so much Chelsea didn't know, but Elizabeth didn't think this was the time to tell her. "He returned to Stoney Creek when Jax was six years old, His marriage had ended and he wanted Jax to grow up in a small town. He started his own company. His son works with his father. Jax loves restoring old farmhouses which is how he ended up with this project." Elizabeth flung her arm out towards her cast. "That was before I did this to myself the first time."

Chelsea's forehead furrowed. Elizabeth could tell she was thinking hard on something. She decided to change the subject. "Apparently, they'll be finished today and they'll all be gone. Now if we can get the media to leave, we'll have the place to ourselves. Jessie is going to talk to them on behalf of the family."

Jessie came to the door to check on Elizabeth. "Hi."

"Come on in," Elizabeth said.

"Just checking to see if you need anything. How's the pain?" Jessie asked.

"I'm ready for some meds and a nap."

Chelsea turned to Jessie. "Is that tall, blond boy Wes Rhyder's son?"

Jessie's eyebrows shot up. She glanced at Elizabeth. "Uh…yes. That's him."

"Chelsea saw the name on the trucks and made the connection." Elizabeth said.

Jessie relaxed. "Oh…I'll get your pain meds."

"I thought I could see a resemblance." Chelsea said.

Jessie returned a minute later, gave Elizabeth her pills and left.

Chelsea suddenly looked lost. "I guess I better go back to my room if you're going to nap. Maybe I'll try to nap too," Chelsea said.

Elizabeth rested her hand on her daughter's arm. She knew Chelsea was feeling strange and she didn't want her to be alone while she and Sydney slept. She made a mental note that one of them would always be close by for the next while. "Would you stay? I'd really like the company. You could nap here beside me."

Chelsea's face lit up. "Okay, if you want me to."

Chapter 41

Sydney woke up with a start. She'd been dreaming. A bad dream about Arne choking her mother. Although she hadn't witnessed it when it happened, her dream had been quite vivid. The clock red four fifteen. She'd slept for three hours. She got up and went into the en suite, shaking off the dream. She washed her face. Running a brush through her hair, she noted that her headache had lessened. It felt good to move her head without extreme pain. *That's a plus.* She left her bedroom to see what the rest of the household was up to.

She popped her head into her Nan's room. She was sleeping with a book laying in her lap. Chelsea was laying beside her fast asleep. She watched them for a few minutes. *I can't believe this is real.* Voices and laughter could be heard from the kitchen area. Curious, she headed there to check it out.

Sydney stopped cold in the doorway. Bea was busy making dinner. Jax sat at the island, his back to her talking to Jessie across from him. Jessie saw her first."There you are, girlie. You had a long sleep. How's the head.

"It's eased some."

"Come and join us." Jessie said.

Jax spun around. Sydney nodded. "Jax," she said. She made a point of sitting further down the island but on the same side rather than facing him. Bea refilled coffee cups and put a glass of juice in front of her.

"No coffee for you with a concussion. Not good."

Sydney smiled at her. "Thank you." She knew better than to argue with Bea.

A writing pad and pen sat in front of Jessie.

"Whatcha' doing?" Sydney asked.

"Your grandmother asked me to represent the family and talk to the news people out there. The others have been helping me to write it. Basically, there will be no interviews at this time and the family asks to be left alone to deal with this traumatic event and heal. And they ask that the press honour their request for privacy.

"Sounds good to me. Thank you for doing this for us."

"My pleasure."

Jax stood. "Well, I have to get home and finish packing. I never thought I could accumulate so much in the short time I've lived in that little house."

Sydney's heart skipped a beat. This time, she looked right at him. *Packing? He's moving out of his house. Is he leaving town?*

Jax caught her eye. "Sydney, could I talk to you for a minute. Privately?" He looked so serious.

"Sure. Let's go outside." Sydney led the way through the dining room and out the French doors. They walked towards the lake. She had no idea how she was supposed to react to Jax. She assumed he was telling her he was leaving. Her emotions were all ready askew and dealing with Jax on top of everything else, was pushing her to the edge.

Jax stopped walking. "You gave us all a scare. I'm glad things turned out all right. I wish I…I could have been here. Things may have happened differently. How are you coping?"

Sydney decided to stay away from that discussion. "I'm okay. My headache's not as severe."

"So you said. I meant how are you dealing with all of this? It's quite a shock for you and your Nan. And I can't imagine what your Mother is feeling."

"It's surreal. I think we're all still numb."

"Everyone says you look alike."

"So everyone says."

"I'm really happy for your family. And that you'll all be okay."

Sydney didn't doubt that Jax cared but he was leading up to something and she wanted him to get to the point.

"I wanted you to know we finished the project today. We're done. The guys are packing everything up. So your family will have their privacy."

They stood side by side, both staring at the lake. Not once had they looked at each other. "You did a wonderful job, Jax. Thank you so much. Forward me the invoice and I'll pay the balance." Sydney paused. 'So you're moving?"

"Yes."

"When?"

"Tomorrow."

Sydney was shocked. She turned and stared at Jax. "That soon?"

"I have something to tell you. Jessie got the results of the DNA tests."

Her face clouded over. She felt angry. "What? And no one told me?"

"Hang on. She got the call a few minutes ago. I asked her if I could tell you because we need to talk."

Sydney felt crushed and turned back to the lake and stared out past the hay fields. She felt hollow inside. "And that's why you're leaving town. I guess I know what you're going to say."

"Huh? I'm not leaving town."

"Then why are you moving? You love that little house."

"Because I'm... wait, enough about the move. This is more important. Sydney, Dad isn't your father. We aren't cousins."

Sydney froze and she forgot to breathe. She didn't know if she should be relieved or angry that a married cheating carnival worker was her father or disappointed that a nice man like Wes Rhyder hadn't fathered her.

"Syd?"

"Wow!" She turned to face Jax. "At least we didn't commit incest."

"I'm so sorry you had to go through this. And then everything else."

Sydney managed a thin smile. "Well… it's all turned out for the best. Thank you for telling me."

Jax seemed awkward. He started to say something and stopped.

Sydney let it pass. "So why are you moving?"

"My Dad is moving to Kelowna to expand his commercial business there. He's helping me set up my own residential upgrades and renovations company here in Stoney Creek. He asked me to move into his house so it's not sitting empty. I prefer my little house but his is rent free."

"That's wonderful, Jax. It's what you wanted."

"Look, I'm not sure that this is the right timing with everything that's happened. And I don't want to overwhelm you… " Jax trailed off.

Here it comes. He's letting me down. "What is it?" She braced herself.

"I know a lot has happened and … Jax paused.

You said that already. Spit it out."Let me make this easy for you, Jax. We shared some good times and we had one great night together. But after everything that's happened, you realize we can't move forward and you really don't want any commitments. It's okay, really. I have enough to deal with right now anyway." Sydney turned back to the house.

Jax grabbed her arm. "That's not what I was going to say at all. Everything I said to you that night, I meant. All these weeks apart, wondering if we were blood, I still couldn't get that night out of my head. I know you're family needs time to deal with all that's happened. You're going to want to spend time with your mother and get to know her. And help her heal. I get that. I don't want to walk away from us but I don't want to put expectations on you that you can't handle right now."

Sydney looked into Jax' eyes. What she saw told her everything she needed to know. "Are you trying to say that you aren't afraid of the 'c' word."

Jax pulled her into his arms. "I'm saying that I love you, Sydney Madison Grey. And I'm not going anywhere." He kissed her with an urgency and Sydney responded back.

Their kiss was long and passionate. And when they were done, he kissed each eye, her nose, each cheek, and claimed her mouth one more time.

"Oh Jax. I love you too."

"So here's the plan. You need time with family and I need time to get my business up and running. We'll see each other when we can. Slow and easy. All I need to know is that we're a couple…exclusivity.

Sydney put her hands on either side of Jax' face. "Damn right we are."

This time, she kissed him. The world around them disappeared. They held each other and whispered words of love and kissed some more. Finally, they stared deep into each other's eyes and laughed. Arm in arm they headed back towards the house.

The French doors were open and Bea and Jessie stood there beaming. Bea gave them a thumbs up and Jessie clapped her hands.

"Omigod…they watched the whole time." Sydney said.

Jax laughed. "They're suckers for romance I guess. And didn't we give them a show?"

Chapter 42

Elizabeth woke up to the sound of crying. It took her a moment to get her bearings. She glanced beside her on the bed. Chelsea was gone. The crying began again. She turned the other way and saw her daughter standing by the window. Chelsea had her hands over her mouth to muffle her cries.

"Chelsea? What's wrong, hon?"

Chelsea turned to her mother. "What have I done?"

Her mother patted the bed. "Come and talk to me."

Her daughter sat down, a concerned look on her face. "Sydney and Jax. They're…together."

Elizabeth could see how upset Chelsea was but she proceeded with caution. "What do mean together?"

"I mean they're hugging and kissing…like a couple."

Elizabeth frowned. "Outside?"

"Yes," Chelsea whispered.

"Well that may mean good news."

Chelsea cut her off. She wasn't listening. "Everything is my fault." She covered her face with her hands. "If I hadn't been such a stupid teenager, getting pregnant by some kid who only wanted to get laid. If I'd told Dad about Arne's advances on me but I didn't because I was leaving. And Mary and Dad dying. All because of me." Chelsea fell apart and began to sob.

Elizabeth took a hold of her arm. "Chelsea, look at me." Her daughter raised her head. "You're not responsible for any of this. We could all go back in time and blame ourselves for things that have happened. You were a victim in all of this. The responsibility lies with Arne. A bad man who interfered in all of our lives and paid for it with his own." She reached for a box of Kleenex and handed it to her daughter.

Chelsea calmed down and blew her hose. But the tears wouldn't stop. "Oh mom…you don't understand…"

"You're worried that Wes may be the father of both of them."

Chelsea's eyes popped. "How do you know that?"

"Sweetheart, there's so much you don't know. Your journals helped us put it all together. Sydney and Jax have been waiting for the results of a DNA test. If they're together right now, the results must have come in. And I think it's safe to say that Wes isn't Chelsea's father."

Chelsea wiped her eyes. "You think? My life has been stagnant all these years while life outside carried on and I caused everyone all this pain."

"You did what you did at the time for what you believed were valid reasons. Second-guessing yourself now is a waste of time. All of us would love to change things we did in our past. We can't. We must all move forward."

"I guess so."

"You might as well know the rest. Jax was adopted by Wes and his ex-wife when Wes' sister and her husband died. Jax was two years old at the time. Biologically, Wes is his uncle but to Jax he's his father."

"I've missed so much."

"And now you're free. It'll take time to adjust but with Dr. Sauvé's help and ours, you'll come to realize that the world is yours. This is your time and you're young enough to embrace it and make something of it."

Chelsea was calm again. Elizabeth leaned over the side table and opened a drawer. She pulled out a bundle of letters with an elastic band around them. "I hope I'm not overwhelming you with too much but you should know one more thing. Wes wasn't using you. He really did care about you all those years ago. He wrote these letters to you in the early months after he moved. Sadly, your father intercepted them and hid them away. I found them after he died. I was going to return them to Wes but now I think they belong to you."

Her daughter stared at the letters her mother held out to her. "Wes wrote these?" She took them in her hand. She shook her head. "Oh Dad. I was so miserable that summer."

"He thought he was protecting you. Don't hate him."

"I don't hate him."

Sydney appeared in the doorway. "Is everything all right? I thought I heard someone in distress."

"Come in, hon, "Elizabeth said. "Chelsea wiggle over and let Sydney sit beside you on the bed. Chelsea saw you and Jax together outside." Her Nan looked at her expectantly.

Sydney glanced over at her mother aghast. "Omigod…I never thought." Sydney glanced over at her mother aghast.

"She knows most of it and about the test. Did you get the results?" Elizabeth asked.

Sydney smiled. "We did…boy, is this weird." She looked at her mother. "Wes Rhyder isn't my father."

Chelsea stared down at the bed. "I'm so sorry you had to go through all this pain."

Sydney took her mother's hand in hers. "It is what it is. And now Jax and I can be together and we're happy. Anything I suffered the past month can't possibly compare to what you've been through the past twenty years. I don't know how you survived."

"I almost didn't those first six months. I was suicidal at times back then. He locked me up in a food bunker built into the hill where the old homestead was." Chelsea's eyes became vacant and she chewed her finger nail. "Once Mary died and he moved me into the house, it was better. Before the kidnapping, I was strong, independent." She smiled. "And as Dad called me, 'wild'. Arne tried to break me and I fought him for a long time. But I was the one who always ended up hurting—physically and emotionally. I learned that if I gave him what he wanted and became the person he wanted me to be, he was happy. That was one of the ways I survived. There were other ways too."

"What ways?" Sydney asked.

"My meditation, yoga, and soul travel. I was so excited when Arne told me you and Mom were back at the farm. Then, I was scared Arne would hurt you. I visited often. Sometimes you saw me, sometimes not. But I clung to the hope that I'd be found. And of course, there was Dad. He stayed with me the whole time after he died."

Elizabeth frowned. "A few minutes ago when you were upset, you said something about your father's and Mary's deaths being your fault. What did you mean?"

"Arne murdered them both."

Elizabeth's hands clutched at her chest. "What? But they both had heart attacks."

"Yes, massive heart attacks."

"I don't understand," Elizabeth said.

"They both found out about me. Mary got suspicious when she noticed him heading to the old homestead a number of times. One day she followed him and snuck in behind him. She saw me. He had me chained to the bed in those days. I begged her to help me. She turned and ran but he caught her."

"And the stress caused her to have a heart attack?" Sydney asked.

"No. Arne had a kidney condition that affected his potassium levels. He used calibrated injection vials of Potassium Chloride daily. His doctors warned him that an overdose could cause a heart attack in a matter of minutes, leading to death. He studied up on it. He carried an intravenous needle full of Potassium Chloride all the time." Chelsea shuddered. "He threatened me with it many times when he was angry."

Elizabeth exploded. "The bastard. But why wasn't it discovered with an autopsy?"

"Arne told me that when tissue dies, it expels the Potassium Chloride into the blood stream where it's dissipated. Tissue samples from an autopsy would be void. He also told me that Mary had a flu shot a few days before and he bragged that he cleverly put the needle into the same pin prick so not to arouse suspicion. He called it the perfect murder."

Sydney was shaken. She knew something was off about Arne but this was beyond anything she'd imagined. "And Papa?" she whispered.

Chelsea nervously picked at threads in her shirt. "He'd come to the house on one of his early morning walks to talk to Arne. Arne had brought me up from the basement room to cook breakfast. I think Dad heard him yelling. Mary had been gone for three years by then and I guess Dad was curious as to who he was screaming at. He walked around the house and peered into the kitchen window. Our eyes locked. I'll never forget his expression," Chelsea's voice cracked and she stared into her lap.

Elizabeth reached out and took her hand. "You don't have to talk about this right now."

"You both need to know. I told Staff Sergeant Reynolds all of this. I asked him if I could tell you."

"Okay, hon."

"Arne ran outside and they struggled. Dad was already on heart medication. Arne knew one shot of Potassium Chloride would be lethal. He also knew Dad injected insulin into his abdomen for Diabetes. He pulled the needle out of his pocket and jabbed it into his stomach." Tears filled Chelsea's eyes. "He left Dad to die on the ground alone while he locked me in the basement. Then, he put him in his truck drove him home and left him...just left him laying on the porch like a sack of potatoes."

Elizabeth spoke in a monotone. "Until I found him an hour later."

The three women sat in silence with tears streaming down their cheeks; lost in their own thoughts; locked in their own grief.

Chelsea spoke first. "When Dad was alive, he and I battled all the time. But after he died, he wouldn't cross over. He stayed with me. When I didn't see him in spirit, I could sense his presence. Sometimes, when I soul travelled to the farm, I'd see him watching over you, Mom, while you slept. And sometimes, it was Sydney. I made my peace with him years ago." Chelsea looked at Sydney. "He never spoke, but I spoke to him all the time, the way you used to talk to me at our pretend tea parties. He was the biggest reason I survived."

Elizabeth furrowed her brow. "I'm still confused about something. We thought you were dead because Sydney saw your spirit. How is that possible when you are alive?"

"It wasn't my spirit Sydney saw. It was my soul. Soul travel means your soul leaves your body for a short time but it can return. You may not remember this, I was studying soul travel during my last year here at the farm."

Sydney picked up the conversation. "And I thought it was her spirit too until I read the journals and realized she practiced soul travel. Something clicked when I found Arne's keys and Papa told Nan I was to use the keys."

Elizabeth held out her hands to Chelsea and Sydney. "We're a family and together we'll find the strength to face all that's happened here and put it behind us. We'll look to the future and celebrate life. Chelsea, one day you'll be able to say you were a victim but not anymore."

The three women held hands, forming a circle.

A circle that sealed their bond—a bond formed from pain, compassion—and love.

THE END

Also by the Author

The Georgia Series

- Winter's Captive
- Chasing Georgia
- Missing Thread

Made in United States
North Haven, CT
07 October 2023